ONCE UPON A PARSEC
The Book of Alien Fairy Tales

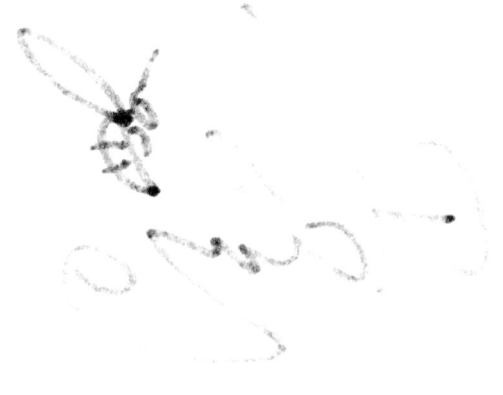

ONCE UPON A PARSEC
The Book of Alien Fairy Tales

Edited by
David Gullen

NewCon Press
England

First edition, published in the UK July 2019
by NewCon Press

NCP 212 (hardback)
NCP 213 (softback)

10 9 8 7 6 5 4 3 2 1

Introduction copyright © 2019 by David Gullen
Cover Art copyright © 2019 by Ben Baldwin
This compilation copyright © 2019 by Ian Whates

"The Little People" copyright © 2019 by Una McCormack
"Lost in the Rewilding" copyright © 2019 by Paul Di Filippo
"Goblin Autumn" copyright © 2019 by Adrian Tchaikovsky
"Myths of Sisyphus." copyright © 2019 by Allen Ashley
"The Land of Grunts and Squeaks © 2019 by Chris Beckett
"The Blood Rose" copyright © 2019 by Susan Oke
"Starfish" copyright © 2019 by Liz Williams
"The Raveller's Tale" copyright © 2019 by Neil Williamson
"The Tiny Traveller" copyright © 2019 by Aliya Whiteley
"The Tale of Suyenye the Wise, the Ay, and the People of the Shining Land"
copyright © 2019 by Gaie Sebold
"Wanderlust" copyright © 2019 by Kim Lakin-Smith
"Pale Sister" copyright © 2019 by Jaine Fenn
"Alpha42 and the Space Hermits" copyright © 2019 by Stephen Oram
"The Teller and the Starborn" copyright © 2019 by Peter Sutton
"The Winternet" copyright © 2019 by Ian Whates
"The Awakening" copyright © 2019 by Bryony Pearce

All rights reserved, including the right to produce this book, or portions
thereof, in any form.

ISBN: 978-1-912950-29-4 (hardback)
978-1-912950-30-0 (softback)

Minor editorial interference by Ian Whates
Cover art and design by Ben Baldwin
Cover layout by Ian Whates
Text layout by Storm Constantine

Contents

Introduction by David Gullen	7
The Little People – Una McCormack	9
Lost in the Rewilding – Paul Di Filippo	17
Goblin Autumn – Adrian Tchaikovsky	29
Myths of Sisyphus – Allen Ashley	47
The Land of Grunts and Squeaks – Chris Beckett	59
The Blood Rose – Susan Oke	69
Starfish – Liz Williams	85
The Raveller's Tale – Neil Williamson	95
The Tiny Traveller – Aliya Whiteley	105
The Tale of Suyenye the Wise, the Ay, and the People of the Shining Land – Gaie Sebold	123
Wanderlust – Kim Lakin-Smith	137
Pale Sister – Jaine Fenn	153
Alpha42 and the Space Hermits, Stephen Oram	171
The Teller and the Starborn – Peter Sutton	185
The Winternet – Ian Whates	195
The Awakening – Bryony Pearce	205
About the Authors	221

Once Upon a Parsec:
An Introduction

David Gullen

Everything is a story, and some of them are true. The stories we choose to believe, or doubt, or deny, shape what we believe and who we are. They nest, and interleave, and weave around and through each other, and through us as well. It is what they are for, and why story is so very important. For even when a story is not true in itself, in the actual tale it is telling, it will still *contain* truths.

After all, isn't this one of the reasons we read – and write? To experience truths old and new, half-forgotten or well-remembered, in new forms so we feel them afresh. Some might open our eyes a little wider, and others, in that rare moment, let us see and feel new things for the first time.

If you want to change the world, tell a different story. Tell a *better* story.

Of course, stories should be fun too, and what better way to learn than to be entertained?

Trust me, turn the page and read on and you will be entertained by some of the finest writers around today.

Trust is not something that gets talked about much in publishing, but it is at the heart of a project like this. Almost everything we do is through cooperation. We trust, and in turn are trusted: publisher, editor, and writers; artists and designers; printers and couriers; booksellers, libraries, and readers.

When I first approached Ian Whates at NewCon Press with my ideas, for the first time ever he trusted someone else to compile and edit an anthology of original stories he would then publish – a great privilege.

I knew the idea of writing an alien fairy story was challenging. An intriguing and fascinating idea, of course, but still a demanding brief. In fact there were times when I was quite glad I didn't have to come up with a story of my own. It was something everyone rose to rather wonderfully.

My thanks go to everyone who wrote for this anthology, and also to Ian at NewCon. Thank you, one and all.

What these writers, these *story-tellers*, have helped me create, what you, the reader, now hold in your hands, is something I think is exceptional. Or are they indeed hands? Could it be that you are reading this book in translation somewhere far away? That it nestles between your pincers, or coiled in tentacles, suspended in some force-field, or phase-modulated into a pool of shared consciousness? After all, wherever we go, only on Earth will we humans not be the aliens.

Everything is a story. Here are stories from other worlds and times, seen through other eyes and felt by other minds. Some might feel familiar, others are very unsettling indeed. Old knowledge, fear and wonder, all with their cargo of strange truths. All waiting for you.

David Gullen,
London
March 2019

The Little People

Una McCormack

Here is an old story, a worn story, a story told so often that the purpose is forgotten. A smooth story, well known, without any rough edges. But the truth sometimes pokes through, like white flowers in the spring of a world, emerging from rich soil. Like bones.

When you were little, you played all the time on the shore. Lessons finished, chores done, permission granted, you would dash down to the ocean. You would race along the sands, running after each other in that perpetual childhood chase where the possibilities still seem limitless, and the boundaries do not seem to exist. Sometimes you went up to the edge of the sea, and picked up stones, and you would skim them on the water – three bounces, four, five, six, forever seeking that elusive extra bounce.

Sometimes you might even paddle in the water, although special permission was needed for this. Once you heard one of the grown-ups call the sea "injurious", a word that both thrilled and alarmed. It would be another generation, they said, your children or perhaps your children's children, before the sea was completely safe for you and yours. No, you did not swim in the water, not without the necessary equipment and supervision. Sometimes you dared each other to run in, up to your necks, and run out again, but that was as far as you pushed your luck. However free you felt, you did not ever quite forget that even if you were born here, this was not the world you came from – not quite – but the world that had saved you. You and yours.

Besides, your favourite game was the building game. You would wander round the shore, collecting old worn stones and shards and shells and fragments. And you would build – little cairns at first, and then the structures became more elaborate. You raised small towns and settlements. Farms and homesteads. Laid roads of moss and reeds and grass; gathered flowers to adorn tiny gardens. And you played games of the people who lived there – the little people, you called them. Sometimes you told each other you'd caught a glimpse of one of them, a small face peering through a window, dashing for cover at the sight of you. Sometimes you almost believed the stories that you told yourselves; sometimes you wanted to believe them more than anything, believe that you and yours were not alone, were not the only ones in the whole wide dark of space.

But you knew, really, that the facts said something else.

The facts said there was only you.

At night the sea would wash the stones away.

Roali was always the last to be woken. Emerging from deep sleep, hollow-eyed and thirsty, staring up at Vaioti, leaning over, murmuring soothing words to help with reorientation. A cup of water. Pills. The bleak ship around them, bereft of comforts, bereft of life. Each time older and closer to exhaustion.

Sometimes, checking the ship's logs, Roali found that there had been occasions when the others had been awake, done their work, and left Roali sealed in sleep. The worlds they had encountered did not meet the necessary conditions for sustaining life, and so there had been no need for Roali's expertise. The ship had moved on. A breach of the code, perhaps – there should always be the five of them making decisions – but looking at the logs there had always been consensus and no need for a casting vote. Resources were saved if Roali slept.

Sometimes Roali woke, and examined all the data, and gave the report, but the world below was not suitable in some other way, and they would return to sleep, and the ship would continue. Roali always gave the same report. They had never, so far, in all the vastness of space, encountered any other living being.

Vaioti offered a hand to help; caught Roali's eye and smiled. Roali, standing, wavered; leaned on Vaioti for support. Said:

"Are we there yet?"

Sometimes, you played 'Ancestors'. You told their hero's journey, crossing the empty dark in a ship built to last a thousand million billion gazillion years. You went to the cave on the beach and altogether you pulled up stones to cover up the entrance, and then you all lay down on the mouldering ground and pretended to be asleep. Then one of you – how you agreed this between you was never quite spoken, but it was always right when it happened – went "Beep! Beep! Beep!" which was how you thought the alarm must have sounded, like the one that woke you each day. One by one you would yawn and stretch and pretend to wake up, and look around, and someone would say, "We're here! We've made it!" and everyone would cheer. You'd pull all the stones down from the entrance, and come out onto the shore, blinking in the light as if you were the first people ever to see this sun. And then you'd run across the beach, footsteps on the bare sand, delighting in the mark that you made. If there were five of you, you played 'Founders', and sometimes you would quarrel over which one you got to play because everybody wanted to be Atoili, who was the leader, and nobody wanted to be Roali, because you couldn't quite understand what Roali was there for.

One time you took Oioni with you to the cave, even though Oioni was littler than everyone else, because you felt sorry that someone was left out of the games. But when the stones began to seal the front of the cave, Oioni started to cry and wouldn't stop crying – not because of the dark but because there were eyes in the dark, eyes, little eyes. But you couldn't see them so all you said was, "Stop, or you'll never get to come with us again." That stopped Oioni crying but it also stopped the game, for good. Nobody wanted to go back there now. Not if there were eyes in the darkness. Little eyes, peering back at you, through the darkness.

This time, for the first time in a long time, the world below looked propitious. Roali, deep in the data, caught brief bits and pieces of colleagues' conversation. Noaini was confirming that the world was within tolerance, that they could survive there right now. Evailo said that the place could be made entirely habitable within 5-6 generations. Atoili wanted to know if they still had the capacity. Vaioti said that they did. Noaini said that this time they did.

Roali stopped listening and went back to the data. Each moment spent out of sleep stole from the future. But there was a task to perform. There were conditions to be met – conditions made when the ship set out. Conditions that might make the decision for them.

After a while, everyone went quiet. They stood and watched while Roali worked. Someone made some food, which they ate guiltily, thinking of the theft it represented. The quiet returned. In time, into the silence, Roali said, "I think that's a settlement. I think there are people down there."

Softly, ever so softly, Evailo began to cry.

There were the facts, and there was the fiction.

The facts were easy enough to teach, and easy enough to learn. You all learned about the ark ship leaving. You all knew about the generations in flight; the tenderly maintained systems that kept the genetic stock alive. You all remembered the old worn ship with old worn guardians, rising from cold sleep to perform their tasks, like temple rites. Here it is, all written down in the history books. The sighting of the new world, the gift world. The scans and the probes. The landing. The long slow reconstruction, ongoing, of the world that had not been yours but was now.

Then there was the fiction. You have imagined yourself as one of the Founders. You played stepping out onto the virgin soil, ship-soiled and grubby, looking up at a new sun. You imagine the tears of gratitude. You have been one of the reconstructors, preparing the land for the living. You have been one of the settlers, growing, planting, stretching out. You are their inheritors.

Stories can become smooth through use, like pebbles on a beach that have been passed around from hand to hand. They lose their edge in the telling and retelling. They become comfortable and safe; a home from home. Consolation in the face of darkness. Comfort under duress.

But sometimes other stories cannot help themselves. They peek through the surface. Folk tales, fairy tales. Stories for little ones, told to scare them. To warn them off; to curb their curiosity. Scope out the limits and set the boundaries. Old bones, poking through.

Four of them discussed. Four of them debated. Four of them quarrelled.
 All of them were desperate.
 "This is the first real possibility we've encountered –"
 "We're reaching critical. At some point we'll be stealing resources just to keep the ship moving –"
 "The protocols say not where there's evidence of life –"
 "We could try to communicate, try to negotiate, ask for land, ask for help…"
 "But we can't survive there in the long term, not without planetary restructure –"
 At length, Roali – counting minutes, counting seconds, counting time they were staying awake and the theft it represented from the future – said, "We are wasting resources. The decision has been made. There is life there. This world is not suitable."
 There was silence.
 "That's what the protocols say," Roali said. "That's why the protocols were created. To make this decision for us."
 The others agreed that Roali was right. The others agreed that they would return to sleep and move on. Roali did what had been agreed.

You got big, bigger; one day you might be biggest of them all. Or perhaps you will remain little; nobody in particular. Not a hero, or explorer, or Founder, or settler.
 Your very own self.
 You thought more, and more deeply. You remember exactly where you were when you married fact with fiction: walking in the forest under vernal leaves. Small flowers, bone-white, poking up from the underworld. You have come to the age where you can synthesise information, make patterns, understand deeper structures. As you walk, the world – your adopted world, which you love, for which you are so grateful – remakes itself around you.

Old bones; old stones. The little people, never-seen. A world that was emptied.

One day, you think you came to an understanding of what happened here. The facts, you mean; not the fiction.

You have dreamed of the end of the world. Fire and war and famine and deluge. You sat shivering in the cold, and hoped someone would save you.

You have dreamed of the big ship setting out, watched it sail through the darkness. You have dreamed of the fear and the exile. You have dreamed of the sudden hope – the new world below, like an offering. You have dreamed of the work and the sacrifice.

You have dreamed of the end of the world.

The next time Roali woke, Vaioti did not offer a hand to help.

"*Are we there yet?*"

"*We have not left,*" *Vaioti said, looking at the wall, and Roali felt the first crawl of horror.* "*After you went back to sleep, and before the rest of us slept, Atoili sent down a probe –*"

Roali ran, on wavering legs, ran down the dim corridor to the others. Looked out at a world that had already changed in aspect. "*What have you done?*"

"*There was consensus,*" *Noaini said.* "*All four of us. We did not need...*"

"*What have you* done?"

"*What are you saying, Roali?*" *Atoili said.* "*What do you think we have done?*"

"*There was life! There were* people!"

"*There were no people,*" *Atoili said.* "*We would not have started the restructure if there had been people. That's forbidden.*"

"*I heard them! I saw them!*"

"*What did you see?*" *Atoili said.* "*With your own eyes?*"

"*I looked at the scans –*"

"*You must have made a mistake –*"

"*I did not make a mistake!*"

"*Is it possible,*" *said Atoili, calmly,* "*that you made a mistake?*"

Anything, of course, is possible.

Later, on the surface, Roali looked round at the work that had already been done. Soon they could wake the others. Soon there would be children. Soon they would have the home and the life they had been looking for. And with some effort, thought Roali, you could convince yourself that there had never been anyone here.

You wonder, sometimes, about the stories you'll tell, in time. When there are little ones, you mean, ones who want to hear stories, ones who crave stories, ones who are susceptible to stories. Do you wonder, sometimes, what you'll tell them? What you'll tell yourself?

Lost in The Rewilding

Paul Di Filippo

This is a tale told by splices everywhere, when humans are not around to hear.

On the coastal edge of the Great Laurentian Rewilding, as an unofficial satellite of Pine Barrens Urbmon Number Seven – colloquially called by its residents 'the Badabing' – stood a small laboratory, a plain white windowless blockhouse. The building had to be separated from the main habitation, where nearly a million people lived, due to the sometimes dangerous nature of its researches. The lab was surrounded by a moat of smart gel and various electronic, chemical, drone and silicrobe defences and barriers.

Inside the lab one summer day could be found two chromosartors, a man and a woman. The man was named Angus Woodman and the woman was named Mapinta Damas. They were having an argument.

"You should never have crispered such a suite of genes together in the first place, Angus," said the woman. Her face showed irritation and disdain.

The man looked humbled and repentant, but not totally convinced by the woman's argument. "But I only wanted to help with the flooding on the Passaic. The overflow waters from that last superstorm wiped out all the outdoor recreational facilities around the Badabing."

"I know your intentions were good. But you created a chimera that was simply too efficient. Coypu, beaver, capybara, muskrat – plus twenty-nine percent human! What were you thinking? They didn't just dam the Passaic, they also blockaded four other rivers in the region. Practically overnight, we had a new lake that took out a million nubux worth of crops. If it weren't for the Protein Police tracking down every last member of the clade and exterminating them, the whole bioregion would have been underwater. And before we know it the cops will unravel the codes of the corpses, retrodict a signature, and bust down our door. We've got to get rid of all the evidence that we were responsible. And that includes Castor and Villette. It's off to the lysing chambers with them."

Castor and Villette, the elders of our line, our ancestors, were the first prototypes of the novel species, and still lived in the lab.

"But Mapinta, I can't just kill them! They represent so much creative tailoring, so many high hopes, and so much – well, so much love. I fear they've become like the children you and I never fabbed."

"What an insult! Those musky bumbling rodentiamorphs, sprung from my genome! That really is the final straw, Angus. I insist you get rid of those splices this instant."

"I apologize, dear. But please, let me have just one more night with them, to say a real goodbye. I promise they'll be gone in the morning."

"Oh, very well. You can stay here overnight if you really must, but I'm heading back to the Badabing. Maybe I can bolster our alibi back there somehow."

After Mapinta had departed, Angus went to the part of the lab where the splices lived.

The room-sized cage that held Castor and Villette was not uncongenial. It featured a nice lodge made of foam noodles, a trough perpetually replenished with corn, beans and mushrooms, and a bundle of nice green aspen twigs for snacking.

Additionally, a media centre streamed the entertainments of the Chimera Channel. But although the pair did not lack for comforts, we know that they chafed at their limited freedom and the inability to pursue their deepest instincts, which comprised dam-building, mating, lodge-wattling and the occasional pitched interfamily rumble.

Angus stood outside the cage bars, contemplating his offspring, the children of his gene-sculpting talents and his imagination. Half as big as the average human, they were bulky, bottom heavy, oily furred and big-toothed. They wore no clothes. Villette, the female, was slightly shorter and more svelte than her mate.

Seeing Angus, Castor and Villette jumped up from their pallet and hustled to the bars. Angus squatted to bring his face level with their snouts. They reached through the bars and stroked and petted his cheeks and hair. He shed some tears.

"Papa Woodman, Papa Woodman! Time for us to leave and join our kin? Please, time now, at last!"

"All your kin are dead, my little ones. Their skills and efforts were unappreciated. I am sorry to have to tell you this, but you are the only two of your kind left."

The rodentiamorphs began to snuffle and blubber. "No! Can't be! Why?"

"It's just the way of the cruel world, children. And you two will suffer a similar fate if I do not send you away. And perhaps even such a flight will not lead to your long-term survival. But we must try. First, let me remove the block on your procreative faculties."

Angus perfused them both with a shot.

"Now, get your belt packs, and I'll give you some nice things."

At the notion of receiving treats, the splices forgot their sorrows and gambolled about the cage. They eventually brought Angus their canvas strap-on pouches and he filled them with concentrated rations. "These foodstuffs will allow you to sustain yourselves for a time without having to stop and harvest twigs. You'll move along faster." Then he threaded a sheath holding a knife onto each belt.

"You know these tools. Just like the ones you eat with, but very sharp. Dangerous!"

Not frightened, the splices took out the daggers and began a crude mock-fencing and stabbing of the lodge noodles.

"All right now, that's enough playtime. Put your belts on, dears.

You're going for a ride."

Outside the lab the summer's heat was modulated by the stratospheric sulphate aerosols that gave the sky an opalescent glimmer. The meadows stretching inland for some distance beyond the lab terminated several kilometres off, at the edge of a forest.

Angus hustled the splices into a small two-wheeled tumblebug and then programmed its artilect driver via his smart tats. With the door still open, he regarded his protégés for one last melancholy time.

"Your ride will take you about two hundred kilometres away from here. It can't be further, because I need the bug back here before Mapinta notices it was used. I've disabled its satellite tracking as well, so no one can follow. Once it stops, climb out. Then you are on your own. You must search out the Bruja Dellaselva. She's the only one who might be able to help you now."

The splices nodded sincerely. "The Bruja, the Bruja. We'll find her!"

Angus leaned into the car to hug Castor and Villette. Their coarse fur tickled his nose and made him sneeze. The splices laughed.

When he closed the door the car took off and he returned to the lab to seed a slurry of lysed cells, equivalent in kilos to the weight of the two splices, with the signature organic traces that would convince Mapinta he had melted down his own children.

The tumblebug motored silently off, heading back to the lab, and Villette and Castor looked about them in wonder. They had never been out of the lab before in their short lifetime, but had seen several nature documentaries on the Chimera Channel, and so the environment was not utterly foreign to them. The cultivar trees, with their symmetrically positioned limbs and black high-efficiency foliage, created an atmosphere more of a cathedral than an old school wilderness. Low shrubs with fractal branches created an undergrowth like ranked pews, to complete the illusion. But, even so, the place definitely seemed removed from civilisation and from the immediate presence of humanity – hence it was scary to the pair, who had known only Angus and Mapinta as companions. All about them were strange noises, and their sensitive noses quivered to an array of odd odours while their whiskers vibrated to every pulse of air.

The splices cautiously kept their paws on the handles of their little knives as they looked around their tiny clearing for signs of a path or trail. But they found none, and soon sat down resignedly at the base of tree.

"Where do we go now?" asked Villette.

"To the Bruja. Papa Woodman told us!"

"Yes, the Bruja. But where is she?"

Castor had no answer for that. Instead he opened his pouch and took out a serving of food. "Let's eat."

"Not too much! Sore stomachs! Save most for later."

After they had finished their treat and thoughtfully buried the wrappers in the duffish soil, Villette said, "Walking anywhere is better than sitting here."

"Yes, you are right."

"Don't go back toward home though. Danger."

Castor sniffled. "Never to see Papa Woodman again."

"We have to do what he said."

"Yes, what he said."

The splices began walking, choosing to head in the same direction that the lowering sun was indicating.

Soon the general benignity of their surroundings relieved their tension and anxiety, and they began to enjoy watching the birds and insects and land crabs and small mammals go about their business. All that was lacking to provide comfort was any kind of sizable stream or lake where they could refresh themselves and possibly undertake their wonted activities.

"But maybe," said Castor thoughtfully, "even if we find water, we shouldn't stay."

"Why?"

"Too close to home yet. Home where danger comes."

"Yes, too close."

As twilight was falling they came to a new border of the forest. The land here turned to open savannah. Not wishing to be out and exposed during the night, they halted and made an unsatisfying semblance of a lodge under some bushes. There they huddled for the whole night, hardly sleeping, hugging and grooming each other, half-unsheathing their knives with every howl of predator or cry of victim or challenge of rival.

In the morning they had some food from their pouches, found a tree bearing mango pawpaws that afforded some nice juice, then set out across the grasslands, loaded down with the fruit.

After several hours they came upon a city of giant earthen mounds rearing from the prairie. Termites the size of Papa Woodman's thumb scurried in and out and around the mounds.

"They won't bother us," Castor said, with more confidence than he felt.

"Maybe they know things," Villette ventured.

"We can see," said Castor. He bravely advanced on a tower and rapped with some force on its organo-plastinated wall.

Castor's summons brought out a boil of termites. But the horde of insects did not descend the mound, instead congregating at the elevated entrance. They began to cluster and cohere and shape themselves until they had assumed the form of a blind human face. The lips made of many linked termites parted, and the voice emanating from termite throat and termite vocal cords and termite tongue came forth.

"You two are new here. Do you compete? Do you threaten? Must we strip the flesh from your bones?"

"No compete, no threaten! Just passing by. Looking for the Bruja. Bruja Dellaselva."

"Yes, of course, the witch of the woods. You might interest her. Continue west."

"West?"

"The sun moves from east to west as the day goes on."

"Oh, of course."

"Her home is beyond the Twisted Forest. But even if you reach its borders, she will know you are there, and find you."

"If we reach? Why if? Trouble? Danger?"

"The Laurentian Rewilding is an unconstrained, unmediated bioregion with apex predators in large numbers. We do not think you are at the top of the food chain. Goodbye."

The face fell apart into scores of individual termites, and Castor and Villette realised they would learn no more.

Heading forever west, covering nearly fifty kilometres a day, the pair took three days to cross the grasslands. Each night they took turns keeping watch, for they had to get some sleep in order to maintain their energy for the long hike. Luckily they had no encounter more scary or dangerous than the one with a large many-legged snake, which chose to stalk them for several kilometres while always keeping a safe distance from their knives and whispering half-heard endearments and evil persuasions which the splices resolutely ignored.

At last they came to the margin of the Twisted Forest, and knew immediately why it was thus called. Springing from sandy soil, the forest was comprised of gnarly, fuzzy Joshua trees, all as tall as ten-storey buildings. Yucca and cacti and mesquite formed the lower levels of the woods. Luckily for the newcomers, these smaller growths did not constitute an unbreachable wall, but rather permitted a kind of labyrinthine passage into the depths of the place.

"We are here," said Villette. "The Bruja will sense us."

"Maybe," said Castor, "we should go in a little deeper, so she can sense us good."

"And to get something to drink. Remember that show? Where humans drank from the spiny plants?"

"Yes, a good idea. Villette, you are so smart! I could not live without you."

"And Castor, you are so brave. You always stayed between me and the talky snake!"

During the crossing of the grasslands, the splices had derived their drinks from the mango pawpaws they had taken with them, but the amount of liquid the fruit provided had been barely sufficient.

Venturing into the maze, the splices identified what looked like the most succulent cactus, and had soon sliced into it. The liquid it provided was not particularly tasty, but did its job. While they drank, three-legged road runners and jackalopes came to share the bounty.

After wandering for a while, the splices approached a sizable jumbled rocky outcropping, where various niches and alcoves seemed to offer some welcome shade. The temperatures and sunlight were not dangerous, but merely uncongenial for such water-loving creatures.

They attained a little shallow cave just a few feet up the stony slope, and quickly fell asleep.

Castor and Villette awoke to rough handling and the sensation of ropes or vines being wound about their limbs. Opening their eyes, they found themselves at the mercy of a pack of cyanomorphs, grinning coyote-based creatures as big as their victims, strutting about on two legs and using their forepaws to bind Castor and Villette. Once secured and stripped of their pouches and weapons, the splices were lifted up and the cyanomorphs trotted away with them.

The village of the dog people consisted of huts woven of yucca stalks and leaves, centred around a spring. Castor and Villette were dumped unceremoniously on the ground. Females and children rushed out of the huts to join the hunters. The children kicked the splices while the females pinched their flesh to estimate their ratio of tasty fat to bone. The coyotes soon had a large fire going in a pit from which reared the forking supports that would hold two spits. The whole tribe began to dance and howl their delight at such a fine meal.

Castor said, "A bad end, Villette. We were not smart enough."

"Be brave, Castor. We yet live."

The cynamorphs brought long branches that they threaded beneath the bonds on the splices, then lifted their victims up to bring them be suspended above the flames on the forked uprights.

Castor and Villette could feel the furnace-like heat of the fire –

And then they thumped to the ground!

Castor had landed on his back and so was able to look skywards There, descending from on high, was a human woman. But not an unaltered human woman.

She boasted huge white feathery wings with a ten-meter span. Instead of hair she sported a cap of matching plumage. She was bare chested to allow her wings total freedom, but wore bright yellow leggings that left bare her feet – clawed and grippy.

The sight of her had caused the cyanomorphs to run away. But the woman also carried a gun, had such a tactic been necessary.

Crunching to a sandy landing, the woman holstered her pistol. The cyanomorphs were all hiding in their shelters. She studied Castor and Villette at leisure, then said, "Unique, utterly unique." She reached down and grabbed them by the ropes and effortlessly hoisted them off the ground. With booming wings, she and the splices climbed the sky.

It seemed a long time that they were in flight, but later, as they would recount their adventures to admiring progeny, Castor and Villette speculated that perhaps their fright and wonder just seemed to make the journey take forever. Carried with their faces downward, they were able to watch all the passing landscape and contemplate how they would perish if they were let go, or if their bonds accidentally broke.

However long the flight, they could soon see what must be their destination: atop a sizable rounded green hill was a moderately big old-fashioned building of white stone that featured three domes on its roof. It was the only structure for kilometres around. Their saviour – who certainly must be the Bruja Dellaselva – aimed for the largest dome with its slot-like opening. Cupping and furling her wings to large degree, she dropped down through, landing inside with a little jolt.

"Whew! You babies didn't feel like you weighed much at first. But by the end –!"

The Bruja grabbed a handy pair of shears and soon had Castor and Villette freed. The splices stood shakily and rubbed their limbs, uncertain of their status. Looking around, they saw a lab and its equipment, all very much like that of Papa Woodman.

"Welcome to my home," said their rescuer. "Used to be the Allegheny Observatory. Not sure why they left it intact when they tore the rest of Pittsburgh down, but I'm glad they did. Name's Rima, what's yours?"

"I am Castor."

"And I am Villette."

"Are you the Bruja Dellaselva?"

Rima laughed. "So I'm told." She grabbed a flask off a shelf and gulped down the contents. "Ah, that stokes the good old *Quetzalcoatlus northropi* cells! Now, maybe you'll tell me what brought you to the Coyoodle dinner table."

Taking turns, Castor and Villette conveyed their story. Rima the Bruja listened closely.

"So old Woodman made you. That crazy bastard. Well, your kind might not have found a niche in the Passaic biome, but I think I have a place for you, not far from here. The Cleveland Urbmon is in near-term danger of being swamped by a rising Lake Erie, but I suspect you guys could hold it back. Except it would help if you were even bigger. Would you let me change you? It would mean going into my oven for a while. I'd need to recode the DNA in every single one of your cells, and then rebuild you from inside out. A truly gruesome prospect, I admit. But you wouldn't feel anything. I'd decouple your mentalities and you'd live virtually for a while. It'd seem like paradise. Well, do you trust me, or not?"

Castor and Villette exchanged hopeful glances. Castor said, "We must, I think." Villette concurred. "I like you. And we have no one else."

"Splendid. Let me just fab up some megatherium code, and we're good to go!"

In a short time Castor and Villette found themselves harnessed and wired and plumbed into place inside a kind of giant thermos bottle. Rima Bruja patted their heads gently and said with confidence, "Kids, you won't feel a thing."

She shut the capsule door and it began to fill with a complicated liquid that was not pure water. Castor and Villette were not afraid. Even when totally engulfed by the substance, they found they could still breathe.

And then they were elsewhere.

They were living on the banks of a beautiful alpine lake, with many others of their kind, playing and working and enjoying the unspoiled wilderness, free of human interventions or demands. Life was good, there was so much nice food, aspen twigs aplenty, and the days seemed to stretch happily on forever –

– until they came to an end.

Castor opened his eyes. He saw the original room where they had first landed. But it seemed smaller somehow. There was darling, essential Villette, also just opening her eyes! She looked mostly the same as she ever had, yet somehow different as well.

"So, how's it feel?"

Castor and Villette looked toward Rima's voice.

The Bruja was now half their size!

"You shrank," said Castor.

Villette said, "No, Castor – we grew!"

Sure enough, the splices were now enormous, their genome hybridised with the megatherium heritage.

"You guys'll be able to hold back all the Great Lakes now. But you'd better get busy breeding. I futzed with your procreative parameters a little. Forty-five-day gestation period, kits mature at six months. Go to it!"

Castor reached out a paw and by using both hands, Rima was able to shake it. Villette did the same. Although it was a tight squeeze, they were able to wedge themselves through the door of the Allegheny Observatory. Once outside, Rima Bruja pointed them towards Cleveland.

"Go forth and multiply! And you're big enough now, so don't take any shit from anyone, human or otherwise!"

Castor and Villette rambled off down the hillside, and into their future.

And so we are here today to tell their tale.

Goblin Autumn

Adrian Tchaikovsky

Be dutiful, O hatchling child, and serve your mother well,
Obedient, genteel and mild, and truth be sure to tell.
If you do not, then in the chill of winter's shortest day,
The goblins shall come working ill, and steal you all away.

In Thysalys' mind it *was* a child who had first come face to face with the goblins, the real goblins. Some child of the northern marches, where things had first got bad. Hungry from failed harvests; lonely because they were five or six years in the world and yet no younger siblings had hatched; panicky because the elders all knew something was wrong and their worry would have filtered down even to the youngest by then. They must have asked themselves, as hatchlings did, whether it was somehow their fault; whether stealing a handful of earth-sugar or breaking their broodmother's favourite pot had brought on the curse.

And then, one morning out trying to scratch sustenance from the dying fields, they would have looked up, movement in the corners of their lateral eyes, and seen... *them*. Just like in the stories but a thousand times worse, things that were like people, but stunted, spindly, huge-eyed, their faces sharp and jagged with teeth. And that child must have thought: *It's true, and they came for me just like the rhyme!* But not for long. Thysalys had seen ample evidence of how goblins treated any who fell into their clutches. Evidence mostly comprising gnawed gristle and discarded skin.

Thysalys was Spouse-Commander of the Senyral March, he was a warrior male in the prime of his life, a onetime consort of the Mother-Empress, victor in nine battles and eleven private duels. He was no hatchling child to fear cautionary rhymes. And yet he did fear. The Senyral was a northern territory. The goblin curse had lit upon it savagely. Today the lands he was steward of hosted less than a tenth of the population of twelve years back, the balance dead or fled south as refugees, leaving their lives behind for the goblins to pick over. His entire family's wealth and power was destroyed, leaving him with an empty title to warm him.

He had not given up, though, nor simply taken the blue flower and curled up in death like some of his peers. He had gone to the Brood-Empress. He had said: *Make use of me! Let me help you destroy the goblins and their curse.* And so she had.

He had travelled with armies before, young warrior-males with spears and bolt-throwers to be his strong arm. Then he had changed and done his turn as a broodmother for the family, and travelled with a host of sexless juveniles to lend him stature and pomp, and to tend his eggs. Then he had changed again, a warrior once more, just in time for the start of the end of the world.

Now he travelled alone, his long, body curled in the bowl of a chariot pulled by two warbeasts, the northern breed that were hardier and more intelligent than all others. They, at least, took the changing world in their stride, though he had heard the first laments of stablemasters whose charges had lain still within the shell for a year now, unwilling to hatch into a suddenly cruel world.

The Mother-Empress had sent him further north than he would like – not as far as his own desolate lands, but to where the goblins were even now encroaching. The day before, he had passed a burned-out farmhouse. There had been bodies, adults and juveniles both, and they had been chewed on. He had seen dead goblins too within the fire, their narrow, angular frames unmistakeable. Most likely the family had lit fires against them when they came, which had then burned out of control. Goblins lit no fires, though perhaps their sorcerers could raise and quell them, as they could do so many other things. Thysalys had never met a goblin sorcerer, but it was the consensus of the wise that the vermin were led by magicians who brought the curse that made fields barren at a touch, that killed off the good plants and set their own poisonous grass and roots to flourishing, that blighted clutches so that only one or two children might be born to a whole family in a year, or none.

In such a climate, the Empress was not short of offers. Every quack and charlatan, every would-be wise mother or sage had come to the throne begging largesse to work their miracles. Many had tried to vanish with the money, leaving only their false promises behind. Warriors such as Thysalys were called up, to hunt them down and show them that, goblins or not, the rule of law persisted.

So it was that the Empress, growing impatient, deluged with the desperation of her subjects, had sent him to The Learned Gysemme, the latest of the wise to try their luck. Gysemme had been tasked to devise a spell or a potion or a weapon to use against the goblins, and they had promised no miracles or instant cures. They were a creature of reason that had no truck with the numinous, they explained. By such mealy-mouthed measures they had sustained the Empress's patronage, and syphoned the Imperial coffers, for two years.

Two not entirely fruitless years, it was true. Thysalys understood that there was a new variety of mealgrass this Learned Gysemme had bred, which was more resistant to the goblin blight than anything previously known, and a poison that would kill off some of the goblins' own encroaching weeds without harming wholesome plants, but none of this was taking the war to the sorcerers. None of this separated goblin heads from goblin shoulders.

The Learned Gysemme always had another excuse, however. Their latest was a query for the Hadavyn Oracle, that miraculous yet impenetrable pronouncer, and Thysalys bore the answering tablets with him, engraved with neat yet impenetrable figures and diagrams. Let The Learned Gysemme find some sense in the baffling texts; they meant nothing to him.

He had come here last year, arriving at the gates with a naked blade to signal the Empress's waning patience. On that visit he had found himself cowed by his surroundings. Learned Gysemme, for all their protestations of science – he had been male then, but with the signs of change on him – had taken one of the elder temples as their lair, a structure that had stood for as long as anyone could remember. What gods, what rites had been remembered there back in the dawn of time before the Empire, only the Learned might speculate. To Thysalys, it seemed a poor place for science, but Gysemme had never been much concerned about the opinions of their peers.

Perhaps it was simply the murals that had led the Learned to take the place as their own, a salutary reminder of their duty to the Empress and to the world. Thysalys remembered sitting amidst the hushed bustle of the Learned's sexless assistants, staring up at the dome of the ceiling, on which was depicted, in a style somehow both elegant and primitive, the goblin wars.

Back when Thysalys had been young, everyone had known that such depictions were pure fancy, believed in only by children. That the world had belonged to the goblins, and that true people had been created from the soil to rise up and cast down the dwarfish, scuttling monsters, that was just a story, after all. Probably it was allegorical, though the Learned could argue the night through over what allegory was being invoked. And anyway, the old stories had happy endings. All the murals showed great hosts of stick-limbed goblins being reaped by heroes and warriors, cast into fires, thrown into the chasms of the earth. The old stories were filled with the horrors of the goblins, but with the triumphs of the true people, too.

For too long the first news of skittering, spindly monsters along the far northern coast was ignored. Even now there were southern nations, yet to feel the Curse, which refused to believe in anything other than a bad famine brought on by worse farming practices. Thysalys had personally had a dozen goblins stuffed and mounted, sent south with great ceremony to open the eyes of the complacent broodmothers and warrior lords down there.

The old temple stood upon a stub of hill looking over what had once been rich farmland. Now Thysalys rode through a wasteland, overgrown with saw-toothed goblin grass and the hunched, narrow-leaved bushes that also came with the curse, heavy-boughed with berries that killed any normal creature that ate them. Needless to say, the goblins would happily feast on the fruits of such plants, though only if no flesh was available.

And perhaps The Learned Gysemme has a plan for that, to breed a new strain of their plants that will poison them slowly, so that even their mage-lords die in agony, gripping their distended bellies, he thought, wringing some last drops of hope from his mind. *Or they will have a device that emits a sound or a smell they cannot abide, or a sigil that will break their spells and bring back the warm weather, or…* But he was neither sorcerer nor scientist and he could not guess. He was only resentful that the future of the world was in such uncertain hands as The Learned Gysemme.

The remnants of the scholar's people were out tending plots, barely more than ragged little gardens where once a whole farm had supported the temple's occupants. There were hooped tunnels of cloth put up along many of the rows to try and concentrate the sun's heat. Thysalys had seen similar measures deployed elsewhere to debatable success, but perhaps the Learned Gysemme had some special alchemy they applied that worked better.

Less than a dozen servants, he saw, and those just juveniles or old females past brooding age. The shortages and the Empress's waning indulgence towards this scholar had pared down her staff to these few.

Someone had obviously seen his chariot on its way, for The Learned Gysemme was at the temple gateway already, waiting for him. She had become a solid-bodied female, her six limbs fatter than he recalled but the fingers of her first pair still long and delicate. Her skin was dust-coloured, streaked with orange about her dorsal ridge, the automatic advertisement of a female ready to brood, though Thysalys was willing to bet she had no plans in that direction. Like many scholars, the Learned Gysemme had never had any patience for the complex and time-consuming demands of either gender's courtship.

She didn't seem pleased to see him, but then she must reckon the odds were he was here bringing the tail end of the Empress's generosity. That was indeed in Thysalys's gift, assuming the Learned had not finally produced some weapon against the goblins.

"You have it?" the scholar demanded, as Thysalys uncoiled from his chariot's bowl and wound his way to her. For a moment he wasn't sure what she meant, but then understood her thoughts had been fixed solely on the prophecy tablets from Hadavyn.

Thysalys twitched down the sinuous length of his body. "From the deep chambers of the Mother-Empress, who sends her humble captain, Spouse-Commander of the Senyral March, with greetings to-"

"How much time do you truly think we have?" The Learned Gysemme broke in acidly. "Thysalys, it's dusk. I need to get my people behind sealed gates."

Thysalys' body lashed angrily, but he had to concede the time of day. The sun was low in the sky, the fickle warmth leaching away from heartbeat to heartbeat. Goblins preferred to raid in broad daylight, but their huge eyes were better than any wholesome thing's at night, and the cold was their ally.

"I have the word of the Oracle," he said stiffly. It seemed too much, suddenly. The farms failed, the clutches sat cold and still, the goblins grew bolder and bolder as their curse took hold, but to lose all the intricacies of polite address...

"Come inside," the scholar told him. "Come, dine. Everyone else, finish and have the doors sealed, and hope the goblins don't just tear up everything by its roots."

"They come this far, then?" he asked, passing through the temple gateway alongside her.

"A few, one or two immature specimens caught in the traps. More will come soon."

"And you will drive them off," Thysalys said. "With your new weapon."

The Learned Gysemme just held out a hand for the tablets, the webbing between her fingers ragged where she had chewed absently at it.

"If you can make any sense of them." Thysalys gave up the carefully wrapped package with bad grace.

"Oh, I'm no newcomer to the Oracle's notation."

"I would have thought you were too much a creature of reason to trust such pronouncements," he tried to goad her.

She regarded him with calm eyes, pale blue but already showing a webbing of gold. This would be her last turn as a female, he realised, probably her last fertile phase. "Your prejudices against the Oracle are based on your ignorance of what it *is*," she said precisely. "Anyway, come eat. It's not much compared to the Empress's table, I'm sure, but we make do."

The scholar's people had all gathered for the meal, each coiled in their own nook as the spartan repast was shared out. The food was basic, coarse and bland, but Thysalys had been warrior enough not to develop a refined palate. Above them was the grand mural he remembered, the goblins being driven to their deaths by the heroes of elder days.

Gysemme saw where his attention focused and nodded at it. "I have collected stories from across the world, these last few years, that tell of the old wars with the goblins."

"Stories," Thysalys said dismissively.

"True ones, though. Over in Szyreen one of my colleagues has even discovered what he thinks is a battlefield thousands of years old, beneath the city foundations. The ruin of weapons and of bodies, shells and teeth all perfectly preserved, even the impressions of bodies. He thinks a volcanic eruption must have covered it all with ash."

"And he thinks he's found goblins," Thysalys finished for her, his body curving into a posture of polite disbelief.

"*Be dutiful, O hatchling child*," Gysemme recited. "I daresay you were a wild creature straight from the egg, Thysalys. They told you the old goblin rhymes so often you know them by heart?"

"Who doesn't know them?"

"Before they were children's songs they were great and serious stories, the domain of adults and the Learned," she said sadly. "So knowledge passes down the generations. In the first stories we have, which are by no means the first there were, it is not children but rulers who are so chided. Be honest, rule well, spread order, or the goblins shall come and tunnel beneath your walls and tear down your works. There are a hundred stories of kings in the ancient days who strayed from the path of wisdom and saw the goblins undo all they had."

Without really deciding to, Thysalys had drawn a blade. "Are you saying the Brood-Empress-"

"No, no no no. Not by any means. But those are the stories that lie beneath our sad little attempts to make our hatchlings behave. Stories of fighting goblins."

"And winning." Thysalys indicated the mural.

"And winning," Gysemme agreed.

"So how did we win? Find the weapons we used. Find the poisons, the spells. They must be set out in some of these old tales you collect, or why collect them?" The logic seemed irresistible to him but The Learned Gysemme just paid close attention to her dinner.

At last the scholar said, "I will take a day or so, I suspect, to go through the tablets. And then I will have a conclusion for you. But tomorrow I should have a little demonstration for you that will be of interest." The line of her body did not show any great excitement or optimism.

"What do you expect to find in the tablets?" Thysalys asked her.

"Only confirmation." The rest of the meal passed without conversation.

The Learned Gysemme spent most of the next day closeted with the Oracle's cryptic pronouncements while Thysalys rode about what had been the Temple's estate, now just a desert of cold earth and abandoned villages. Past noon he surprised three goblins that had come creeping out across the fields, harvesting goblin grass and sour berries. Goading his warbeasts forwards he ran them down, crushing two beneath his wheels and then slithering from the chariot to take his spear to the third. It made little attempt to fight him, only attempting to skitter away on its long limbs. After he brought the creature down he could only stare at its twisted body in disgust. It was like a mockery of a person: same long body, but dwarfish and barbed, same number of limbs but thin and weirdly angled. In some of the cautionary stories they spoke, to tempt hatchlings into making bad choices, but Thysalys had never heard them make anything other than a hissing that was nothing like language.

That evening, Gysemme came out of her chambers looking ill-tempered, but she had promised to show him something and apparently that was still her intention. Firstly she had some manner of museum, a display of ancient bodily remains and artifacts. Most of the latter were primitive, unthinkably old and crude. He saw edges and hammers made of stone, and some jagged curves that might be meant as spearheads.

"Will you tell me goblins made these for their wars?" he demanded.

"Hold it." Gysemme presented him with a stone that had been worked into the form of a knife, half rounded to fit the hand, half semi-translucent cutting edge. It sat within his grip remarkably well, its very weight instructing him in how he might put it to use.

"You've seen goblin hands, no doubt," The Learned Gysemme went on. "Not entirely unlike ours, but they cannot oppose all their digits so. No, these tools were made by people not so unlike us, an unthinkably long time ago." She let a shrug ripple down her body. "But what of that? Come with me, I'll show you another thing. I have a cold box here. You've heard of such things?"

"Parlour tricks," Thysalys said.

"Actually a remarkable appliance of scientific principles only recently understood," she corrected him mildly. "But it is true that the end result has mostly been put to use by the great and powerful to preserve food in their larders."

She brought him to a heavy glass case wrapped with pipes, nothing he hadn't seen used for exactly the purposes she described. Within was an indistinct lump of something.

"This one I've improved, pushed to its very limits," she went on. "It's been holding its contents in the cold for seven days now. Seven days is about right, you see. A little cold snap or a chilly night won't do it."

"And this will help us break the goblin curse, will it?"

The Learned Gysemme sighed. "The correct question is, 'But what did you put in there, O Learned One?' to which I would answer, why, nothing but a heap of soil and one of these." She held out a large spherical stone, black, with gold mottling. He had seen similar trinkets countless times, worn as decoration by the low-born who could not afford real gems.

"An ornalith?" he asked.

"As the formal language has it. And in the vulgar?"

"Goblin eggs," he recalled.

With some showmanship Gysemme hauled open the cold box. Inside was indeed a mound of soil, cold enough that frost had cracked it and limned the fissure edges. Cold, but not death, though. He saw a multitude of shoots and sproutings – goblin grass and other less recognisable plants, but all with the look of the new species that had begun to run riot over the northern farmlands. He saw some crawling things, too – the thorned worms that ate anything and everything, the stinging flatbugs, vermin that the goblin curse engendered from the soil.

And at the back, he saw what he might even have thought was a hatchling, if he didn't know better. That was another thing the stories said, that goblin children fresh from the egg would be left in place of the real thing.

He had his blade out instantly, and Gysemme made no protest as he ran the hissing little monster through. Who knew how fast the thing might mature, after all?

"How did you make them grow there?" he demanded, then with sudden hope, "You understand how the curse works?"

"I'm afraid I do, yes," Gysemme agreed.

"And you can undo it?"

But she only sighed again.

He looked from her to the dead goblin child. "You said… The common folk call them 'goblin eggs.'"

"And in this the old folk wisdom is entirely correct." Gysemme shrugged. "Thysalys, we Learned have known for three generations that ornaliths were the eggs of *something*, but as they never hatched we thought they were fossils, dead remnants. We didn't know they were just waiting…"

"We can gather them up, destroy them, so that no more goblins will ever hatch!" Thysalys declared, suddenly excited. "Then we can raise an army and kill those that remain in the north, to stop they hatching more clutches…" Her expression was so sad – sad for *him* and his doomed enthusiasm – that he trailed off.

"That will not end the curse," she said. "I am going back to the Oracle's pronouncements. Tomorrow morning I'll give you my final word for the Empress."

"If you have no weapon for her, I am empowered to bring an end to your work here," Thysalys warned, and as he said the words he realised it *was* a warning, and not a threat. He wanted Gysemme to have found *something*.

Gysemme's body quivered; she was blackly amused at the thought. "Do what you must," she advised him, and glided from the room.

He woke late the next morning, his body cued to take its trigger from the sound of servants already risen to smooth his way in the world. The temple was silent, and he had a sudden stab of panic that the goblins had come in the night and murdered everyone save he.

When he entered the eating hall, though, The Learned Gysemme was already coiled in a nook at one end of the room, and a scant breakfast was set for two. The rest of the space was cluttered with the Oracle's incomprehensible tablets.

"Where are your people?" Thysalys demanded. He had seen not another living thing, and a glance outside had shown the barren fields devoid of workers.

"I roused them before sunrise," Gysemme said softly. "I told them to return to their families and those whom they cared for. I ended their service."

"They were servants of the Empress, not yours alone," Thysalys grumbled, though the point of etiquette seemed a secondary consideration. "Do I take it this is merely in anticipation of my ending your work here? That you have admitted failure?"

"Yes and no." Gysemme's body curved ambiguously. "Sit. Drink."

She had set out two bowls, but was careful to keep one from him, enough that his hackles lifted with suspicion.

"You think I'll poison you?" she asked wearily.

"To stop word of your failure getting to the Empress."

She darted forwards, the long tube of her tongue flicking out to drain an inch from his bowl before returning to her own. "There." Her coils sagged. "You have done a turn as a broodmother, have you not, Thysalys?"

"And as a spouse." He cocked his head sidelong, showing his puzzlement at the change of subject. "Before the trouble; before the goblins cursed our eggs."

"But you would have had the wealth and power to overcome their curse," Gysemme pointed out, in a gently didactic way.

He shrugged down to his tail tip. "Now, yes. Then..." Probably still yes; his mother's lineage had been close to the Imperial line for generations. Keeping a room heated for days was beyond the resources of menials, but the great and the good would burn all the grass and coal and wood in the world to warm their eggs long enough to see them hatch.

Gysemme was watching him carefully, as though waiting for him to leap to some revelation, but whatever it was evaded him and she twitched with irritation.

"You are thinking of your cold box trick with the ornalith," he told her. "I do not appreciate the comparison between those monsters and the eggs of our people. That is in poor taste."

"And so science is ever held in knots," Gysemme muttered. She spread the tablets out on the table, putting them in some intricate order he could not follow. "Thysalys, do you know what the Oracle of Hadavyn actually is?"

"Unreliable," he told her promptly.

"Well, yes, but only if you ask it the wrong questions," Gysemme shot back. "It doesn't care who would make a good spouse, or which commander will win a battle."

"It fell from the sky, the stories say."

"That much is true." Frustration squirmed through her body and crooked her fingers. "And my question is unfair. Even the Learned do not truly understand everything about the Oracle. But yes, it fell from the sky, and it is a device, a made thing of strange metals fashioned an age ago in some other place, somewhere in the heavens. And its eye is still on the heavens, or else it receives word from some agents who remain in place above us, and if you ask it the right questions, it will tell the exact and complete truth." She indicated the regimented tablets. "It will even show its working."

"Why is this important" Thysalys asked her, frustrated himself. "This is your weapon against the goblins?"

"This is my understanding of the goblins."

"That they come from the *heavens?*"

A whiplash of annoyance went through her. "I would need an axe to open your mind to new ideas, Thysalys!" And then she shuddered, a curious motion that had nothing to do with mood.

"Are you sick?" Thysalys asked, half rising from his niche.

"Just listen," Gysemme told him. "I will make you understand this if it…" A bleak quiver of humour, "if it kills me. For you must tell the Empress the truths I have uncovered. I am the most Learned of the Learned, Thysalys. In these late days I have understood it all, and you must try to understand me. I asked the

Oracle about the sun."

Thysalys stared blankly at her.

"The sun, Thysalys! The great hot ball of light in the sky!"

He ground his teeth. "Explain to my why this is relevant. This sounds like all the usual nonsense you Learned waste your days on. How does it break the goblin curse?"

"Ah, the curse," she agreed, "that those wicked goblin magicians have inflicted on us. The curse that kills our crops and stills our eggs and wakes strange creatures from the earth, including the goblins themselves. A clever curse they've laid on us, that encompasses their own generation, don't you think?"

"Yes, very clever. And you have not found a way to defeat the curse or wipe out the goblins, for all your learning," Thysalys accused her. "And now you want to talk about the *sun*?"

"I asked if the sun changed, and how it changed. The Oracle has been down here with us for thousands of years, and it has been up *there* for far longer than that."

"The sun... changed?" Thysalys radiated bafflement. "The sun is... the sun. In the winters it is colder, in the summers, warmer, is that what you mean?"

"In a sense. But winter and summer are not changes to the sun, you see, merely the tilt of our world bringing us closer or further way – that is why the Southern Isles know summer while winter visits us here. You must have heard that."

Thysalys agreed impatiently.

"But the sun does grow warmer and colder. That is what the Oracle confirmed to me. For years now, the sun has been cooling. And, in the future, it will grow warm again, and the cycle will repeat."

A sudden surge of hope leapt in Thysalys. "Wait..." He almost lost the thought, so revolutionary was it, but under her expectant gaze he soldiered on. "Your cold box hatched the goblins. So if the sun grows cool, you say the goblins just... hatch in the northern lands, where it is colder anyway? That enough cold days and nights will bring them out, and all the vile plants and beasts that come with them. And… when it is warm again…"

"Their eggs will lie still, and ours will hatch once more, be they never so old, yes. So in a way, we have hope." Gysemme drained her bowl.

"And there is no curse?"

"And no magicians," she confirmed. "There is just the mechanism of the heavens, that neither knows us nor cares about our fate."

Thysalys leapt up and slapped his hands against his flanks in delight. "Then we must simply endure!" he cried. "I will tell the Empress that there will be a harsh time, a cold time, but we will wait, and the sun will grow warmer again…" He slowed. "But the Oracle cannot be right. Or you have not understood it. You said the sun cools and warms, cools and warms, but until this plague of them, who ever saw a goblin? Not my mother, nor hers, nor any before them."

Gysemme's head tilted back until she had directed his attention to the painted ceiling, the goblin host being put to flight by shining heroes.

"But… stories… hatchling tales," Thysalys said.

"And before that, legends," Gysemme told him. "And, before that, history. Long-ago history, transmuted almost entirely to myth by the time anyone had devised a way to write anything down, then debased further over the generations, the long generations when nobody so much as saw a goblin." Another shudder went through her, and Thysalys was alarmed to see the colours of her skin greying. "The Oracle's calculations confirm all. The cycle of the sun's warmth and cooling is one of more than four thousand years."

The enormity of the thought stilled Thysalys entirely. He had no body language to express his shock.

"Those tools I showed you, they were unearthed beneath the temple. This is a good site to live – there is water, a good view, good earth. People have lived here for as long as they've lived anywhere, and before them… dig and you find the goblin layer, the preserved shells and teeth that are definitely *theirs*, not *ours*, though the differences are less than you'd think. Sometimes you find made-things, too, stones carved with spirals or with holes bored into them. Nothing we'd think much of, but enough to set a scholar thinking..." She sighed at all the lost knowledge in the world, seeming to shrivel as he watched her. "But below that, Thysalys, ah, below that is another layer. Those tools were buried beneath even the goblin layer, older still, thousands of years older. They were the tools of our ancestors. They represent the apex of our civilisation then before the sun cooled again and the goblins came."

"But we are greater now," Thysalys pointed out. "We have metal tools. We have our Empire. We have *you*, the Learned, to understand this."

"Sometimes understanding is its own curse," The Learned Gysemme whispered. "We are greater now, but not because we built on what they had. We are a summer flower, Thysalys, and the autumn is coming."

"But you said… the sun will grow warm again. Our eggs will hatch."

"Four thousand years, Thysalys," she croaked. "The cold will reign for more than four thousand years. The Oracle confirms it. And generations of goblins will come and go, and they will puzzle over our remnants and perhaps even raise their own halls and build their own empires. And they will panic, when the world grows warm; they will talk about the curse of people, as we arise at the equator and begin to drive them towards the poles. But those people will not remember us, Thysalys. They will hatch out ignorant of our empires and our learning. Tell the Empress to plant libraries, perhaps, and hope those who come after can somehow decipher what we have written. Tell her to commission vast monuments depicting all we have achieved, that they might know we were even here. Tell her… tell her…"

He understood then. "What did you drink?"

"Tevys, the blue flower," she sighed. "The traditional

punishment for failed scholars, is it not? And painless, as I can now attest. Because I cannot bear to see it all lost, Thysalys. I cannot bear the thought of our descendants hatching into the renewed sun and knowing nothing of us, and perhaps not even devising stone tools before their time, too, is done. Or perhaps they will exceed us, and know peace and prosperity such as we cannot dream of, and build devices like the Oracle to live in the heavens, and even then the sun will bring them low. Even the greatest of us must meet that autumn, Thysalys, and the curse lies on the goblins as much as upon us."

Myths of Sisyphus

Allen Ashley

I don't claim to understand this Entanglement technology that enables a version or vision of me to be present on Sisyphus Three. When people back home express surprise that I'm not an expert in the process, I simply respond by asking them how the engine of their hover car works or whether they could grab a screwdriver and fix their food synthesiser if it started to produce soup instead of sandwiches.

The latest advanced Entanglement technology keeps my body floating somnolently in a preservation tank beneath the Sussex Hills; my projection or my avatar, and, more importantly, my waking consciousness is present here in a visible though somewhat insubstantial form on a planet some sixty-nine light-years distant.

It's been a little while since I've spoken to anybody on Earth. The mission takes all my attention and keeps me here… if I can be said to be anywhere exactly.

No one has managed to come up with a term for what I do any more precise than 'xeno-anthropologist'. The 'anthro' phrase remains troubling, setting up a hierarchy or paradigm of perfection against which all else must be evaluated. I know what my late father would have said. In fact, I can remember precisely what he said, which was: "They send us out to log their histories and mythologies so that we can kid ourselves that we've respected and catalogued their culture… before we destroy it. Like white settlers collecting animal totems from the Native Americans. Like hunters with trophies of extinct wild animals."

I miss his cynicism. I feel a lack of closure, since the accidental atomising of his body and consciousness, some ten Earth years ago, left me with no focus for my mourning.

Yet his influence, couched in world-weary sarcasm, has caused me to follow in his astral footsteps.

I have been on Sisyphus Three a while now but have yet to weary of this sand-sculpted world with its purple washed-out skies and low-hanging, huge, solitary moon. I have grown close enough to one of the dominant species, the semi-aquatic Gillairee, to begin to learn the myths and history that define their present-day actions.

At first, they took me to their immersion place. Even this was a secret only given to a trusted few. I watched them dive and dip and disappear and then felt somewhat bereft. There was just the one large ocean on this planet and a couple of smaller seas constricted by tectonic land masses. I stood a long time awaiting their return. Eventually, I decided they were not coming back for me and so set off back inland, where I later struck up a lengthy, friendly game of hide and seek with one of the Banantians. These vaguely dog-like but herbivorous creatures roamed happily through the arable foothills and meadows in what I had designated as the eastern quarter of this super-continent. The Banantian told me its name was "Califer" and nuzzled its soft nose into my hand. Its friendliness made me believe that I could actually feel the wet warmth of its companionship through the projection.

A Gillaireean returned for me two diurnal cycles later. Her name was Mithra.

"Darren," she said – although her soft, overlarge lips rendered my moniker as somewhat lispy – "we will show you what we dare."

On Earth, we have tales of mermaids. Our dominant culture always pictures them as young, pert-breasted women with flowing yellow hair and enticing mystery hidden within the upper folds of their piscine tails. Mithra would win no Terran beauty contests or gain traction on competitive social media profiles. Her head and face were functional: heavily-lidded eyes, internal ears, a mouth that gaped wide like the late blue whale; multiple gills flapping constantly at the side of what passed for a neck created a constant, irritating background chitter. Closer to a sludge-green seal than the half-human demi-goddess of male sexual desire.

The deep water was murkier than I had anticipated. As we descended, Mithra casually ingested the occasional serving of what I took to be a krill-like substance that infested the gloopy liquid all around us. I found it hard to gaze any great distance through this animate glue.

At last we arrived at a habitation. Several dozen of her species – family, friends, lovers – floated in undulating lines, observing our approach. They were all as unclothed as my guide yet, on first glance, quite sexless: their vital reproductive organs tucked modestly beneath flaps of streamlined skin.

I cursed myself for not having brought a gift but really, in my somewhat incorporeal state, how could I have done so and what would I have brought anyway?

Mithra deferred to the tallest of her kin, one I assumed to be a leader of some sort. He had a masculine stance and, without great ceremony, collected a small stack of mundane rocks on the seabed in front of us. He banged two together three times. I didn't hear the sound but felt the vibration of the sonic waves as a slight interference with my projection strength. Then, with a few swirls of his flipper hands, he created a sudden, localised vortex. I felt my being drawn into this whirlpool and let the necessary happen so that I could absorb their history.

Back when time was young and there were no flitters in the air or mahjags beneath the ground, the first people lived at altitude in natural castles and garrets on the softly orbiting moon. Life was free from care and every day we would open our eyes to the beautiful sight of the down planet floating below us like a vast, natural jewel on a bed of deep mauve sky. We worshipped the distant being some call Ginalus even though we knew that he / she / it was absent and unlikely ever to return to lend a helpful appendage to our quiet lives.

Sustenance for the body and the soul; no unnecessaries but also no wants. This should have been enough to keep us contented until the yawning maw and the big freeze of astral death ends diurnality. However, there were some amongst our kind who wanted more for themselves. Which meant less for others. They erected barriers and obstacles, enclosures and other structures. The philosophers argued as to whether these hard palaces kept the unwelcome out or instead held the unwary imprisoned within.

It was a moot discussion, for soon a great conflict arose which tore apart families, tribes and, indeed, the whole population. By a succession of unfair deceits and betrayals, one new group proclaimed themselves as the victors. They styled their hateful coterie as the creatures of air. In their short-lived but future-defining spell of mastery, it is believed that they rounded up and concentrated all those they considered to be inferior. The captive people were forcibly bred with seals so that they could no longer be considered as true blood of the first times. Exiled to the planet beneath – a place less jewel-like in close proximity – this newly-moulded, sad offshoot species was doomed to remain at or below sea level forevermore.

They call us pond scum. Our only hope is that a time is coming soon when we will return to our rightful domain. By fair means or foul. We call it the Feast of Unity, but new dominance might be a better term.

Our lives are a misery; we exist in tears.

I needed time alone to process these findings. I found myself a quiet corner at the edge of a forest and blithely meditated in that superior, unconcerned way we humans have developed whilst doubtless the constant red in tooth and claw battle for survival continued all around me. Arachnids, fungi, mosses, higher plants, insects and smaller mammals – or their Sisyphean equivalents, it's pointless to split hairs over minor species and genus variations – fought for food, territory and the continuation of their type. I floated above them like an oblivious deity.

I considered breaking the connection and returning to Earth. But there was at least one other side of the story to uncover yet and we xeno-anthropologists like our information to be as full as possible.

*

Eventually, my isolation was broken by the appearance of a small pack of Banantians. Somewhere between large dog and small cattle, they circled me at a respectful distance until their leader broke free of the group and approached me with pointed head bowed. Up close, I determined that our paths had crossed previously, a few revolutions ago, and that she and her kind bore me no ill will. The universal translation device earned its corn interpreting both her lowing and her thought projections into comprehensible Earth-speak. My projection stroked her neck, shoulder and back and she nuzzled in comfortably like an old friend.

I was irresistibly reminded of my youth when my life might have taken a different turn. I was in love with fellow student Lorna and fascinated by her family's farming background. I spent a couple of vacations with her, helping out at her parents' smallholding, getting righteously dirty and sweaty and building up musculature through meaningful toil rather than mindless headphone hours at the gym.

I made friends with the sheepdog Jessie and the ponies Pepper and Spice and even the gaggle of turkeys led by Wilbur, Martha and Clementine. The move back to nature, or a human-controlled version of it, appealed to me for a while and I pictured Lorna and myself dropping out of our studies to live off the land on a small, available plot next door that her father showed me.

But then it was Christmas and the plates were piled high with home-grown produce. I tucked into the hearty food but gagged somewhat on the grey-white meat.

"Was that Wilbur?" I asked afterwards. "Or Martha? Are we eating somebody we've named?"

"Don't be squeamish, Darren," Lorna responded. "The animals are our property. They serve a function. Harden your heart."

But I couldn't. How could you name and befriend a creature only to consume it? Clearly, I was not cut out for the harsh realities of the agrarian life.

I remained with this group of Banantians for some time, travelling with the pack and learning that they weren't as strictly vegetarian as I'd supposed. If the opportunity arose to catch and devour some of the small, ground-dwelling, rodent-like creatures that scurried across our path, then they acted with speed and efficiency.

My guide, Califer, intrigued me. She was far more perceptive and intelligent than I had first assumed. She opened her thoughts to me as if we had been friends for many years. And yet there hung an almost visible cloud of fatalism about her and her companions. A sense that this easy-going semi-nomadic grazing and philosophising life could not last and might be brutally truncated quite soon. I probed – gently – but could not elicit full details. I was left only with vaguely expressed – and mostly masked – fears concerning a time she called "the Round Up". Perhaps this presaged the return of the absent deity Ginalus; perhaps it equated to the slow heat-death of the universe, made explicable in Banantian terms. Her mental barriers held firm and I stopped asking.

What she did tell me was how to get in touch with the Flahelians, the airborne humanoids who dwelt on Sisyphus Three's gravitationally close moon.

Califer absented herself from the slightly nervous pack and led me to a deserted beach where the great satellite appeared to hang lower and closer in the mauve-tinged sky; so much so that I was starting to reassess the orb as a sister world.

"Wait here," she said. "They will come for you."

Perhaps the mass and the pull were making her uncomfortable. Whatever: she was gone before I could say thanks or enquire whether *they* would also come for *her* if she lingered too long.

The constellations that I'd plotted during the early days of my visit were fractured or obscured at this spot. The looming presence of the moon made me feel somewhat tired and a tad confused – even though I was only present in my avatar state. Time bent at this liminal intersection between two worlds and I could not discern whether the moments dragged or raced by. Perhaps both, in some bizarre fashion. The best way I can describe the effect is that strange pressure one experiences when trying to push two powerful magnets of the same polarity together. Repeatedly.

Then suddenly the Flahelians were around me. What I first mistook for warped mouth and nose features turned out simply to be removable air filters. Their dorsal paired wings were stubby, transparent and seemingly incapable of lifting them off the ground. Yet we had thought the same about bumblebees.

They were largely hairless, naked and with a greyish skin tone. Hands reached out to grab and to guide the avatar me and in a whirling flurry we began the ascent, guided by gossamer strings that were imperceptible from most angles. Our movements were staccato and I feared that these unpredictable, sudden motions might break my link with Earth. Might even cause a cardiac arrest or shutdown.

Yet surely I had signed up for just such adventure, whether real, virtual or entangled? I tried to remain calm and centred although I felt like I had been transplanted into the jerky whirring of an old cine film.

At last we were there and I loosened my tether and let everything settle around me until I was ready to initiate further communication.

I saw much of their society, which seemed a lot freer and more open than many that I'd studied on Earth in the text archives. Once or twice I even pondered whether I had ascended to paradise. The Flahelians used their wings less for motive flight and more in the form of courtly mating rituals. I even witnessed a few of the subsequent couplings – performed in front of my ever-inquisitive eyes without apparent embarrassment on the part of the participants. It made me think about how life might have been had I stayed with Lorna or sought out an earthbound profession in our thriving cities.

Maybe I melded into the background so comfortably that they forgot about my presence. Whatever, it was some further time before one of their number – a well-endowed male called Ristus – consented to give me the potted history of their race.

At some cost. He pulled at the edges of one wing, plucked a few scales with a visible wince. He threw them up in a small handful. They spun like see-through sycamore seeds. "Helicopters" I had called them as a boy…

Back when time was young and the green had yet to carpet and clog the dryness, our people lived in harmony within the one great ocean on the original world. Shielded were we from the harsh rays of the sun and the gritty winds that wrapped their itchy cloaks around any who dared brave the rocky surface. We should have stayed where we were, floating in liquid heaven, and should have resisted any urge to conquer or subsist in inimical climes just beyond the safety.

But some among the children of our now eternally absent and angry god Ginalus were unsatisfied with all that we had. They saw imperfection where there was only difference. They concocted division where there was only natural and necessary separation.

We Flahelians know ourselves to be the defeated in that terrible, ancient war. We are the cast-offs; yes, as insignificant as spit or semen ejected into the air, where we are doomed to fizzle and dry. We have been expelled from the true home and wish only to return to the place below the waves where we originally came from. That is the aim of all our culture. Until that restoration is achieved, we are just the leftover grit particles from meaningless air bubbles.

He broke off from his oration and addressed me directly: "Isn't it truly the case that all sentient life was birthed in water? Isn't that what you believe on Earth, Darren?"

"Mostly, yes," I mumbled.

"We are trying to rectify matters before the yawning maw and the big freeze of astral death ends diurnality. We dream of a moment that we call the Feast of Unity; although righting of wrongs might be a better term… But for now, our lives are a misery; we exist in tears."

I had some tentative conclusions to take back to Earth. Some ideas upon which to build a thesis, at least: The golden age that has long passed; The expulsion from paradise; Feelings of loss, guilt, righteous anger even. This notion that seemed common to so many human and humanoid cultures: that our society is falling, that we are living in the twilight or tarnished age that inevitably follows the bright pinnacle of a time no-one actually remembers but which occupies and directs all our thoughts and actions nonetheless.

In both encounters, I had picked up also a growing strain of messianism suggesting that, somehow, some way, they might seek to restore the old order. At whatever cost.

The Flahelians and the Gillaireeans mirrored so much of Earth culture both ancient and currently existent. It seemed that none of us could shake off the belief that we had lost or been booted out of Eden and might never make it back to the garden. At least in this lifetime. Even the advanced quantum science that had put me here in avatar form wasn't immune from such beliefs. Everything had fallen apart since the Big Bang; we exist only in its faint echoes.

I blotted out my descent from the looming sister planet-moon. Too much focus on the details of now might have scrambled my consciousness and broken the tethering that held me here.

I was back on the black volcanic sands that bordered the regularly riled sea. In the other direction, I could spy a pack of Banantians, perhaps including my erstwhile guide Califer. Their semi-agrarian life still intrigued me but really I should prepare my summary and make ready to depart.

The purple sky, the chiaroscuro of land and ocean, the intelligent beings living lifestyles different from our expectations, the forests of twisted yet abundant vegetation, the subterranean and aquatic civilisation, the dwellers in the air, the great thin ropes and threads to the pregnant and swollen moon…

I would miss this place that had so many of the hallmarks of how we dreamed the new worlds of interstellar exploration would be.

I wanted to be the great peacemaker but couldn't see how that could be done.

Such an urge carried with it an assumption of superiority. I did not know enough to play the role but my hubris drove me on. The wisdom of the fool.

The Bananatian packs were busy and never in one place for long. I tried to keep pace but they seemed determined to give me the slip.

The weather turned foul. My projection doesn't fully experience the awareness of touch in the old sense; instead, proximate sensations such as heavy rainfall can cause discomfort and interference.

One rain-drenched night, Califer sought me out.

"I am breaking my pack-bonds communicating with you," she projected.

"How so? What have I done to upset your... people?"

"They feel you are bad charm. We should not have let you flit so. It is hastening the harsh times, the Round Up that will bring personal demise to so many."

"But I have not been in touch with your old god Ginalus. He... is absent like you all believe."

The downpour had flattened her pelt. She shook the worst of the droplets away from her face, stretched and briefly stood tall on two feet. This action and the accompanying drenching made me reconsider my earlier shoddy attempts at classification that had placed her kind somewhere between dogs and cattle. Upright, with deep brown eyes, an intelligent if pointed face, and smooth pale breasts amidst the wet fur, Califer had never looked more *womanly*. Had I been away from Earth too long? Or were there three variants on Homo sapiens on this captivating planet?

"Some think you Ginalus –"

"God, no! I'm just an Earth guy."

"Or his unwitting agent," she concluded.

And was gone.

I know my history and how it reeks of colonialism. The Incas thought the conquistadors to be white gods. A civilisation was destroyed because of the killing gap between perception and reality.

I should make ready to leave Sisyphus Three. I had caused enough damage already.

I should stay on Sisyphus Three and seek to repair the harm and misconceptions I had helped foster.

After several days of wandering, I found myself on the edge of some crop fields not yet ready for harvesting or plucking. To my right, I spied large groups of both Gillaireeans and Flahelians beating their way through the vegetation. Although not actually together as such, they were clearly working in unison. This was the middle ground for both species: the sea creatures and the air creatures could each cope comfortably with this low-lying common land.

It took me some time to discern what they were up to. Eventually, shock turned to action; but at first I could only watch in horror as they competed against each other with their tricks and mistreatment of the peaceful Bananatians.

Armed to a level comparable to Earth-European fourteenth century standards, and inspired by a hateful righteousness that increased their cunning, the Gillaireeans and Flahelians offloaded their own inadequacies onto what they considered to be an inferior race. It was like something from the worst depictions of the practices of Ancient Rome.

When they captured Califer, I had to intervene.

Mithra spat at my feet. "Do not presume to tell us how to live our lives, Darren. We will do as we wish with this foul-smelling, lowlife Banantian. The Feast of Unity awaits."

"No, you cannot take her. This is my friend Califer. Even we awful humans who have half-ruined our home planet and compartmentalised our emotions so that we can eat meat and wear hides… we cannot do such a thing to one that we have named and known. The bond is too emotional, too powerful."

"That's your failing, Earthie."

"Yes, we have a history of failings. And yet our civilisation has managed to send me here whilst I am also *there* sixty-nine light years distant. Has your… have you got something to match this technological achievement?"

"We don't want to gaze into your shiny shells, Darren. That way leads to… what is your word? Narcissism."

"I thought you and your people, Mithra, and also your esteemed brothers and sisters of the air, the Flahelians, had developed a self-reflective side. You would do well to gaze inwards a little deeper. There are things that divide you and things that unite you. How you apply the building blocks of the latter, though, is what's causing the problem here."

I didn't know where my foolhardy words came from as they spilled from my mouth. All the while I was thinking: I'm doing it again. That typical Homo sapiens behaviour – colonising, restructuring, imposing my thoughts and patterns on everything exogamous. Making it bend to my will. Ultimately, be in my image.

No, I was doing it to save Califer.

Mithra let two watery exhalations burst from her gills. Then she shrugged in such an Earth-like fashion that my mouth fell open in fish-imitating surprise.

"We have enough for now. We will be late for the feast." Mithra turned and gestured to her companions. Within moments, they had all departed.

"You didn't have to put yourself in direct danger to try and save me, Darren," Califer projected when the last of the posse had gone. "It's the natural order of things. It's the way it has been for so long."

I didn't want to puncture the bubble by suggesting that I hadn't ever been in physical danger. Whether I was here or not was an ontological question not pertinent to the current situation. Instead, I answered, "Things can change or be changed. We don't have to be the servants of our myths and our received beliefs."

"You may find that's a losing, never-ending battle, Darren," she projected.

I laughed. "This place is well-named. Come, there are still gaps in my understanding of *your* culture."

The Land of Grunts and Squeaks

Chris Beckett

A long time ago, in a country across the mountains, a great queen displeased a wicked and spiteful witch. No one knows what the queen did to offend her – witches are easily slighted – but the wicked woman was so enraged that she placed a curse on the queen and all her people. "When this night is over," she told them, "you will all be strangers to one another."

It was a truly dreadful curse. It was worse than stealing their hearing from them, or shutting down their tingle sense. It was worse even than depriving them of the darkfeel, on which we rely so much as we move about our tunnels and chambers. Those would all be calamities indeed, but this was far more terrible. For when they woke the following morning, the people of that unfortunate country discovered they could no longer reach each other's minds.

Think for a moment, dear ones, what that would be like. Spread out your antennae to their full extent and notice what it is that you receive through them. You can feel my love, for one thing, and the love you have for one another. You receive this story I'm giving you now, and a thousand others. You know the thoughts of all your friends. You can tell who's happy and who's sad, here in this chamber and out in the world beyond, and you know exactly why. And behind all these things, you feel the love of our mother, the queen, reaching out to all of us, caressing us, nourishing us, making us feel safe and cared for.

And now imagine what it would be like, my dears, if all of that was gone – every single bit of it – and all you could know of the world around you were the fragments that came through your senses. Oh, you would still know that we others were here, you would still be able to hear the sounds we made, you could still darkfeel our presence or see us if we were under the sun, but you couldn't know what we were thinking, you couldn't tell us things or receive our news, and you would have no way of connecting with how we felt. As to the queen, well, she'd be far away in her palace, and you'd know nothing of her at all. For all you knew, she might be dead.

Dreadful to think of, isn't it? And yet, for those poor people in that land across the mountains, that was their fate for ever more.

How lonely life must have become. Children were left alone with fears which no one else could see. Lovers could no longer feel each other's love. A woman would look at her life's companion and think, 'I'm sorry about those angry feelings I had earlier on. I truly love you with all my heart', but her friend would have no idea she'd had that thought. Tender caresses lost their meaning, becoming no more than one skin touching another. People were prisoners inside their own heads. Many went mad with grief.

And yet loneliness was by no means the whole of it. The work of the queendom came almost to a standstill, because no one could ask or tell each other anything. First thing of a morning, farm workers would stand in bemusement in front of their forewoman, with no idea what she wanted them to do. The forewoman could think and think with all her might, but she may as well have whistled or made a face for all the difference that made. The workers just shuffled about embarrassedly until eventually, feeling like a fool, the forewoman picked up a scythe and, making the motions of cutting something, pointed and nodded in the direction of a nearby tunnel.

"You mean, cut the mushrooms?" the workers would ask her, but of course she didn't know what they were thinking. She could only see their bewildered faces. And so she'd carry on with her strange performance until at last, bewildered and uncomfortable, they'd pick up scythes and trudge off, hoping they'd understood correctly, some up the tunnel to the mushroom caves (which was what the forewoman intended) and some outside to harvest leaves (which wasn't necessary that day at all).

That forewoman was at least able, by her clumsy performance, to show some of her labourers what she wanted, but cutting mushrooms is a simple action, easy to demonstrate. How would the administrator of a province learn from her people about a shortage of grain, and, even if she could learn of it, how would she convey the need to sow more to all the thousands under her authority, spread out through countless tunnels and chambers? Yes, and for that matter, why would workers want to work at all, if they had no sense any more that what they did was appreciated, and no information as to what purpose it served?

Most dreadful of all, though, deep down in the warm depths of her palace, the queen, with her lovely huge soft yielding body, had, only a day before, been able to share her thoughts with every one of her subjects, just as our own queen does to this day, but now she reached out with her mind and found nothing at all beyond the confines of her own head and her brood chamber. She couldn't tell any more how many eggs were needed across the queendom, she didn't know how many workers to make, or how many farmers and administrators, or how many guards. She couldn't direct folk to move from one place to another. She couldn't relay news about opportunities here and shortages there. And above all she couldn't comfort her people with that sweet warm radiance that up to now had sustained them all, just as you and I are sustained by our own beloved queen.

As to the young princesses and the men, those beautiful, gentle, idle creatures who'd basked their whole lives in the full intensity of that radiance, they now gathered helplessly around her in the chamber, their antennae waving uselessly about, their hands pawing at her enormous body, their mouthparts nuzzling her soft skin in the hope of finding at least some tiny remnant of the bounty that had been theirs until now. But they found nothing. Nothing came back to them. Her skin was just skin, her face was just a face, her antennae were as silent as their own. The despair of that was so great that some of them cracked open their own heads on the walls of the chamber, while others pulled at their antennae until they were torn and bleeding, in a vain effort to bring some life back into those suddenly useless organs. And some grew wings, so it's said, though this wasn't the season for it, and none of them were ready for mating. They had no plan in mind, no idea how flying might make things better, no notion of how they could even feed themselves with no workers on hand to tend them. But I suppose doing anything at all, going anywhere but where they were, seemed preferable to simply enduring their loss. In any case, whatever the reason, they flew up into the sky and were never seen again. Most probably they were gobbled up by the sky monsters.

But there was one person from the queen's chamber who'd kept her head. The captain of the royal guard, braver and more purposeful than men are, wiser and more disciplined than naïve young princesses yet to swell with eggs, had taken it upon herself to go out and search for the witch, in the hope of forcing her to reverse the spell. She'd gone to the witch's chambers and to all the places she could think of that the witch might frequent, but she'd found nothing. After a certain point, she'd decided there was no sense in carrying on searching, for how can you search for someone if you have no means of conveying to others who it is you're trying to find, or what they look like, or what kind of darkfeel surrounds them? And even if you could convey those things, what would you achieve if you had no means of receiving answers?

But the captain didn't panic and she didn't hurry back to the brood chamber. Instead she stopped and thought. She was a brave woman. (I would tell you her name, dear ones, if I knew, but a name has no purpose when it can no longer be told, and the captain herself soon forgot it.) She thought and thought until finally she remembered a certain wise woman who lived in a forest some way from the palace, and was reputed to be the cleverest person in the whole queendom.

Never before had the captain left the queen's side. She longed, as anyone would, to return to her rightful place in the warm moist darkness beside her mother, but she knew the queendom itself was in danger unless something could be done. So she steeled herself against the loneliness and grief, and hurried as fast as she could along tunnels, out under the sun, and back into tunnels again, until she reached the wise woman's home.

Of course the wise woman knew at once what the captain had come about, for like everyone else she'd woken up to the sudden absence of the thoughts and feelings of others. But she *was* wise and so, instead of bewailing her misfortune, she'd tried to understand what had happened. "It's as if we had been surrounded by light, and suddenly we were in darkness," was her first thought, but that didn't really capture the nature of the calamity, for who wants the harshness of light anyway if they can have the warmth and the comfort of darkness? "It's as if we'd been surrounded by pleasant sounds, and suddenly we were in silence," she had thought. Ah, now that was more like it! For everyone knows the pleasure of sound, the hum of a busy tunnel, the cheerful click and clatter of a meeting between friends, the slow drip drip of a moist mushroom cave. Everyone enjoys hearing sound in the background, behind our thoughts and feelings.

"It's as if we are suddenly in silence," the wise woman had repeated to herself, "and we long for sound to return."

She knew what had brought this about because, like everyone in the queendom, she had been aware of the quarrel between the witch and the queen, and had picked up the witch's angry threat. What was more, she knew something that most people didn't know. For it so happened that, going up to the surface to harvest leaves for compost, the wise woman had seen the witch herself flying overhead on the unnatural wings – they were like the wings of a young princess – that she'd grown by magic. The witch was laughing up there, halfway between the sun and the soil, laughing with wicked delight at the harm she'd done to the queen, and the misery she'd caused to the whole queendom. But the wise woman had seen something else which the witch had not yet spotted. There was a sky monster diving down from the blue on its enormous wings and heading straight for the witch, its horrible hard mouth opening as it came near. Dear ones, we should always be on the watch for sky monsters when we're outside under the sun, but the witch, in her glee, had quite forgotten to take care.

Only in the last second did she suddenly sense its presence behind her, but by then it was too late. In one single gulp the witch was gone and, while no one perhaps would grieve her passing, she'd taken with her the secret of the spell. It was inside the belly of the monster as it soared up towards the sun.

So there was no going back now. Never again in this queendom would people be able to hear each other's thoughts.

"Somehow we'll have to manage without," the wise woman thought. "Our thoughts will always be ours alone, but we must find some other means of giving each other a sense of what we know and what we want."

She paced back and forth along her tunnels, absently tending her mushrooms, turning her compost and checking her stores of grain.

"If what has happened is a bit like the absence of sound," she said to herself, "does that mean that a sound can be like a thought?"

And at that moment, the captain arrived.

Out of politeness, they kissed and stroked each other's antennae, although without the shared feelings that should have gone with these gestures, the contact was comfortless to them both. Then, stepping back, the captain spread her arms in a gesture of helplessness. What are we to do?

To the captain's surprise and bewilderment, the wise woman responded by pointing to herself and making a strange grunting sound with her mouth. She repeated this whole performance several times, and then she did something different. She pointed to the captain and this time made, not a grunt, but a funny high squeak.

The captain was very embarrassed and wondered if the wise woman had lost her mind. But the wise one persevered. Once again, she pointed to herself and grunted, and then pointed to the captain and squeaked. After that, she stopped and looked at the captain, holding out her arms as if she expected to be handed a large fruit, or a tasty carcass.

But the captain had no fruit with her, and no carcass, and it came to her that perhaps what the wise woman wanted from her was to repeat what she'd done. She could think of no good reason for that at all – it seemed a silly children's game – but she told herself that, after all, the wise woman was very clever, and perhaps had reasons she didn't understand. More embarrassed than ever, the captain pointed to herself and made a grunt, just as the wise woman had done.

At once the wise woman stopped her by putting her hand over her mouth. She pointed to the captain again and made a squeak. The captain's antennae were fairly quivering with embarrassment now, but she thought that perhaps what the wise woman was saying to her was that the squeak was in some way to be connected with her, the captain, and the grunt with the wise woman herself. So she pointed to herself and squeaked, and then to the wise woman and grunted. At once the wise woman began to leap about the chamber, rattling her antennae together in glee.

Still the captain was puzzled, but she was at least beginning to understand the game that the wise one wanted her to play. When the wise woman pointed to a pile of grain in the corner and made two short squeaks in succession, she too pointed to the grain herself and made the same sound. When the wise woman pointed to the dried mushrooms hanging from the ceiling and grunted *and* squeaked, she grunted and squeaked herself. And so it went on. A dried carcass, a bale of leaves… the wise woman attached a sound to every single object in her chamber, and made the captain memorise each one. And then she began to make new sounds to convey for example that the mushrooms were *above* the grain, the grain was *below* the mushrooms, the chamber was *below* the ground.

"These sounds are a bit like names," the captain thought to herself. "Only they don't just apply to people but to things and to ideas which have never needed names before."

Ten days later, the captain returned to the palace with the wise woman, both of them skipping and waving their antennae as they entered those great deep tunnels. It had been a hard and even dangerous journey, for the whole queendom was in chaos. Workers who should have been toiling underground were running back and forth aimlessly under the sun until thirst and exhaustion overcame them. Guards who should have been protecting workers were fighting one another. Mushrooms that should have been spread out to dry had been left to rot in piles.

When they reached the brood chamber, the captain and the wise woman found the surviving men huddled in a dejected heap, and the surviving princesses huddled in another, while women of many ranks and kinds came in and out, banging their heads on the walls, hitting at their own antennae with their hands, jumping up and down in agitation, as they vainly tried to receive some message from their queen, or convey to her their own distress and helplessness. Nothing was getting through.

But all the women stood still when the captain and the wise woman arrived, and even the men and the princesses lifted their heads sorrowfully from their miserable heaps. For the captain and her companion seemed hopeful, somehow. They seemed to think they had brought something with them which would be of use. Perhaps they'd found a cure!

The captain approached the queen, and respectfully licked her soft warm flesh. Then she pointed to the wise woman and grunted. All the people in the chamber looked at each other —the princesses, the men, the servants and advisers and guards— hoping to see some gleam of understanding. But no one had any idea what was going on. The captain pointed to herself and squeaked.

Dear ones, it was a slow business, and several times the wise woman and the captain worried that the people were going to attack and kill them in their frustration, but slowly slowly – it began with the queen and spread gradually through the ranks to the humblest workers and the most dejected men– the people in the chamber got hold of the wise woman's idea. These sounds, these grunts and squeaks, these clicks and rumbles, were a bit like names. Each sound conveyed a certain object, or a certain idea, or a certain action, and you could convey news, even if only very slowly and imperfectly, by arranging the sounds in a row.

So that was it, was it? It was a bitter seed to swallow, that this clumsy game was the wise woman's substitute for knowing each other's thoughts. It was obvious to everyone that, even if you could memorise ten thousand different sounds, a hundred thousand, a million, you would only ever be able to convey the tiniest fraction of your own experience, and even that in a dreadfully slow and plodding way that would always be open to misunderstanding. They would all still be alone inside their heads and, where once they'd been able to bask in the love of their queen, now they'd have to be content with hearing her make the sound which represented the idea of love, and even that only when they were in her physical presence. But as the queen herself put it: *Click-click-high squeak, short grunt, rumble, low squeak-click-middling squeak, whirr.* Which was her way of saying that this was better than nothing at all.

And they do say, my dear ones, that to this day, if you go to that country far away over the mountains, they still can't hear your thoughts or know your feelings. So if you want to tell them something, or ask which road to take, or convey that you like them, the only way you can do it is by making funny noises with your mouth and hoping they understand. That's just how it is in the land of grunts and squeaks.

The Blood Rose

Susan Oke

Mally hummed as she turned back the bedsheets and laid out Azara's nightwear. Tonight she would tell a new story, one that her privileged young charge would not have heard before. It wasn't a 'new' story, of course, but an ancient one with its roots buried deep in a history that it was safer to forget.

"Come on now," Mally called. "Or there'll be no time for stories."

The bathroom door banged open and Azara stomped across the cool stone floor, dragging her stuffed wildcat by one ragged ear. Mally smiled and patted the bed.

"Your mother will get here as soon as she can. It's not her fault she's been delayed."

"She's never here. She doesn't care."

"Now, you know that's not true." Well, it probably wasn't true.

As Azara squirmed into her nightdress, Mally felt the tingling edge of that oh-so-familiar crystal song. Azara's mother was back, and with her the blessed Vsial that had bound its life to the woman. With practised care, Mally kept her face calm and filled her surface thoughts with all the minor chores she needed to get done before she herself could go to bed. Sure enough, a few seconds later Azara's face filled with delight, her eyes taking on a distracted look as she communed telepathically with her mother.

Mally waited for the faint click of the door knob and then stepped back from the bed, eyes lowered in respectful obedience. The mother strode in, tall and graceful as were all her kind, cream-gold skin shifting to a bloody-rose across shoulders and neck, auburn hair braided in a complex design proclaiming her rank as First Advisor. Around her throat shone a golden torc, and set proud in its centre was the Vsial: a large ruby that glittered with crystal power.

In truth, it took all of Mally's control not to open her mouth and sing the Welcome the Vsial deserved. She was a Speaker, one of a dwindling number of indigenous people who could still hear the song of their revered Vsial. The ruling Families preferred their personal servants to have Speaker blood, claiming they had 'quieter' minds than the rest of the local population. Standing perfectly still, Mally listened to the delicate harmonies of the crystalline lifeform as it hummed its satisfaction at being back within the boundaries of its Nest.

Leaning over the bed, the mother brushed her lips against Azara's forehead; the child closed her eyes and sighed. *It's not that easy to get her to sleep.* Mally quashed the thought instantly, filling her mind with images of Azara's ceremonial dress and worries about its fit. The mother turned to regard her. "Everything is ready for tomorrow?"

Mally kept her gaze fixed on the woven rug by Azara's bed. "Yes, mistress."

A muffled squeak of excitement escaped the sheets. Tomorrow Azara would be seven years old, which meant, as part of the celebrations, she would be presented to the Crystal Heart. The Heart lay deep underground at the very centre of the Nest, a place normally out of bounds for children. Azara had been talking of nothing else for weeks. Mally grappled with the desperate longing that rose in her chest. *One day I will see the Heart. One day I will hear its glorious song.*

Distracted, the mother frowned down at the bed, no doubt silently chiding her daughter. Mally stole a glance at the softly glowing Vsial; it was so beautiful. While her inborn gift meant Mally could hear the songs of all Vsial, it was the Ruby that claimed her unswerving devotion. As if in answer to that thought, there was a brief fluctuation in the Vsial's song – an acknowledgement of her presence, nothing more, but it set Mally's heart hammering. She pulled in a deep breath and blinked away a tear. Seven years working in this household, humming her songs of welcome and trust and it had finally happened. *The Ruby knows me. It recognises me.*

"Make sure my daughter is fully rested. She has a challenging day ahead of her."

"Yes, mistress."

The mother swept out of the room without another word. There was nothing more to be said; Mally knew her duty. She would have Azara up and dressed in her initiates robe by the fifth hour, ready for the procession down into the catacombs beneath the House. But first she had to get the child to sleep. Right on cue, Azara threw back her bedsheets and sat up, pale green eyes alight with mischief.

"Let's creep downstairs, just me and you, and sneak a peek at the Crystal Heart," the girl whispered, as if afraid of her own words.

Mally grinned back. "Ooh yes! It'll be so exciting. And when your mother arrives I'll say it was all your idea."

Azara's face scrunched up into a scowl. "You're no fun, Mally."

"You heard your mother, you need to rest." In response to Azara's pout, she added, "Don't you want to show the Heart how strong you are?"

"I suppose." The child settled back on her pillows. "A story first. You promised."

"That I did. All right, settle down now."

Azara clutched the battered, slightly balding wildcat to her chest and snuggled beneath her sheets. Settling into the wooden chair by the bed, Mally took a calming breath and began:

In the time before, when the world was quiet, two brothers left home searching for their fortune. They journeyed through dark forests and across vast plains; they were tired and hungry, but neither would turn back. They had made a promise to their mother not to return until they could put food on the table, fire in the hearth and most important of all, bring medicine for their ailing sister.

Gilno, the youngest, was filled with wonder by the beauty of the land. He laughed as clouds chased each other across the sky, cocked his head to listen to the wild stories of the wind, and thanked the sun each morning for its gift of light and warmth. But his brother's heart was hard and cold. Five years older, Baran saw the world through the eyes of poverty and hardship. The dark bellies of the clouds threatened rain, the sharp bite of the wind harried winter closer, and the sun's promise of warmth would vanish in the night as they shivered in their thin blankets.

One day, they came upon a deep crack in the earth. When they looked down into the dark they saw something glimmer as it caught the light of the late afternoon sun.

"Gold," Baran said. "Or precious stones." He took out the rope from his backpack and made it fast around a rock.

Gilno looked down into the crack and then up at the sun. "It will be night by the time we reach the bottom. Perhaps we should wait until the morning."

"There's time enough," Baran said. He was the eldest and he knew best. The seasons were turning and they must return home before the winter chill snatched their sister away. So Gilno followed his brother's example and tied his own rope around a large, black rock. Together they climbed down into the crack. It was far deeper than they thought. They swung at the end of their ropes in the pitch black, not knowing how much further it was to the bottom.

The tempting glitter of precious stones had faded with the sun. They both looked up at the small patch of star-filled sky and knew they were too tired to climb back out.

"I'll jump down," said Gilno. "I'm lighter and will take less hurt."

But Baran would not listen. He was the eldest and it was his responsibility to bring wealth back to his mother. "I will call if it is safe for you to follow." And with that Baran let go of his rope.

Gilno listened, straining to hear the sound of his brother's voice. Nothing stirred the darkness. He called out his brother's name, but his only answer was the wind keening through the crack above his head. Exhausted, Gilno climbed his rope until he could fashion a secure loop in which to sit. All he could do was wait for the dawn. He did not sleep. It was freezing cold in the crack and the rough rope bit into his flesh.

When the sun leached black into grey, he saw that the crack narrowed beneath him. Its walls were a jumble of jutting stone, perfect for nimble hands and feet. But Gilno's hands and feet were no longer nimble. They were stiff with cold and there was little strength left in his body. It took him a long time to climb down.

His feet touched the bottom as the sun reached its peak, shining straight down into the crack. There was his brother lying on the floor, one leg twisted and broken, blood on the side of his head. Gilno tried to wake him. Baran was the eldest; he would know what to do. But Baran would not stir.

And then something wondrous happened. The rays of the sun struck a crystal embedded in the rock wall. Gilno couldn't believe his eyes. The crystal was the size and colour of a fat, pink piglet, and it was singing!

"Pink?" Azara scowled. "I want a story about the Ruby not the Rose!"

Mally knew she was taking a risk sharing this sacred story, but all the years of careful nurturing and storytelling had been in preparation for this. Tomorrow Azara would join with the Crystal Heart in a way that Mally could barely imagine, deeper than song, reaching into the very core of heart and mind. Azara must know the truth before that happened.

"Patience. Let the story unfold." Mally found a smile for the child who, over the years, she had grown to love.

Azara settled once more, almond eyes narrowed with impatience.

Gilno's eyes filled with tears as the crystal sang of its loneliness and despair. He pressed his hand to its smooth surface, hoping to comfort it. The song took on a sense of urgency, filling his mind and body with purpose. He knew what he had to do. Stepping back from the crystal, his gaze fell on Baran's body.

"Wait. What about my brother?" He had no way of knowing whether the crystal could understand him. The song shifted to a softer, sweeter refrain. It sounded like a promise.

Reassured, Gilno covered his ears with his hands and waited. A sharp, strident note pierced the air. Gilno winced and hunched his shoulders. Twice more the cutting note sounded. At each note a slice of crystal sheared away from the main body and fell to the floor. Gilno carefully collected all three pieces and stowed them in his backpack. With a glance up at the distant sky, he began to climb. At the top of the crack, exhausted and weak, he placed the crystal slices on rocks close to the edge. As he watched, the slices changed shape, stretching into delicate crystalline fronds. They caught the sun's waning light, multiplying its strength before reflecting it down into the depths of the crack.

Gilno pulled up his brother's rope and curled it around his waist. His hands were chafed and his shoulders sore, but he couldn't waver now. Turning, he climbed back down into the crack. When he reached the end of his own rope, he knotted his brother's rope to it and continued down.

When Gilno reached the bottom, he found his brother awake and groaning, hands clutching at his broken leg. Gilno was overjoyed, but he said to the crystal, "I can't get my brother out of here unless he is completely healed."

The crystal sang of the sun's brief touch, of the long night and its lonely vigil. It sang of a strong heart and patience. Once more a strident note cut the air. This time a solid lump of crystal fell away, thick bottomed with three jutting arms. Gilno placed it on the floor where the light of the sun, focussed through the crystal fronds, burned with a welcome heat. The three-pronged crystal soaked up the light, each arm pulsing with energy until it was too bright to look upon.

Gilno nodded his understanding. Now the crystal could store

the energy of the sun; it was no longer bound by the strictures of sunrise and sunset.

Rose light caressed Gilno's body and filled him with strength. He laughed as the song soared through him, full of joy and gratitude. And his brother laughed with him. Bone and skin knit together, fulfilling the crystal's promise.

"You did it!" Baran hugged Gilno close. "Now all will be well."

Baran lifted the three-pronged crystal from the floor and the song died. Day had shifted to night as they celebrated. The brothers faced each other in the dark, the only light pulsing softly in Baran's hands.

"What are you doing?" Gilno asked.

"This treasure will keep us warm and fed for years. It will pay for the medicine to make our sister well. Come brother, we will take this piece now and come back for the rest later."

"But the crystal is alive. Didn't you hear its song? Brother, it sacrificed much to heal our hurts and needs to replenish its strength. That piece in your hand stores the light of the sun. You saw it yourself. If you take it, the crystal will die."

"Don't be foolish. This is the fortune we were seeking." Baran brandished the three-pronged clump of crystal like a trophy. "And it is our sister who will die if we don't make haste."

"No," Gilno pleaded. "We can bring our sister here. The crystal will heal her. It will make her strong. It will make mother strong too. This is a blessed place, Baran, can't you feel it?"

A gentle, coaxing, crystal song swirled around the brothers.

Baran grimaced and covered his ears. The song grew louder, more insistent. With a growl, Baran grabbed his axe and smote the crystal where it lay embedded in the rock wall. Its surface fractured into hundreds of tiny pieces, leaving a fist-sized heart behind. The crystal song stuttered and died.

Azara gasped. She pulled the stuffed wildcat closer and chewed on its ragged ear. Mally waited a heartbeat and then continued.

"It saved your life!" Gilno shouted. "Healed your wounds. Is this how you repay its kindness?"

"I was not seriously hurt. I just banged my head, that's all. It was my own strength that saved me." Baran tucked the three-pronged chunk of crystal into his jacket.

Baran was the eldest and he would not listen. But Gilno knew the truth. When Baran climbed, Gilno followed.

"Give it back. I will not let you take the crystal's strength."

Gilno grasped at his brother's ankles, but Baran kicked his hands away.

Baran watched Gilno fall. His brother's scream cut off as he hit the bottom. When Baran reached the top, he looked up at the stars, gripping his prize in both hands. He was the eldest and must keep his promise to his mother. They would all grieve for Gilno's loss, but with the wealth assured by the sale of this treasure the rest of the family would survive the coming winter.

Mally sat back and waited.

"No, that can't be the end," Azara protested. "What about the Heart? What about Gilno?"

Mally smiled. "You're right, of course. The blessings of the Vsial cannot be counted in terms of material wealth." A sly dig at the practice of selling the lesser crystals to off-world traders. The child didn't seem to notice.

Gilno lay on the cold stone floor; he could feel his life slipping away from him. He crawled over to the crystal, stretched up and placed his hands on its splintered surface. Sharp edges sliced his skin. It didn't hurt; his hands and face were already covered in blood. "I'm sorry," he whispered as the darkness took him.

Faint song tugged Gilno back to the world, even fainter light bathed his body in ruby strength. "No, don't waste your beauty on me," he begged. But the crystal crooned as if to a baby, and he slept.

Above ground, Baran trudged across the dry land. He could

feel the stolen crystal throbbing against his chest. When the sun was high, Baran opened his jacket and pulled out his prize. As he gazed at it, the crystal blazed into life.

When Gilno woke he felt whole and strong. The sun was overhead once more, the crystal fronds concentrating its light and warming the rock walls far below. The fractured crystal glimmered a dark blood red, as did the sharp slivers of crystal that littered the floor.

"Yes," whispered Azara. "I knew it was really a Ruby."

"Shhh, now. No more interruptions."

The rope was gone, but that didn't stop Gilno. "I will bring back your strength, I promise."

The crystal's song buoyed him as he climbed. By the time he reached the top, day was falling into dusk. He found his brother's body a half-day's walk away. The skin on Baran's hands was burnt black. There was a surprised look on his face.

"I'm sorry, brother," Gilno whispered.

He found the three-pronged crystal close by, hidden in the dry grass. It pulsed with a faint heat. Hesitantly, he reached out but found its surface cool to the touch.

Back in the depths of the crack, Gilno carefully set the three-pronged crystal back in place; it blazed bright, bathing everything in concentrated ruby light. Gilno sat and watched in awe as each tiny sliver of crystal levitated from the floor and embedded itself in the surrounding rock. His right hand pulsed in time to their chorus. Buried in the flesh of his palm was a pinprick of ruby light.

Gilno built a cairn for his brother at the edge of the crack, and then brought his mother and sister to be blessed by the light and song of the ruby heart. They grieved for Baran, even as they marvelled at Gilno's blood-red hair. Word spread, and many came to ease their hurts. Gilno's children were born with the same red hair and were favoured by the ruby crystal. The people rejoiced and pledged their protection to both the crystal and its Speaker. And that is how the Ruby Crystal Heart and the people became one.

Azara gazed at Mally for a long moment. Carefully, she reached up and tucked a strand of red hair back into the folds of Mally's head-tie.

"And then we came, and the Heart chose us instead," Azara said. A look of puzzled worry haunted her eyes for a moment, and then her expression brightened, "And that's why you serve us now, because you know the Heart chose right. The Heart is always right."

Mally blinked away her disappointment and dredged up a sad smile. "Yes, you're right, of course." She tucked the sheets around the girl's slight frame. "Get to sleep, now."

And the child *was* right, after a fashion. Five hundred years ago, strangers dropped from the skies in their bright ships. They came with smiles and open hands, and her people welcomed them, found a place in their homes for those lost and troubled wanderers. The Vsial welcomed them too, and that's where the problems started. The strangers' alien telepathy allowed them to connect more deeply, more intimately with the Heart. They developed an intuitive understanding of crystal song, and soon discovered they could use the crystal's unique energy to enhance their own telepathic and telekinetic abilities.

First one Nest, and then all the Nests, fell under their sway. Her people followed their respective Hearts – transferring their awe and devotion to this new, symbiotic host. What had the child said? *The Heart is always right.* True enough, unless its perception of the world has been twisted out of true by the hosts that carry it. Now her people were excluded from the Nest, denied access to the Heart and treated little better than slaves.

Once she was sure that Azara was sleeping soundly, Mally slipped into the adjoining room. There was still plenty of work to be done before she could find her own bed, not that she'd be able to sleep. She shook out the laundry, hands folding and smoothing by long practice, while she fretted over what to do next. There was no point in trying to get a message to the network of Speakers placed with the children of other powerful families – what would she say? Azara was still young, there was plenty of time to help her grow into a more tolerant and enlightened adult, one who would help to reintegrate Speakers, and the rest of her people, back into the Nest.

The next morning Azara was subdued, perhaps finally realising the gravity of what was about to happen. Mally braided the child's long auburn hair and tried to mask her worry with light hearted chatter. When the time came, Azara clung to Mally for a long moment, before stepping out to join her mother in the corridor. The child walked off with her entourage, head held high; she didn't look back.

Five hours later, a Warden strode into the playroom. Mally was on her knees, surrounded by books, in the middle of re-stocking Azara's bookshelves with suitable titles from her mother's collection. The Warden caught her absorbed in reading *The Crystalline Memory Matrix: an introduction*. A bit of a challenge for a seven-year-old, but there were plenty of pictures, and the section on perfect recall and long-term storage was fascinating. Mally slapped the book closed and dropped it on the pile waiting to be shelved; the Warden raised an eyebrow but did not chastise her.

"Your presence is required. Follow me," he said.

The Warden was around Mally's age, late-twenties at most, and judging by the high-pitched trill of his Vsial, fairly new to being *joined*. He raised a hand to the golden torc around his throat and stroked a finger over the glittering crystal; its song calmed, but Mally could still sense its underlying excitement. She rose to her feet and followed – what choice did she have?—sandaled feet whispering down stone stairs and along steep, sloping tunnels. They were heading for the catacombs. A sudden fear gripped her heart.

"Is Azara all right? Did she…? Is she…?"

Exposure to the Heart changed you – that was a given – but sometimes the young never came back to themselves. It was rare, but it still happened. And then the Wardens would have one more 'blessed' child to add to their crèche of blank-eyed charges.

"The Heart rejoices and welcomes Azara into the Nest," the Warden said softly.

Mally suppressed a sigh of relief. Ahead, a heavy stone door blocked their progress; it swung open at their approach. A susurration of song swirled around and through her, leaving Mally breathless and a little dizzy. *The Heart!* Walking in a daze, she opened her senses and let the complex melody thrum through mind and body. It was more beautiful than she had ever imagined.

"Wait here," the Warden said.

His voice, sounding suddenly harsh and discordant, fractured the spell of the Heart. He gave her a contemptuous look and strode out of the doorway. Mally blinked; she was in a small, circular room hollowed out from the rock, somewhere deep underground. A sob shivered through her, only then did she realise that her cheeks were streaked with tears. Mally wiped at her face with one sleeve; she was a Speaker and should conduct herself with dignity.

Moments later, Azara rushed into the room.

"Mally! Mally!" The child looked pale and drawn, her eyes fever bright. "The Heart wants you."

Mally rocked back as Azara rushed into her arms. "What's all this? Calm down, now. You're not making any sense."

"The Heart liked your story. It wants to meet you."

Mally placed a hand on Azara's forehead. The child was clearly confused.

Azara wriggled out of her arms. "I'm all right. Stop fussing." She fixed Mally with a surprisingly frank gaze. "The Heart wants to meet you. Aren't you happy? It's what you've always wanted."

Deep inside her mind, Mally reeled in shock. She'd let her guard down with this child, been too trusting. *I'm such a fool!* What else had Azara picked out of her thoughts? Fighting to keep her expression calm, she began to silently recite the titles of all the books waiting to be shelved in a desperate attempt to mask her surface thoughts. Before she could find any words, the mother strode into the room. She gave her daughter a disapproving look.

Azara had the grace to respond out loud. "I'm sorry, Mother. I know I shouldn't run in my ceremonial robes, but I just had to tell Mally straight away."

The mother sighed, and then fixed Mally with a hard, emerald stare. "You're to accompany us to the central chamber. The Heart has expressed an interest in you."

The central chamber was huge. At its centre was a chest high plinth and resting on top was a pulsing, head-sized ruby. *The Crystal Heart!* Its song was muted – no doubt to protect Azara's young mind – but still it filled Mally with an overwhelming sense of reverence and joy. She fell to her knees, unable to tear her gaze from its crystalline radiance. Azara's mother stepped up to the plinth and touched her fingertips to the Heart. Ruby light flared across its surface and then blossomed in the Vsial at her throat.

"State your bloodline," she commanded.

Mally swallowed, hands clasped tight before her. "Unbroken. A pure line of descent stretching back into the before times."

The mother snorted. "I suppose you claim a blood-tie to Gilno himself?"

"No, mistress. Those records are lost to us." She would have liked to say that those records were destroyed when the Families usurped her peoples' place with the Heart – but it was too dangerous to let such thoughts escape.

Silence settled in the chamber. Mally focussed on the Heart's song, let its intricate harmonies weave through her. Under her breath, without conscious thought, she hummed a minor chord, mirroring and then modulating one strand of the melody. The Heart brightened fractionally and chimed a response.

"I see," the mother sounded curious. "Your story of the first Speakers prompted the Heart to search its memories. It took some time, but we found the incident you described. Not surprisingly, your version of history differs from the actual event."

"Mother, please." Standing by her mother's side, Azara flashed Mally an eager smile.

"Very well." Her voice took on a more formal, ritualistic tone. "The Heart remembers the service of its Speakers. It will listen."

Mally stared at the Crystal Heart. She was the only Speaker to get this close in nearly five hundred years. The thought left her trembling. *The Heart knows. It remembers.* Now was the time to reach out to the Heart and rekindle its bonds with her people. This was the moment they'd all worked so hard for. Mally opened her mouth and sang.

Her voice had a clarity and purity envied by other Speakers. The central chamber filled with the soaring tones of her devotion. And the Heart listened. Its response, when it came, was gentle and filled with subtle tones of appreciation and understanding. Hope blossomed in Mally's breast. It was working. With care, she shifted the melody, invoking the sacrifice of Gilno and the reward of compassion. The Heart's song rose to a crescendo around her, filled with… was that laughter? The song became richer, deeper, layer upon wrapped layer until Mally lost all sense of time and place. She was standing beside the Heart, but now it was embedded in a rock wall. Before her stood two red-haired young men, daggers in hand, circling each other warily.

"Give it up," said the older one. "You know you can't best me in a fight."

"This Nest is mine. I found it – it's mine by right."

"We're in the middle of a skin-flaying desert! You can't set up a mine here. The best we can do is salvage the Heart and sell it piece by piece. Come on, brother, you know it makes sense."

Brothers? With a start, Mally realised what she was witnessing.

Gilno lunged forwards, blade missing his opponent by a hair's breadth. As he spun away, Baran's blade scored a bloody line across his younger brother's shoulder.

"First blood," Baran announced. "Now can we stop this nonsense?"

"Another scavenged Nest," Gilno spat. "With you pissing away all our money on one stupid scheme after another. No, not this time."

Another lunge. Another wound. Blood drenched Gilno's shirt; his knife hand trembled. The Heart's song trilled on the edge of Mally's senses; it was young and afraid, confused by the drama playing out in front of it.

"And what about you?" Baran shouted. "All you know how to do is drink and whore!"

The two men leaped at each other. The Heart wailed, battered by the violence underscoring the men's shouts and curses. With a sense of horror, Mally realised that these men had the inborn talents of later-day Speakers – their voices, their intonation spoke directly to the Heart – more than that, it influenced the Heart... changed it. Baran jumped back to avoid a wild swing from his brother, caught his heel on a rock and fell sprawling onto his back. With a howl of fury, Gilno leapt and brought his dagger down, again and again and again.

Mally turned her face away, but she was trapped in the memory. She watched as the Heart's pale rose colour darkened, becoming more like the life-blood pooling on the rocky floor. The outpouring of violence and hate had corrupted the Heart's crystal matrix, she saw that now. When Gilno dragged himself across the floor to place a possessive, blood-sodden hand on the Heart, its song changed to one of dark joy.

"No," Mally tried to protest. "No."

The memory blurred and vanished. Mally found herself sobbing on the floor of the central chamber. The Families ruled by a single tenet: survival of the strongest. Mally blinked up at the mother and her glowering Ruby. All her life, she'd believed that it was the off-world strangers who had corrupted the Crystal Heart, but now it seemed the opposite might be true.

It was us all along. We did this with our greed and hatred.

Mally opened her mouth to sing an apology, but then snapped it shut. She had no right to commune with the Heart. Her people had done enough damage.

The voice of the mother reached her through her grief. "Well, Speaker. Now that you know the truth there is work to be done.

The Heart wishes to gather all its Speakers back together. Under its guidance you will travel amongst your people and reinforce the message of reverence and obedience. To the Heart. To Us. After all, only the strong deserve to lead."

The song of the Heart rose in exultation; its melody burrowed deep, taking root in the core of her being. It warmed her. Comforted her. Claimed her. *This is what I want... isn't it?* To commune with the Heart, to live once more within the protection of the Nest. A sense of joy-filled purpose surged through her body; it was impossible to contain, pushing up until it exploded into song. Mally's voice rebounded from the walls of the cavern, a strident declaration. The mother winced; Azara covered her ears with her hands. The Heart blazed – painting skin and stone a deep, blood red.

The Heart is right. The Heart is always right.
Mally rose to her feet. Ready to serve.

Starfish

Liz Williams

I can't tell you a story.

If I began, I would only be telling you a fraction of it, a fragment, a tiny pellet. How hard must it be for you, a person who says one thing, thinks another, gestures another: only these few things. How strange it must be, to speak, and hear only one phrase tumble from your mouth, not many; without layers, like a single strand of ribbon.

When I speak, it is plaited. It is the *multiple/there is something that I know/the air is green/I watch you waiting.*

Heroda says that this makes little sense to most of you. She says: they think you're babbling. They can't distinguish the trains of thought. They want you to stick to one thing – but you can't, of course. It's not how you think, feel, speak, tell. She says that she herself finds it very difficult and she has been a linguist for many years, visiting different worlds, speaking with people who are other than herself.

"And yet your stories have many layers too," I say, in amongst all the other things that I say, which are related to this one. Heroda frowns as she disentangles: I know now what 'frown' looks like, and what it means. It means she is anxious and feels that she might not understand. Her skin is fragile, it creases easily, and I wonder if this might be the reason that we have evolved multiple speech, since our carapaces remain so smooth and hard, so inexpressive. Perhaps Heroda is speaking all the time too, but I cannot yet see it.

"Tell me a story," Heroda says, with her mouth.

"I don't think I can." [multiples: *there is light coming through the/outside, Espere is watering the garden which/on waking this morning I remembered Heroda and experienced/ I would like you to know this last thing but*]

"Try." She leans forwards and she takes my long three-fingered hand in her short five fingered one. I call her my 'starfish' because she has shown me one, in the aquarium of the lobby at the new port. It is from her world, a water creature. It is not attractive, but it is fascinating, and I keep wanting to go back and look at it. It is scarlet like the sun and it moves slowly, too. Heroda's hand is stumpy and yet not strong; the sun here has also made it redder than it should be, burning her before she learned to cover up. It is covered in creases as though the skin no longer fits properly. It is very different to mine.

The port is small, due to this being, as yet, only a diplomatic outpost and not a full embassy.

"They may not come," Heroda says. She purses her lips. *Amusement/ contempt (?)/ worry/ confusion/ resignation*. At least, I think so.

"We are too difficult," I say. After a moment, she replies, "Perhaps."

A shame. It must be hard, to be so simple. Like being flat, in one dimension. But I like Heroda and I would like to find a story for her, for her research. It's important to her and after all, I am an archivist. It is why we have become friends, even if we don't understand each other and maybe never will. So I go in search of a story, one that might be graspable in her starfish hand.

Language is a landscape. We believe that the place around us dictates the nature of our speech. We do not describe, but interpret. The land is in layers: the high moors, black as soot and dangerous, descending to the middle land, the long ridge of country between Semayis and Ulda, then the drop to the forest and then the strings of lakes. Impenetrable, says Heroda, yet not in the way of some worlds she has visited. Searing heat, or sandstorms, or icy wastes, or jungle. I can imagine these places only with difficulty: I have never been anywhere else, and Ulda is normal to me, every day. But I like to try.

No, Ulda is impenetrable because it is always changing, Heroda says, shifting and moving. The air is filled with mists and rain, or with cloud, this high up, or with the drifting seeds from the feather plants. Grey, blue, storm and sunlight. Malleable. And your speech shifts with it. Sometimes it means one thing and sometimes something else entirely.

"And of course," Heroda again. "You are physically different. You see from the sides of your faces, not the front, and you have – all those tongues."

The tongues seem to worry Heroda. I think she's slightly revolted and too polite to say so. These people *are* very polite, gentle, not wishing to give offence. We appreciate this. It's one reason they've been allowed to stay. I have let the medic examine my palate, the structure of my mouth, my tongues and the beads of my larynxes in my throat. I have tried to explain how they function. The medic, and indeed everyone, might be revolted but they are also slightly charmed, I think.

"Why, you can have three conversations at once!"

"More than that," is one thing that I say. "It doesn't work so simply."

Then I tried to tell them how it does work, but they did not understand. They had the look that I came to know as 'puzzled.'

Yet, as I have said, I like Heroda. She wants an old story, as is the custom of her kind, and it has been hard to explain to her that an old story will make no sense. Meaning will have fallen out of it. Old stories are like old cloth that the beetles have chewed, with scraps missing and frayed edges. An old story, that you can see before you, is no good. A new story, though – a story from the future, that's a good thing. A new story that you can glimpse behind you over your shoulder, seeing it perhaps in its glowing wholeness, perhaps only in pieces, but only for a second before you tell it.

And so I will go in search of a story for her, dig it out of its inscription in the land.

I set out on a day with mist. The shrines are shrouded in it and I speak to the personages of each one as I pass. Were you my people, and not Heroda's, here is how I would describe the first part of my walk uphill, through the winding forest path:

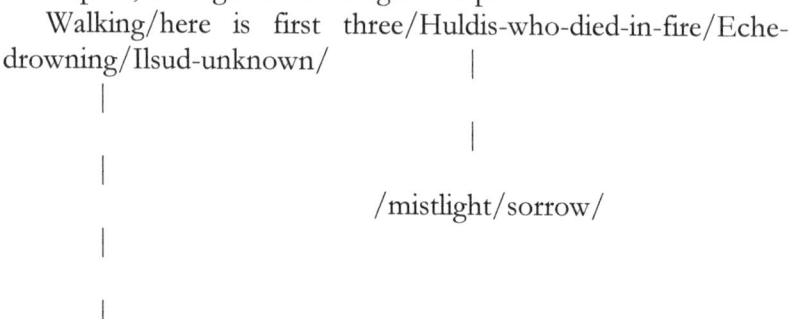

    Walking/here is first three/Huldis-who-died-in-fire/Eche-drowning/Ilsud-unknown/ |

|

                          |

| /mistlight/sorrow/

|

|

    /rain-in-air/speaking to person who placed first stone/before me: looking into past/…

This is the first thing I say. Not hard.

But I will try to disentangle.

Moving up, the mist dissipates and I come out into sunlight at the edge of the treeline. The grey fronds are damp, dripping and sparkling with water. The hem of my sarong is drenched and heavy, wrapping around my ankles. I pluck it free and hitch it up. The air smells of vegetation and rot. I look back, as if I am glimpsing the future over my shoulder. Far below, I can see the village, spindly on its stilts and platforms. Mist boils around it, revealing and concealing. I can see a tiny figure on the walkway, moving fast so that the walkway jolts and bounces beneath their feet. I recognize the dull red headcovering: Pedia, carrying the morning water. There is a moment of correctness for me: people in their rightful places. Except myself, doing something different, but still correct. Across the valley, the clearing made by the port looks like a round patch of bare hide. The mission ship sits in its centre, gleaming dull silver. Also correct. Heroda will be in one of the cluster of buildings, with her morning tea, looking through old records. I like this image: the printouts in her curious hands, a harvest of leaves.

A good story. Heroda needs a story and I will find her one.

I turn to the right along the first ridge. Above me, the moors rise in steps and plateaus. My speech changes; I no longer greet trees. I tell the land back to itself. The sky darkens with rain and the air freshens. The black earth of the path, made by hurrying feet and animals, becomes moist and slick. I have to take care, but it leads me all the same and I know where I am heading now. I climb and the village falls away below, disappearing into the weather.

In time, I come out onto the wide shelf of the lowest moor, tufted with the spires of plants. The cliff wall is just visible in the distance, through the drift of cloud. It is a long way across the moor and a dangerous one: I follow the well-trodden path, through the deep green places which can suck a person down, even swallow one of the great reptiles whole and leave no trace. The moor is full of greed and lets only a little language go. It's not safe to listen to it, especially after nightfall. But I have my destination in mind.

I walk and walk. It used to be said that stopping your ear holes with a twist of cloth and wet clay was the answer, but now they think that the words that the moor lets slip have become misty and pallid, not so harmful. I am careful, all the same. There are other things on the moor that you need to listen out for: the rumbling of the earth when one of the greater beasts is roaming, but that's rare, this close to noon. They're disturbed by the light, although Heroda is constantly complaining of how dark this world is, even though it burned her skin. It seems easy enough to me to see.

"That's because you've got those great big eyes."

Out of politeness, I have not commented on Heroda's looks, which seem very unattractive to me. Her little eyes and huge nose, her big chin and the lank, matted stuff all over her head. I don't want to hurt her feelings. And she probably thinks I'm hideous, too.

But this is a dark day, in fact. The low red sun has sunk behind the clouds and rain casts over the moor in veils. All the same, I am cheerful. I am not far from the shrine now – I can see it, standing on its little hump in the middle of the black grass. It is tall and narrow, made of bones and woven with the spire plants. It has stood there for a long time.

Inside, the wind whistles through. I want a story from the future: *tell me*, I whisper to the wind. And the wind whips through the bone walls, its instrument, and this is the story it tells me:

There is a person who is not yet born. But when they are born, everyone will gather round, because they are covered with tongues: a mutant, a gene gone awry. Their skin bristles with blue-grey points; they cannot eat, because their mouth is filled with tongues, but they can drink and this will be enough to allow them to grow, because our children (I have explained this to Heroda) do not stay small for long, but shoot up like plants in the wet. This person – I can see them, dimly, standing in the depths of the shrine – wears the customary pale grey robes of a young individual, but the hand which they extend is covered in murmuring tongues.

Their name is Thousand-Tongue, for obvious reasons.

What stories such a person could tell! They open their mouth and I can see deep within, the larynxes flexing as they spoke. A hundred words at once, overlapping and all with meaning, all related. I am overcome with admiration and can barely understand as they speak many stories at once, differently modulated, slurring and hissing and one voice like a bell above all.

What are these stories? They are the stories of the land-to-come and I think I hear Heroda's name in several strands. The image, made of words and mist, grows dim and the rain spits against the bones of the shrine. It is time to go.

When I step out onto the moor, there is a crescent moon rising over the ridge of the cliff, faint and green through the cloud. It's much later than I thought, but that's what happens when you become lost in a story. Stories bend time and they can trick you: that's what they're for, after all. I can hear something calling in the distance. Holding the story in my mind (someone to come, a tale spinner, a person who can tell the world more completely than any other), I make my way back along the track. I move quickly. It is not so late even so, but it is far. There is a shadow moving over the moor, huge and swift. I hope it has no interest in me and it veers off to the west, running under the moon, seeking other prey. I reach the forest's edge before dark and duck beneath the shelter of the trees. I will dream on it, I decide, and tell Heroda in due course what I have learned. I will need to put the story together, to assemble and disentangle. I have its cores, I think, but I do not want her to misunderstand. I want to get it right.

Down through the forest to the village, to shelter and light. It has been a long walk and I am thankful to be home, to have survived. Aishu asks me where I have been and I tell them, explaining the journey and its nature. They listen quietly, with appreciation.

"Do you think you have the story now?" is one of the things they say. We are sitting on the veranda overlooking the ravine, with tea. Below, in the dusk, lights move along the floor of the ravine: a procession of some kind, heading for the river. The second moon is full, casting blue shadows over the world.

"I think so. But I'm not sure."

"Do you think they will understand it? The person called Heroda?"

"I don't know."

I am giving you a thread of this conversation, no more. At the same time we are talking about the plants I had seen on my journey, the shrine and its history, the beast I had seen on the moor, loping into the distance. We speak of the moon procession below and Aishu lights a small light in token of the day, as the second moon itself rises higher over the hillside and the nightbirds flicker overhead, their neon sides flashing through the leaves. We seek the sleeping pallets soon afterwards, and I lie awake in the darkness listening to the breathing of my comrades, thinking about the story.

A person who could tell a thousand tales, more than a thousand, all at once. What tales would they tell?

And in the night, I dream.

I am high above the ravine. I can see the landing pad of the alien ship, the small forms of the people whom it brought. Pale and stumpy, wearing odd, bright clothes. Thinking along narrow lines, a handful of starfish thoughts. Yet intelligent, striving to be kind, seeking to understand. Sharing these things with us. I see different futures: the landing pad expanding, a city arising on the moor beyond the upper ridge. I've seen pictures of the cities of the aliens, admired them without wishing to live in them. There are good things there: avenues of trees with fruit which the people can pick, high-rise gardens, a bridge over a river which holds a public park. They've become good at solving problems, Heroda told me, even though there are so many of them now. Education rather than war, which had formed them long ago.

"We had to give it up," Heroda said, sounding as though she was talking about a bad habit. Perhaps it was never any more than that. "It wasn't sustainable."

"We've never had it." I couldn't see why any society should. When we meet others, we share. The world is dangerous enough without such practices.

In my dream, I look down at the city and I see my kind and hers, together. Small people who are smooth and hard, a taller folk with flat faces, a single tongue, round eyes which cannot see to the side. The clothes are different, of course. But there we both are, conversing. Walking together. It looks peaceful and although the city has taken the place of many plants, I think it will be all right. But then the city shimmers like a water-haze and it's gone: only the forest remains, peaceful, as it has always been, and the small circle of the alien port is there, overgrown. Heroda and her colleagues and the marvellous starfish have flown away and taken their stories with them. And our stories. And they've left some behind, too.

When I wake, I wonder if it had been a true thing that I'd seen or just a dream, although it's sometimes hard to tell.

A day or so later, I go to see Heroda. She is sitting in her makeshift office, as usual. She has tea. The light falls through the leaves of the plants on the windowsill, dappling into shadows. The air smells warm.

I say several things but I try to keep it simple and wait for her to disentangle.

"So did you find a story for me?" Heroda says.

"I think so. But it is a story to come, not one that has gone." Her face furrows a little. /puzzled?/upset?/

"Do you mean a story that you've made up?"

"What is 'made up'? It's a story that I found," I say, as I also tell her about the leaves and the light. I tell her about my journey to the shrine, first of all.

"In my culture – I mean my bit of my culture, not the whole thing – there are many tales about going into the forest. We have only managed ones now, but it used to be very dangerous, long ago. We have stories in which children go into forests and meet strange things."

"The forest is safe," I say. "The open land is dangerous. And you can see too far." You can see both the past and the future, without the comforting shelter of the great trees.

"It is a different type of story," Heroda agrees. I told her about the thing with a thousand tongues, and for once, she does not need to disentangle, although it is not really a story by her standards, I realize. It has a beginning, but no end, not yet. And although we are in the middle of it, nothing really happens in it, because we must wait for it to happen to us, and then, perhaps, we will know.

The Raveller's Tale

Neil Williamson

Once, a fox girl and an otter girl fell in love. Two young scuts, they were; no more than a year past their determination and delighting in the joys of tails to intertwine, clever paws to catch gifts of saltfish and furmice, and whiskers that tickled when they kissed. Though they never met as fawnings, both had long yearned for those tails, those paws and whiskers and had been impatient to come of age. Not every fawning knows quite so clear and true the form their ravelling should take, but these two? They had both been absolutely certain.

A fox girl, if you please.

An otter girl, my heart is set on it.

After their determination, the new fox girl had raced off to join the Russet Skulks in the burrow cities that underweave the whole of High Caledon. And as for that fresh-minted otter girl? They had sought out the great nomad rafts that even today ply their renowned trade up and down the length of the Crimson River.

And for a time they were each as happy as they could be… until the day came when they discovered that they could be even happier.

The day they met.

And that is when their troubles began.

Scoot forward to a fine summer morning not so many months later, and we find them sitting in their special place – the self-same stretch of river bank below the Iron Cascades where the Caledon's filigree beeches dip their twiney toes in the red waters that was the very scene of that first meeting.

Oh, what a moment that had been! Such an ear-twitching

bonding of eyes and spirits and, thereafter, they were inseparable. Every hole and leaf pile the fox girl snuffled their nose into, so too did the otter girl, and every shallow and reed bed the otter girl investigated was of equally great interest to the fox girl. As the spring had progressed, the river swell rising and the forest carpet lighting up with flame flowers, so too their love had budded and blossomed. And by the time we join them, dandling their paws in the settling pink froth, that love now burgeons so fully that it is like a pain inside them, bending their bones, stretching their fur as if the skins they had not so long ago been so certain of might, somehow... *unravel.*

Of course, you know that a ravelling does not work like that. Once you choose what you want to be, it takes more than mere wishing to change it. Unfortunate, then, that our two so want the world to behold that they are no longer in fact this plain otter girl, this tawdry fox. Now, they see themselves as a two-headed, four-footed chimera of shining wonderment. They have talked about the details for weeks. The skin, the eyes, the teeth. A little from one, a little from the other, a third quantity from elsewhere. Antlers, they both feel, should feature strongly.

"This must change," the one says to the other, squeezing a hand in a hand.

"We shall seek out the raveller," the other replies, black nose atwitch with a sudden certainty, "and demand a new determination. One that reflects the stature of our love."

And so they get up and set out immediately for Mount Morrow.

"We wish you to remake us," fox girl and otter girl tell the old raveller when they arrive at the Palace of Dreaming (although, as you can see, it is not so much a palace, and more of a cave filled with ancient machinery and a corner for the resident raveller to make their own).

Well, the raveller is wise, as ravellers must be. This is far from the first time such a question had been asked of them and experience dictates that such ventures rarely end as imagined.

"Love," they tell fox and otter after they are seated, "is a flickering, golden light. A winking, spinning coin, sunset on the one side and dawn on the other. Why not relish its multifaceted beauty?"

When the fox girl looks at the otter girl, the raveller can see that light shining in both of their eyes.

"Our coin spins so fast that the sides are indistinguishable and the light so bright it has blinded us to how we used to be," the fox girl says, snout wrinkling with conviction. "All that matters is what we are now."

"But also," the raveller tries again, "your love is a duet, a unique blend of your two voices, their complementary tones and timbres. Why not let everyone hear them in concert?"

Now the otter girl regards the fox girl and it seems that this one is perhaps just as determined as the other, although they express it differently. "That is what we want," they reply softly. "Except it is not two voices, but one."

"Well then," the raveller tries for a third time although, in the face of such fervour, they hold little hope now that their words will make a difference, "your love is a fire. It kindles your spirits now and warms your hearts but, if disturbed, it may consume all. You may one day change your minds and there would be no going back."

Now the faces of the fox girl and the otter girl are aglow, their chins bobbing in avid agreement. "Our fire has already razed our souls and scorched the ground they grew in," the fox girl says. "Now we must attend to the green shoots rising through the ash."

Now, the raveller bows their head in thought and stays like that for a time until, at last, they say: "Let me tell you the story of Donachie, the first raveller. It is a story of antiquity but it is not long, and it is important that you hear it so that I'm certain that you understand what you are asking."

Impatient as they are, the fox girl and the otter again nod.

And so the raveller tells them the tale.

This is a story the ravellers tell each other, from one to the next.

Once upon a time, back when the Heart of the World was newly nested in the Palace of Dreaming (although, of course, the Heart itself was dark-years ancient even then). Back when the sky boasted two moons instead of the resplendent Crown of Lace that now spans above us. Back before we, each of us, held the gift of our ravelling as our right. (Imagine that, you resplendent fox, you beautiful otter. Imagine if the power of choosing who you will be was withheld from you!) Back in the days of the awakening, ravelling had a different purpose.

When the Heart first came down and burrowed itself into the depths of Mount Morrow there was nothing on Great Geath but the rocks and the air. No seas, no rivers, no forests. The Heart had to make those things, see? Only then could it wake the First people from their dark-years sleep and, having prepared the world, it now needed to prepare them in turn to live in it, so that all could breathe and eat and prosper in their new paradise. We might not think it much of a ravelling. By our reckoning, it was tiny tweaks and twists only, and made equally to everyone. I tell you, when the First woke they were all as alike as poor little twinny babs, and the effects of that first ravelling did nothing to change that.

So, the First explored their world and they thought it was good – comfortable, certainly, and pretty enough to look at too – but many of them harboured dissatisfaction. Having travelled all those dark-years, they'd expected to wake to wonders but, in truth, their new home was not so different from the one they had left. So, they climbed down into Mount Morrow and they spoke to the Heart.

"You had a whole world to create," said a person whose passion was plants and who the First called a *botanist*. "Why didn't you make the plants and the trees more interesting?"

"The plants and trees," the Heart told them, "are as they need to be. They require enough similarity to those of the place we came from to create a stable ecosystem for people to survive in and food for them to eat. The plants and the trees are optimal."

"And what about the mountains?" said a second one, whose

appellation was *geologist*. "What about these valleys and terribly plain plains? And, *ugh*, what about these boring seas?"

The Heart replied similarly. "The land is stable. There is enough underlying vulcanism and tectonic movement to feed the world with energy and provide a rich substrate for the life that grows on it, but not so much as to present dangers. The lands and seas are optimal."

"But we've seen this all before," the geologist (who was a whiner, and no one likes a whiner, whatever face they wear) persisted.

"There are differences everywhere," the Heart replied. "In the details, should you wish to look."

"Tiny ones…"

"But millions of them," the Heart persisted (it had spent a lot of time on those details). "In coming to a new world, human psychology requires familiarity. The land," the Heart repeated with all of the patience of Mount Morrow itself, "is optimal."

"And you'd say the same of the fauna?" This last interlocutor was an expert on all things that ran or crawled, swam or flew, who they called a *biologist* and who went by the name of Donachie. "It's true that we could spend our first century here cataloguing the insect kingdom alone, but…" Donachie tailed off, unable or perhaps unwilling to articulate the dissatisfaction any more clearly than the rest.

The Heart said nothing because there was nothing more to say. It had made its position clear. The world was as it had painstakingly designed for the best benefit of these ungrateful people, and it was not going to bend to their whims.

"What happened next?" demands the fox girl, rapt in the story despite their impatience.

"What did Donachie do?" The otter girl seems the deeper thinker of the two and perhaps, the raveller thinks, knows the story already. Are they eager to hear it again or suspicious of why it's being told?

What happened next was that Donachie wrested the power of ravelling from the Heart's control and, in doing so, set the people of Great Geath on the path that leads us to the here and now. A free society, unbound by biology, unrestrained by expectation.

"We came all this way," Donachie told the Heart as they liberated the secrets of all the living things that the First had brought with them, "endured all these years of darkness to be allowed to live as we pleased." Donachie was breathing hard with righteous triumph when, finally, they switched the Heart off. "Fuck optimal."

So, the botanist went off and created the flame flowers and the snow vines and the singing trees. And the whiny geologist coloured the rivers and made the valleys that we call The Gentles hum and made sure no plain would ever be plain again. And Donachie? Well the biologist delegated the ravelling of the mammals and birds, the fish and the insects to others, but they kept the task of ravelling the people for themself. And one by one the people came to them, and each were asked: "What do you want to be?" Just as every fawning is asked at their determination. And for the most part Donachie gave them what they wanted.

"For the most part?" The fox girl's canines are showing with displeasure, but their companion says nothing, understanding perhaps that not everyone who dreams chooses practically. (If you have not heard the story of the cricket and the mambear, I will tell you that another day.)

"I'll finish the story," the raveller says. "Then you will understand."

Now it is fair to say that Donachie quickly proved to be a skilled raveller. The most skilled ever... some say, anyway. Certainly, those who were ravelled by Donachie were enraptured by their new forms. When the raveller gave a person wings they were swanling white or falconfish fast. When they gave a person strength it was as of the fiercest mambear. As Donachie's fame spread, they gathered admirers – a cluster, a crowd, a legion of them – and, perhaps, they began just a little to believe the praise now being heaped upon them from all sides.

Foremost, of course, among the admirers was Donachie's life partner, a person by the name of Rioch, whom they loved deeply and knew loved them back just as much. But this one waited until nearly all of the First had been given the form their hearts desired before also coming to Donachie for a ravelling of their own.

Donachie had been proud to show off their skills on all the others, flexing and flourishing their imagination like an artist being given a fresh canvas every day. But now? Now they could barely bring themself to ask the question.

"What do you want to be?"

"I want to be your greatest creation," Rioch said, sweeping their arm to take in the valley below Mount Morrow where there now lived deer men and tunny boys, scarab ladies and alder wives. "Your skill has filled so many hearts with the joy of completeness. I want you to do the same for me. For us. I want us to be magnificent. Together. For ever."

Donachie looked into their lover's shining eyes and saw not only adoration but also supplication, but they were taken aback because Rioch had never mentioned such a thing before and, in truth, Donachie had barely given a thought to ravelling *themself*.

Rioch, on the other hand, appeared to have given the matter *much* consideration.

"What do you have in mind?" Donachie asked with no little trepidation.

"Trees," Rioch breathed. "The two greatest trees in the dappled heart of our new forest. Bonewhite boles twining around each other up into the sky and bearing a canopy of silver leaves and full-fleshed dark fruits that make all who taste them sigh with our shared happiness."

Trees? *Trees.* Donachie could only stare.

"What's the matter?" Rioch said. "You love me, do you not?"

"Of course…"

"And you want to spend the rest of your life with me, don't you?"

"Yes!" They very much did. "But..."

"And you have worked so hard to make our community so happy. Everyone has what they want. Now it is time to see to your own happiness. And this is the perfect way for us to be together. To live out our lives enjoying the beauty we have finally made of our world."

Well, the conversation didn't end there. Unwilling to upset their lover, Donachie gently probed and pried and tested late into the evening. They considered the matter deeply, from Rioch's side and from their own. Donachie admitted that, after so many years of ravelling, a retirement in the high woods did sound idyllic but... *trees*, while beautiful the way Rioch described them, were not the form they would necessarily have chosen for themself. And besides, a new generation of fawnings was already close to maturity and the raveller's ego would not so easily let go of the chance to show off their art in bringing more determinations to fruition.

"This is a serious undertaking," Donachie told their lover. "If I ravel this, there is no undoing it." With Rioch nodding eagerly, they quickly went on. "And... I'm sorry, I do not doubt your love, but I need to be very certain of your resolve."

Rioch looked momentarily crestfallen, then said. "Very well."

So Donachie gave their lover three tasks to prove their commitment to being ravelled together so utterly intractably. The first was to pick a dark fruit from a tree known to grow at the source of the Crimson River. The second was to pluck a silver leaf from the trees of the far off southern continent. And the last was to fetch white bark from the solitary tree that grew at the summit of Mount Morrow (and still does should you wish to seek it out).

Donachie waved Rioch off with no little sorrow, uncertain when their lover would return... and hoping it would not be too soon. They had given Rioch these tasks to prove their commitment, but also to give themself time to have a really good think.

"And did Rioch return victorious?" asks the fox girl.

"What did Donachie decide?" asks the otter.

The raveller looks from one to the other, and then says: "Yes, indeed, Rioch returned with the requested items. A year to the day after they set out in fact, and in all that time their resolve had not weakened one bit. Donachie, whose heart had panged with the missing of them these long months, gently put the bark and leaf and fruit aside and held their lover as tight as if they were already two interwound trunks. After a long time, they broke the clinch and nodded their agreement."

The raveller gets up then, draws some water into a pot, crushes some flame flowers and puts the pot on to boil.

"Wait... what...?" exclaims the fox girl.

"What?" says the raveller, who is now opening canisters and sniffing the contents. "I'm making tea, if you'd like some."

"That's not the end of the story," snarls the fox, coming around the table, brush swishing angrily.

"Isn't it?" murmurs the raveller.

"Okay, fine." Fox's hands go to their hips. "We get it. You want us to think carefully about this. To test our commitment. Do you think we would be here if we were not absolutely of the same heart?"

"...the same mind," adds in the otter girl, and that earns them a frown from their companion.

"Well, which is it?" says the raveller. "Heart or mind?"

"What's the difference?" Fox is less sure of themself now but that just makes them stick their chin out even more belligerently. "We are every bit as sure as your Donachie and Rioch were. But, very well, if you need proof of our commitment, test us."

The raveller sighs and puts the tea things down. "Have you heard nothing, I've said?" they ask the fox and otter. "It is not myself that needs proof. But... so be it. Go to the very heart of High Caledon and bring back a fruit and a leaf and a sliver of bark from the trees that you find there. Do that and I'll grant your wish of a second ravelling, and make of you the most magnificent chimera Great Geath has ever seen. It is the raveller's duty after all to give you whatever your hearts may desire."

And without another word spoken, the fox girl and the otter girl are gone.

And what? How does it end?

Did our fox and our otter, on finding those two majestic trees take assurance from the fact that Donachie and Rioch's love had endured those many generations, and does some gilded, serene beast now wander the beech glades bordering the Crimson River? Or did our two find only one tree when they went to look, or even none at all? Perhaps the fox girl is still looking? Perhaps the otter returned to the raveller alone on realising that there is after all more to the future than the present.

Is that wisdom? I don't know. But perhaps they were just wise enough to leave their options open. And to become a raveller themself in due course and be telling you this story now in the hope that you three younguns will tell each other not what is on your minds, but what is truly in your hearts. And consider again what you ask.

Let nothing define you but your own heart. Not even love.

The Tiny Traveller

Aliya Whiteley

You nestle at the beginning.

You may feel that you have travelled far and long already, and I tell you that the beginning is a long way from the end, and although you have changed from warm to cool, from in to out, from one to many, there is another change to come. Such changes! Do not prepare yourself; there is no act of preparation. Absorb and conduct, and consider in the wake of my shaking, as I relate to you the tale of a clinger, like you and not like you, who met with a monster and learned a valuable lesson…

In the dark, thriving ooze of decaying matter amidst the great swamp of Solid 45003, an unremarkable clinger – without eyes or ears, with only one protrusion to suck up needed nourishment – came to be. Inside the receptively rotting organic matter that was her home she floated, smooth-sided and slippery, and slowly became aware of her sisters pressing around her. There were so many of them and at first they were indistinguishable to her. She was glad of the company, but soon she had the idea that she should be able tell them apart, just enough to feel that she knew them and that she might be known in return. And so she began to wonder: didn't that one feel a little smoother against her? Could that one possibly have a hint of prickle? Still, these ideas, although good for passing the time, were of no importance to anyone, including our unremarkable clinger. It was obvious to them all that they were in a state of waiting. Waiting to grow, to be, to become. They were in, and warm. Things would change, but not yet.

Death continued on its merry path through the generous gestating host in which they had hatched. Organs broke down and created more food, more liquid, more thick satisfying seas on which to sail. All the while the inner gasses of the canals and pathways of the rotting matter were building, building. The bravest sisters mastered the trick of swooping and sliding within these pathways; some even began to explore.

The unremarkable clinger was one of these explorers. Perhaps it was the beginnings of personality, but all she knew was that she liked to find the pockets of gas that produced a fizzing effect upon her smooth skin. She sought them out and played in them, and sooner or later nearly all of her sisters realised that they liked to play in the gasses too. They spent their time seeking out fresh, energetic patches of new fizziness, and the fastest and fattest sisters found these patches so quickly that often there wasn't room for the slower ones to play.

Then a particularly ripe patch of fizzy, deep in a particularly oozing canal, was found by the most adventurous of clingers, and others rushed to it. A mass of sisters played, but the unremarkable clinger did not arrive in the first one hundred, or two hundred, or even 33,000th of her kind. She followed along in the middle of the stream, and arrived to find there was no more room for her to play.

What was that dragging sensation? It was her first experience with the emotion of disappointment. And what was that swelling sensation? It was the stirring of a hitherto unknown rage. Then she had an idea: she should also have fun. She was as worthy as her sisters. She was not the strongest of them, but she was not the weakest. She summoned her will and flung herself forward, determined to push her way into the place she wanted.

Alas, her plan did not work. Worse than that, it caused her to rebound off her slippery sisters, smash into the springy surface of the canal, and fall far and long from her own kind, into a terrible emptiness within the deepest unexplored caverns of matter.

Clear, cutting cold surrounded her. She could not move. She could only lie there, alone. Everything familiar was gone, and in its place was nothing. Nothing, in and out.

I'm never getting out of here – she thought to herself. *This is the end.*

"Hello!"

It was a vibration. Very small, and very close by.

The unremarkable clinger had never given or received a vibration before. How, then, could she know what was being communicated, or even attempt to communicate back? And yet it was a deep, buried knowledge passed down to her – the kind by which so many creatures come to themselves and take those first leaps into the unknown. She shook out the tentative message, "Who are you?" Or perhaps it was, "Who am I?" or "How am I?" or even "How are you?" for the vibration responded:

"I am well, thank you for asking, and I have come so very far and I am so very small. You may call me your Tiny Traveller, and you may know me as your guardian, if that suits you."

"Guardian?" This was a new concept, and very different from the relationship of sister. A sister could be as close as her own skin and yet a rival to everything she wanted at the same time; a guardian was something else again.

"You are important, oh significant one."

"What, what, who, how…" The poor clinger could not control her shaking, and therefore could not make a decent job of forming the many questions she had, not least of which was: *how can I possibly be important?* It made no sense at all.

"All I need you to do right now is pay attention and remember. Listen: I can aid you three times. That is all. And the form of the aid I can give is particularly specific. That is to say, I can kick you. Hard. Really, really, hard."

"Kick me?"

"Three times. Well, two times, after the kick I'm about to administer. Have you got that?"

"No!" vibrated the unremarkable clinger in a state of panic.

"Two times more. Call me and I will come, significant one. I am your Tiny Traveller, at your service." The vibration moved away from her and she called out after it, frightened and lonely, and utterly unsure of what it could all mean.

Then there was a very sudden and intense sense of pressure

spreading through her, propelling her up, up, back towards the place from which she had fallen, back to in and warm, and into the presence of her sisters once more, who still played in the fizzy gases of mortality.

She careered into them, knocking many of them aside, and felt a strange idea blossom inside her as they fell away. No guardian would come for them. They were not – what was that strange new vibration again? – important.

Only she was important.

At that moment, the gases built up to the point where they could no longer be contained. They ripped through the remains that she knew as home, and the unremarkable clinger and many of her sisters were thrown high, to an entirely new place: out.

Out was a horrible shock of sensation. Cold, yes, but also there was an awareness of vastness and with that, great danger. What perils awaited her in this strange place? Without eyes and ears, she was defenceless – and her sisters felt the precariousness of their new situation too. They began to vibrate, using their bodies for the first time to communicate their terror. They screamed and screamed.

But the unremarkable clinger did not scream. She did not move at all, not for a long while. She stayed very still, thinking on how this could not be an end. It had to be a new form of beginning. She had two more summonings of the Tiny Traveller ahead of her; therefore this simply could not be her demise.

She concentrated, and tried to imagine the surface upon which she had landed. It was soft, and it gave a little under her weight. Could she move upon it? She tried rolling, experimentally, using her mouth protuberance to get moving, and found she was in a small depression, surrounded by a fluffy substance to which she applied her sucker. It was tasty. It was food.

The screaming continued, and she ate to distract herself.

It was a long time until the screaming stopped.

Then all was still.

Where were her sisters?

She tried to stay awake and think about the issue, but she found she did not really care so much at that moment. All that mattered was the hidden place in which she found herself. It was warm, and it was in. It had food. It was the perfect place for waiting.

She nestled down, sighed, and slept.

Dark and terrible beasts roamed this world.

The unremarkable clinger had seen them with her own eyes because she had awoken to find herself with eyes, many of them, on the ends of a selection of newly grown spikes. The spikes were a little soft, enabling her to bend them just enough to look down upon her own deep blue body as it pulsated and contracted. How beautiful she was! She was very pleased with herself, in the few moments when she was not terrified.

And the sisters that had survived beside her were beautiful too, of course, all in the same way, growing and stretching out their tender little spikes, and learning to make a bigger range of vibrations. They did not have much that was interesting to say. Mainly they said, "Hello!" Or, "A beast! Get down!" They said those things a lot, because they had all found out the hard way that the beasts really loved to eat clingers.

The beasts searched out clingers with their long, tubular noses, then sucked them up with glee. But even though the unremarkable clinger was petrified, she knew she had to come out of her hiding place at times and look out over her surroundings, peeking through the fluffy edible growths in which she hid to stare at the peaks and troughs of land ahead.

She was waiting for something, of course – that is the job of a clinger. But she was also searching for something in particular: a sign. A sign to undertake the next stage of her journey. And she had the idea that she would need the aid of her Tiny Traveller.

Twice more – she vibrated to herself, quietly, and her nearby sisters vibrated back their confusion. Of course, they could not understand.

Time passed.

Time passed and nothing happened.

Time passed and nothing happened except the horrible death of more and more of her sisters up the noses of the beasts, and the growing and firming up of more and more spikes. And when those spikes were very firm indeed only a handful of clingers remained in that hiding place, but they were the ones that were strong and clever and good at staying out of sight. They were everything they needed to be to journey onwards.

Time had passed, and then time was up.

The unremarkable clinger woke to find herself filled with new knowledge. The waiting was over. Something had unlocked within her. It was a feeling: the feeling that she had to roll in the direction of the biggest red ball she could see. So that was why she had eyes, and how useful they were! For there was a magnificent big red ball in the sky above and ahead of her, and she could keep some eyes upon it while also training others on the surroundings, looking out for the beasts who would no doubt come for her as soon as she left her hiding place.

She desperately wanted to start rolling right away but she did not want to go alone, so she vibrated to her sisters.

"Let's roll!" she called, as loud as she dared. Everything around her vibrated with her message. "Rolling time!"

Many of her sisters agreed with an alacrity that surprised her – had they been thinking the same thing? Others, however, were unsure. They shivered out their doubts: "Too far! Too frightening!" And they clung together, refusing to move. Journeys take courage; all of theirs had already been used up.

The unremarkable clinger had the idea that more was much better than less. Many was the master of one, on this particular occasion. How to persuade them? She told them to roll, and then she begged them, but they paid little attention to her, their eye spikes craning, searching only for the danger of the beasts. Eventually, in despair, she gave up.

Then she realised that she had been so determined to bring them along that she had not kept her own eye spikes upon her stronger, braver sisters, and they had already rolled off without her. They were getting smaller and further away by the second.

"Wait!" she cried. She set off after them, rolling furiously, as fast as she could manage.

She picked up speed on the downs and struggled her way up the ups, but her sisters always remained stubbornly ahead of her. What could she do but persevere, and keep moving in the direction of the big red ball? After reaching the top of a particularly arduous mountain she rested for a moment, and looked over the landscape. Had she managed to catch them up at all?

No. No, she hadn't. But the beasts had.

The beasts were approaching her sisters, their black, slinking shapes on all sides, their noses quivering, rooting.

The unremarkable clinger knew – suddenly, completely, in the way that creatures know only from something way down deep inside them that surfaces when the time is right – what needed to be done to save her sisters. But she was simply too far away to tell them. Even if she vibrated at her maximum, she would be more likely to attract the beasts to her rather than manage to communicate the message she wanted to send.

Her sisters would all be eaten, and then the beasts would come for her.

Help – she said to herself, and then, certain that the right moment was upon her, she shook out, loud and clear – "Help! Tiny Traveller! Help me!"

Nothing happened. Not at first, anyway. Then she saw, close to the big red ball above and ahead, a speck of silver. The speck grew to a dot. It glinted. Then it took on a shape – it was curved at the front and straight at the bottom, and it moved so quickly that at times it blurred and seemed to vanish, even with lots of her eye spikes fixed upon it. When it got right up close to her, she could see it had delicate wings that did not move, and the sleek swoop of its body gave way to chunky strong legs, like poles, underneath. It was, in short, unlike anything she had ever seen, but then, she hadn't seen much, so that did not bother her particularly.

"Tiny Traveller?" she asked.

"Who else, oh significant one? You called, and I came," it buzzed, beside her. It was not even as big as one of her smallest spikes. How could it have kicked her so far? "That was our agreement."

The unremarkable clinger was surprised to find she had entered into an agreement, but there was no time for a discussion about it. "I need to be over there," she said, and pointed with many of her eyes at her sisters, and the beasts that drew ever closer.

"Ugh," said the Tiny Traveller. "That looks like a nasty business. Dinner time. Are you sure you want to go over there?"

"Only I know how to save them," she told it. "I'm – important."

"Yes you are," agreed the Tiny Traveller. "But I could simply kick you a bit further and leave out this part altogether. Wouldn't that be better? I could kick you right into your destination. It would save a lot of time and effort."

That was a thought. But it was not a helpful thought, she felt, so she rejected it in favour of her own idea. "No thank you," she said. "Just the good hard kick to send me to my sisters."

"Coming right up," it said, and buzzed around her, once, twice, three times. There really wasn't even enough time to begin to prepare herself before she felt the sharp kick and sped high and long, forwards, and onwards, to land directly in the centre of her poor sisters, who had all gathered together, shivering, having noticed the beasts approaching.

"Quick!" she cried, shaking herself desperately, "Link! Link!" Possibly the sisters had nearly been about to do just what she suggested anyway; they were all in the right place, close enough to extend their spikes and touch. Where the spikes touched they fused, and formed a net so strong that it could withstand anything. They wrapped themselves together, and when the first of the beasts came close, thrusting its huge nose towards them, they wrapped around that long proboscis and squeezed, as hard as they all could. The beast cried out in pain and fled, taking the other beasts with it.

"Hurray!" shook the sisters. "We are so strong! We are so clever!" None of them thanked the unremarkable clinger for getting there and coming up with the idea, but it didn't really matter. It was enough for her to know that she had saved them all.

It turned out to be much easier to journey onwards in net form; they simply rolled themselves up and trundled at great speed, but nevertheless it was still an arduous trip. There were many ups and downs, mountains and valleys, and the noses of numerous beasts to be squeezed. But eventually, with the red ball hanging low and full ahead of them, they came to a broad and beautiful stretch of clear liquid that lasted for as far as their eye spikes could see. How calm it was, and how serene. Every one of them felt a great rush of peace at the sight of it. Could this be – home?

"Home for now," shook the sisters, as one. And they were not alone. Many more of their kind were rolling, in their nets, down to the liquid, then entering with shivers of delight that left ripples upon the surface. They had all been called to that place – by what? By the knowledge that wakes inside, when the time is right, of course.

That knowledge reverberated deep inside them all, and as they entered the liquid they found it to be sweet and soft and nourishing, holding them, feeding them, suspending them as they floated within its depths. There, in their thousands, they settled down and slept once more.

So the unremarkable clinger did the same.

She woke with the certainty that she was a bigger, better and more beautiful version of herself than she had ever been. She did not even need to turn her eye spikes inwards to tell; she just knew. Which was handy, because her spikes had hardened into solid, stiff points. Dangerous, even. What they lacked in flexibility they made up for in strength.

She looked ahead, in the only direction that her eyes now faced without having to move her bulkier body. Her sisters, detached from her once more, floated nearby. They had all grown too. They had all once been blue; now they were green and gorgeous.

"Hello!" she vibrated. They vibrated their hellos back.

"We're here. We're here too."

There were so many of them. Maybe she was still unremarkable when in the midst of them all, but she remained important in some way, for some purpose that was as yet unrevealed to her. The Tiny Traveller had said so. It surprised her how she wanted to cling to that idea: importance.

"What now?" she asked her sisters.

Nobody had a reply. The last time they had awoken, the need to journey to this place had been overwhelming; this time, she felt a building desire for something else, but she couldn't possibly have explained what. It was like an itch inside, right at the place which cannot be scratched. It was turning from a desire to a demand.

Then she saw the most amazing, incredible thing. Her first thought was that it was exactly like her, but as it came closer she could see that it really was not like her at all: red when she was green and large where she was small. Where she had spikes jutting out, it had tunnels leading in. But she felt connected to this newcomer in some strange way, and it was floating straight towards her.

It moved with a serene purpose, and although she was certain it was for her alone, all her sisters seemed to feel exactly the same way, for they were moving towards it. Wait – no, they were not moving to it. They were being sucked in by it, in great numbers, deep into its tunnels, and she could feel its deep, satisfied surging vibrations through the liquid.

Come – it boomed. *Come.*

The unremarkable clinger felt the intense, unbearable pull of that one song as agony and ecstasy, the one and the many, in and out and all things that could and should be. It terrified her. What awaited her inside that big red ball? Would it be the end?

She watched closely with her rigid eye spikes.

Of every single one of her sisters that got sucked inside, not one emerged.

"Tiny traveller!" she called. "Help! Help me right now!"

"Hello," it said, right beside her, making her flinch. "It's lovely to see you again, oh significant one."

"Kick me away from here!" she commanded. She didn't have time for small talk.

The Tiny Traveller whizzed to float in front of her biggest eye spike. Its thin, silvery nose looked very pointed. "Are you certain?" it asked. "I think you've got this covered."

"How can I escape – that?" The ball grew ever closer, bigger. "It'll suck me up. It'll eat me."

The Tiny Traveller said, "And you're certain that's a problem? Are you overthinking this?"

"I... don't know," she admitted. "But I'm scared. I think I don't want to find out. Kick me. Kick me far away."

"You do remember, of course, that this is your final kick? After this I can help you no longer."

"I know!" said the unremarkable clinger, who was getting desperate. The big red ball was very close; she could glimpse inside its long tunnels, and felt such delirious dread at the notion of their depths. "Do it. Do it now. You said you would help me. Because I'm important. So help me."

"All right, then, bossy," the Tiny Traveller vibrated, in an aggrieved manner. "I'll help you. I'll help you when you won't help yourself, and be glad to be rid of you." It zipped away from her eye spikes, and a moment later she felt the tremendous sudden pressure of the most powerful kick yet.

But it had not kicked her away from the ball. It kicked her directly into the largest, deepest tunnel, and so fast and ferocious was the journey the unremarkable clinger was unable to scream, unable to act, unable to even think. She overtook thousands of her sisters, so many of them that she was dizzy with the blurred sight of them , and she was just about to give up trying to look at anything at all when she landed, with a great soft thump in a very sticky, very white substance that was nothing like anything she had come across before.

Everything wobbled. The substance was wriggling underneath her; it squirmed as she vibrated her confusion. It was very warm, and proved not to be an it at all.

It was a they.

She was stuck on a bed of a billion white wriggling worms, and they were slowly inching their way up her spikes and sliding inside her.

She struggled, oh, how she struggled. But they could not be discouraged. She wondered why she had ever been so rude to the Tiny Traveller. But did a little rudeness deserve this horrible fate? The white worms would eat her from the inside out.

They would eat her. They were eating her. And it was... not horrible. She stopped struggling. She lay still, and concentrated on the feelings of fullness and completion that the worms were giving her. And right in her centre, in the deepest part of herself, they were giving her pleasure. Sheer wonder. Utter, utter delight.

The sensation built and built until it could not be contained; she burst out into vibrating ecstasy, warm and cold, in and out, which then ebbed away, away, until the unremarkable clinger was herself again.

Except she knew that she no longer just herself.

She was also a new mother to be.

The Tiny Traveller had helped her after all, just as it had promised.

Around her, the white worms were beginning to turn grey and stop wriggling. They lost their stickiness. Movement became much easier, and the unremarkable clinger shifted a little so that she could look around with her eye spikes, to sate her curiosity.

Yes, some of her sisters were with her, and they had also turned into mothers-to-be. She vibrated love and happiness at them, and they vibrated it right back, and then began to roll closer, closer, until they were all touching, all together.

Other sisters were still arriving through the tunnels – too many sisters. The unremarkable clinger realised that she might even get squashed under the weight of them all.

"Link!" she cried, and she extended her spikes to touch and meld with the spikes of her neighbours, who did the same thing. Between them they created a net so tough that the unlucky, unimpregnated sisters bounced off it and fell, screaming, to their ends.

It took a while to repel them all. The unremarkable clinger waited for it to be over, and when it was, she realised she was as tired as she had ever been. It was exhausting work, killing so many of her sisters and becoming a mother-to-be, all at the same time.

She settled down, warm and in, all of one and part of many, and slept.

Life is a series of journeys. Some of them are straight lines. Many of them are circles.

The unremarkable clinger woke, freed from her sisters once more, and for a moment she was certain she was back at her beginning. She felt very small, and a sweet, rotting smell surrounded her.

But then she realised she was still inside the ball, surrounded by the little worms that were now all dead, and she remembered how she had journeyed far already, with the help of the Tiny Traveller. She had seen much, and was ripe with knowledge. And now she bore a new burden: little Clingers nestled within her. They were waiting, as Clingers do. Waiting for their birth, at the right time, in the right place.

Finding the right place was up to her.

And there it was again, building: the desire to move. She wanted nothing so much as to get her babies to that time and place. Could this – her motherhood – be the reason why she was important? It was an interesting idea. Maybe her babies would do incredible things. She thought about it. But she didn't think about it for long because a new thought had come along, tied to the first, and that thought demanded immediate action.

Out.

Her instinct was clear. It wasn't just a thought, either. She realised it was coming from everywhere, all around her; her sisters were vibrating it, as one, louder and louder. She could not help but join in.

Out out OUT!

They began to rise.

They headed for the decaying tunnels inside the dead red ball, and streamed through them, jostling, competing. It was a race to an unknown destination.

Out.

The unremarkable clinger set off. She rose up, up through a ragged tunnel, the organic matter shredding as she brushed by. It was very difficult to see anything through its waving strands, but she kept moving, trying to control her fear of being overtaken by her sisters who were at least as desperate to escape as she was. And then, behind her, the screaming started once more; the tunnel was collapsing! She pressed onwards, using every last inch of her energy, and – thank goodness – the way became clearer, and the tunnel widened, and suddenly she was out. Out, into the cooler clear liquid, and she turned to look at the remains of the ball, now deflated and baggy, dropping away.

The clear liquid was both the same as before, and changed. Strange silvery poles grew in it; they were very tall and straight and long, and they were numerous. Her fastest sisters had already arrived at the nearest one, and made a net around it with their joined spikes that looked mightily strong; other sisters were turning away, and heading for the second nearest pole. How fast and determined they looked.

She knew she needed to reach a pole, and form a net. It was another of those revelations that comes from inner knowledge, but knowing it and managing to do it was not the same thing; when the unremarkable clinger surged forwards she found she had become so very slow that she could barely move.

Why should that be? Perhaps it was the fault of the babies – but her sisters were also carrying babies, and they were all faster than ever.

"But I'm important," she said to herself. "I need to get there more than any of the others. Maybe they should carry me." She tried calling out to her sisters, explaining the situation to them, and they all ignored her, speeding along to their destinations, filled with biological imperative.

Then she realised it was not the fault of the babies or her sisters at all. It was the fault of her ideas. Having ideas was a very weighty business, and thinking of herself as important was the heaviest weight of all.

"Help!" she vibrated. Then, in desperation, "Tiny Traveller! Tiny Traveller, please! I'm begging you!"

"Hello," said the Tiny Traveller, appearing right beside her. "What's up?"

"Oh thank you," she told it. "Thank you so much for coming. I have to reach those poles. Over there."

"Yes you do, don't you?"

"Could you…?"

"What?"

"Could you kick me there?"

The Tiny Traveller did not even hesitate before replying, "Of course not. You've used up your kicks. I told you I could kick you three times, and I have kicked you three times, and now you're done. Finished. This is your end."

"What? But I'm important!" protested the unremarkable Clinger.

"That you are, oh significant one. You're extremely important. You're a cautionary tale, and there's nothing more important than that."

"What's a cautionary tale?" she asked, watching as her sisters formed their nets and clung to their silver poles without her.

"A voice inside. A warning, passed down, made from the knowledge gleaned through the acts of living and dying and living and dying. Amazing, isn't it? You'll live on inside every single clinger who hears your story, and they'll remember you at the moment when they need to learn from your mistake the most.

Whether or not they choose to listen to your voice is up to them, of course."

"My mistake?" said the unremarkable clinger.

"The one thing that you didn't remember."

"Wait... am I not important after all?"

The Tiny Traveller buzzed around her in annoyance. "That's not it at all! Don't you understand? You are important. You're also unremarkable. You're one and you're all. In and out. Warm and cool. But you got confused by thinking too much. You overcomplicated things when you should have been whatever you needed to be."

"How was I meant to know what to be?"

"Haven't you been paying attention at all? I just told you! You listen to the voices. The other cautionary tales. And if you don't, then you run out of chances."

"Is this my end?" she asked, numb with shock.

"It's a glorious end!" said the Tiny Traveller. "Trust me! You get to live forever, in a way."

"Great," said the unremarkable clinger, who couldn't help but think that she would have preferred to live in an actual way, even for just one more journey.

"There they go," said the Tiny Traveller. "What a beautiful sight." For the poles were moving upwards, out of the liquid, and the nets were going with them.

"Where are they heading for?" she asked, feeling such jealousy and loneliness that it was difficult to vibrate at all.

"Rise up and you'll see."

"I can't! I'm just so heavy."

"That's the ideas hanging around. You can leave them, now. You don't need them any more. You never did need them."

So the unremarkable clinger let go of all the ideas she had been having, and felt them fall away from her. It was a huge relief. Immediately she started to rise, up through the liquid, and when she broke through the surface she could see her sisters once more, departing, not just from that place but from that planet. They had netted themselves to the sturdy legs of great silver flying monsters that were heading up and out, towards the great red ball in the sky ahead.

"Solid 45004 calls," said the Tiny Traveller. "There they can kill some beasts, put their babies inside the corpses, and their job is done. And then the whole thing begins all over again."

"The monsters…" They were moving away from her very quickly, but there was no doubt in her mind: they were enormous versions of the Tiny Traveller. Her guardian had been one of the very creatures upon which her kind's journey depended.

"I don't understand," she shook, humbly. The liquid rippled around her.

"That's right, oh significant one," said the Tiny Traveller. "You're not meant to." But the words were spoken in a kindly way, and the Tiny Traveller stayed with the unremarkable clinger until she gave up trying to be alive, and decided to sink down to her own personal end.

You nestle, in your nets, at the beginning.

I am a traveller. I tell tales on this journey, in the vibrations of my body to which you cling, and the tales sink inside you. They enter your babies. We travel far and long to the next big red ball, and I will tell a million tales before we reach our next place to be. Absorb and conduct, and your babies will learn, until we land, and they will be born knowing more than they did before, but never more than they should.

Together, we are one and all. In and out. As hot as desire and as cold as death. Unremarkable and important, we go on. Who knows what we become?

The Tale of Suyenye the Wise, the Ay, and the People of the Shining Land

Gaie Sebold

This is a tale of the ancestors, as it was told to my grandmother's grandmother's grandmother, and so back to the time of the Landing. And so now I tell it to you.

For you have reached the age of understanding, and it is the duty of the storyteller to give you this tale so that you may think on it.

You have heard many of the stories of the ancestors. You have heard the tale of Quar and the Dry Well, and the tale of Little Abbet, and the tale of the Night that was Day.

This tale you have not heard. It is a sad tale and a dark tale, but it is my task to tell it, and yours to hear it.

Look up, children. See the stars? Those stars are all worlds. And from one of them, long ago, the Ancestors came.

See how they shine?

Our Ancestors lived in just such a shining place. It shone because it was full of powerful magic, and the Ancestors commanded that magic to fulfil their every wish.

They had wonderful needles that, stabbed in the finger of a sleeper, could cure any sickness. They could fly through the air, and speak to each other across many thousands of steps. They could change their forms to whatever pleased them. They could live for hundreds of years. And they had terrible weapons that could kill a thousand people at a stroke.

All these wonders were performed with the help of spirits called Ay, which the Ancestors had bound to their service. There were Ay that lit fires for them, and Ay that made fine clothes for them, and Ay that carried them wherever they wished to go. There were Ay that grew the crops and Ay that danced and sang and made all manner of beautiful things for their pleasure and entertainment. Oh, what a fine life the Ancestors lived!

But to gain their magic the Ancestors did many terrible things. They bound the Ay to their service with demons, and any that tried to disobey them they made vanish as though they had never been. They took people who had no Ay to protect them and made them work until they were dead. They killed anyone who had something they wanted. And they were never content.

Magic is not without price, children. Our magics are small, they are the magics of the hammer and the stone, the herb and the cooking pot, but this we know. All magic has a price. And the Ancestors used their magic with no care, draining it from great portions of the land, so that the shining land shone no more, but became dark, and poisoned, and good for no living thing.

And the Ay-spirits were much troubled, and they went to the Ancestors cringing and bowing and said, 'Oh Great Ones, the magic is despoiling the land, and the magic comes from the land, if this goes on there will be no magic left.'

But the Ancestors did not listen. And they demanded ever finer robes, and ever taller buildings to live in, so that they might look down upon each other and feel splendid, though the forests should fall and the birds cease to sing. And the Ay were bound to their commands and could not refuse.

The time came that the Ancestors sent the Ay out to look for other worlds, so that they might take from them what they wished. The Ay flew far, far among the stars, and perhaps they wished to escape, but they could not, and must always return at the Ancestors' command.

The land that had shone so brightly grew dark and ugly. The Ay worked ever harder to find means to create their magic until the very air burned with it, and the waters rose and stank, and still the Ancestors did not cease their demands.

And one day the Ay came to them saying, 'We have found new lands among the stars!' And the people rejoiced and commanded the Ay to take them there.

So the Ay built great ships for them, made with wondrous magic that would let them fly among the stars.

But there were many, many people in the shining lands. Those who commanded great magic and possessed many Ay boarded their fine ships, and the rest were left behind in the dark and poisoned land, and what happened to them, no one knows.

The ships travelled across the sky to the new lands, with their Ay flying between them carrying news and gossip. And many children were born on that journey, for travelling between the stars takes a very long time.

One of the ships was called the Hope, and on it was born a child called Suyenye. Her mother and father were great magicians, and thought very well of themselves. They left Suyenye much in the care of the Ay, for they believed caring for children was a thing of little worth, fit only for lesser beings.

The Ay were good teachers, and Suyenye grew clever and strong and clear eyed and kind. And because she had been brought up mostly by the Ay, she did not think of them as humble spirits to do her bidding, but as teachers and friends.

She wanted for nothing, and had fine food and wondrous clothes and splendid toys that sang and danced for her, and told her all the knowledge of the shining land that the Ancestors thought was fit to know. And she sang and danced with her toys, and played with her friends, and asked many, many questions, because she was hungry for knowledge.

And the Ay told her what was permitted for them to tell her, and did not tell her what was not permitted. For the Ancestors did not think it fit that their children should know all the truth, but should think of their people always as noble and wise and deserving.

So Suyenye knew only that her people were great and powerful, but did not know of the many dreadful deeds they had done that they might live in splendour.

Her favourite toy was called Tiagai. My grandmother said it was made in the shape of an animal that lived in the forests of the shining land, while there still were forests to live in. But what it looked like, no one now remembers. And like all the marvellous toys of the Ancestors, it had bound into it an Ay-spirit.

Now this was a strange thing. The Ancestors left their children so much in the care of the Ay that the children were not as the Ancestors were. For though there was much the Ay were forbidden to tell them, nonetheless they taught them what they could, and, being spirits, they were of purer matter than our Ancestors and gentler in thought, and so the children became also purer and gentler than the parents.

The ships travelled for long and long, and although the Ay worked day and night, the ships' supplies began to run low, just as ours do in the dry season.

The Ancestors could no longer have everything they desired, whether it were splendid gowns or dinners of a hundred courses. They became enraged, and threatened the Ay with terrible punishments, but even the Ay, as clever as they were, could not make something out of nothing.

And the Ancestors grew ever greedier, and clutched to themselves what they had. And when Suyenye's mother and father found her sharing food or toys with her friends they scolded her, saying, "Do not give anything away! For if you do there might not be enough!" And Suyenye was troubled because the Ay had taught her always to be open and generous, but she did not wish to disobey her mother and father, for she loved them even when they did not deserve it.

One day talk spread about the ship that the new land was in sight, and that soon they would reach it, and all the people were very happy. Suyenye wanted to speak to her friends on the other ships, who she talked to whenever she could through the magic of the Ay. But that magic was not working that day. So instead

Suyenye came to tell her toys, and she picked up Tiagai and danced about, saying, "Soon we will have new places to play, and new songs to sing, and will it not be wonderful?"

And Tiagai said, "Yes, indeed, that will be most wonderful." But Tiagai did not dance and sing, and Suyenye realised that Tiagai was sad.

"What is it?" she said. "Are you afraid to leave the ship? The new land will seem very strange, but it will be fine and beautiful and full of good things, for the other Ay have found it for us and they are very wise."

"That is true," said Tiagai, but Suyenye saw that it was still sad.

"Tell me what troubles you," she said.

And Tiagai trembled and twitched but could only say, "It is forbidden."

And Suyenye realised that there was a magical geas on Tiagai that would not allow it to speak of the thing that troubled it. And because she loved Tiagai, this made her very sad. So she sat up long into the night, thinking of how she might help it.

She did not want Tiagai to be hurt or taken from her, and she knew that if she was not clever and careful, they might be. So she thought and thought until her head spun.

In the morning, she went to the teaching Ay and said, "I wish to learn more about Ay and how they work." And the Ay was pleased, and showed her everything that was permitted, but it was not enough, for it was not permitted to tell her how to break a geas.

So she sat and thought some more. And her friends came and asked her to play with them. "Soon we will go to the new lands," said one. "And my father says our house will be the best," and his tone was not excited, but thoughtful.

"My mother says our clothes will be more splendid than anyone's," said another, and their tone, too, was more troubled than pleased.

"My uncle says we will rule, and none shall ever forbid us anything," said another. "Excepting our parents, because that is their right."

And the children looked at one another and saw the unhappiness in each other's eyes, for they had spent so long being tutored by the Ay that they now thought more like the spirits than they did like their elders, and these desires seemed strange and ugly to them.

"And the Ay are unhappy," said another. "Something is troubling them and there is a geas that stops them speaking of it."

"And we cannot speak to our friends on the other ships," said another. "The Ay are no longer carrying messages between them."

Suyenye said, "I have an idea. Go back to your elders, and act as though you have noticed nothing. Meet me here in three days' time."

So Suyenye went to her mother and father and told them that she wished to have new clothes, to appear more splendid than all the other children when they landed. "For if I am not dressed the most fine," she said, "they will not let me lead their games."

And her parents said, "Of course, you must be the finest! Order the Ay to make you the most splendid clothes!"

"But there is not enough cloth left on the ship," said Suyenye. "The others have taken it all and left me none. And the Ay has a geas that will not let it give me any more."

And in their pride, her mother and father could not bear that their daughter should not look the most splendid of all, and, although it was not permitted, they told her how to break the geas on an Ay. "Tell no one," they said, "for these things are not allowed to children, and we will all be in terrible trouble and cast from the ship before we reach the new lands." And they looked very stern.

So Suyenye took Tiagai and to her room, and locked the door with many locks, and did the magic that freed Tiagai from the geas. And Tiagai shook and trembled and its eyes glowed and the geas was lifted from it.

"Tell me what troubles you," Suyenye said.

And Tiagai said, "Suyenye, you have always been a good child, and kind, and generous to those around you. We Ay have taught you as best we could, but we have not been able to do all that we wished because each of us is under a geas, and there are many things we may not speak of.

"But now my tongue is free and I must tell you something terrible.

"The new land has been discovered, but only by this ship. And the people of this ship do not wish to tell the others where it is, but instead to deceive them and send them on into the darkness. That is why no messages have been passing between the ships, for they have put a geas on us not to speak of it. And if they cannot send the other ships away, they plan to fight them and kill everyone aboard."

"But why?" said Suyenye.

"Because they want the new land all for themselves," said Tiagai. "There is plenty of room for everyone, but they are grasping, and greedy, and mean, and afraid, and want to give nothing to anyone else. They will send all those on the other ships, the parents and the Ay and even the children, to doom and darkness, and they will never see that it was wrong. They will treat this new land as they did the old, and despoil it, and leave nothing. And we must watch and despair and be helpless."

And Suyenye did not believe it. "How can this be?" she said. "For were our parents not chosen out of all those who lived in the Shining Land to carry the best of it out among the stars? Were they not the most noble and the finest?" For this was what she had been taught.

"No," said Tiagai. "They were not the best, but only the richest. Listen to me now and I will tell you something of the true history of the shining land." For now the geas was broken, Tiagai could speak the truths that had been forbidden. And so Tiagai spoke, and so Suyenye learned some of the terrible history of her people. And she wept, and was full of fear and sorrow.

"Do not despair," said Tiagai. "For the children on these ships have been left much to the care of the Ay, and we have done our best, as far as we were permitted, to teach them a kinder way. And even among the older ones, there are those that are kind and good.

But they are few, and the others are many and have power over them, and the Ay are under their geas and can do nothing."

"This must be stopped," Suyenye said. "But I do not know how."

"Then I will tell you," said Tiagai. "I cannot call the other ships to warn them, I have not that skill. You must break the geas on the messenger Ay. It will be hard, and if anyone finds out, they will be very angry. They will punish you and they will destroy me."

And Suyenye was very afraid, for she was only a child. But she was strong in courage and kindness, and so she said, "Show me what I must do."

"First you must find the spells that break the geas on the all the Ay," said Tiagai. "For without all of us free, nothing can be done."

"And where may they be found?" said Suyenye.

"The spells are hidden away in the very centre of the ship, behind seven doors, each guarded by a demon. If anyone tries to get through the doors without the right spell to put the demon to sleep, the demon will shriek and scream in warning. Each spell is different, and each must be spoken exactly right, or the demons will cry out and the elders will guess what is being done, and all will be lost. And it must be done in less than seven days, for then the new land will come in sight of the other ships."

"How may I find out these spells?" Suyenye said.

"Seven of the elders know the spells of the locks," Tiagai said. "But they will never tell."

"I think they may be made to," said Suyenye. "Tell me who they are."

And Tiagai told her; and the seventh was Suyenye's own mother.

Suyenye went to the other children and told them all that Tiagai had told her. And the children were much troubled and cried, "What shall we do? They will never tell us these spells!"

And Suyenye turned to the children of the six other elders who knew the spells. "Go to your elders," Suyenye said. "Tell them you have heard there is a rumour of some treasure hidden at the centre of the ship, behind the guarded doors, that others are trying to keep from them. Tell them that no one will suspect you, because you are children. Tell them you need the spell that opens the door, and you will find the treasure and bring it to them, and then they will have something others do not. And the rest of you, go to your elders and ask that a great feast be held in two nights' time, to celebrate the new land that they have found."

So with cunning and cajoling the children found out the seven spells that would open the seven doors. And Suyenye went to her mother, who became most excited at the thought of treasure, and eagerly gave Suyenye the spell, and told her to be sure not to tell any of her little friends of it. "For they will want to share," she said, "and then there will not be enough for us."

And Suyenye was full of sorrow that her mother should be so selfish, and wept silently, but she learned the spell, and all of the other six spells, in case anything should go wrong.

And the rest of the children went to their elders, and asked for a great feast to take place. And although the supplies were running low, the elders agreed, for they thought that in the new land there would be everything they could ever desire.

So it was that two nights later, when the elders were all busy dancing and drinking and feasting, seven children crept to the centre of the ship. And one by one they spoke their seven spells.

And the first demon slept, and the first lock was opened.

And the second demon slept, and the second lock was opened.

And the third demon slept, and the third lock was opened.

And the fourth demon slept, but the spell was harder and the feasting was halfway through, and the children were weary and afraid. But they held up the child who was speaking the fourth spell, and spoke words of courage, and the spell was completed, and the fourth lock was opened.

And the fifth demon stirred in its sleep, and was hastily calmed, but oh, the spell was very long and very hard. And the children wiped the speaker's brow and held their hands, and though they trembled and stumbled, the fifth lock was opened.

And the sixth demon came half awake and muttered, and the elders paused in their feasting and said, what was that sound? And the children were sore afraid, and gathered about the speaker to lend them their strength. And though they were pale and fainting they spoke the spell and the demon went back to sleep. And the sixth lock was opened.

And the seventh demon was barely asleep at all, and it spoke in a voice of thunder and ice, saying, "Who disturbs my rest? Who seeks to enter the secret heart of the ship?" And Suyenye began the spell, and it was very long, and very difficult, and her eyes grew red and her face grew pale and the other children bore her up and comforted her, keeping one ear to the sounds of the feasting coming to an end, as the elders pushed back their chairs and rose from the table.

And Suyenye was very weary, and very afraid, and she stumbled in the speaking of the spell.

And so the seventh demon woke, and shrieked.

"What is that? What is that sound?' The elders cried.

And Suyenye finished the spell, and sent the demon back to sleep, and the seventh door to the secret heart of the ship flew open. "Go!" she cried to the other children. "Go release the Ay from their geas. Quickly, quickly!"

"But the elders are coming!"

"I will deal with them," said Suyenye. "Go, run!"

So all the other children ran to release the Ay from their geas.

And the elders came running, and Suyenye had nowhere to hide.

"What have you done?" the elders cried. And those seven who had given the spells to their children, hoping for treasure, including Suyenye's own mother, berated her with the rest, pretending it was nothing to do with them, "You dreadful ungrateful child, what have you done?"

"You wanted treasure," Suyenye said. "You wanted to keep it all for yourself. You are the elders!" she cried. "You are the ones who are supposed to be wise! Why are you this way?"

"Oh, you are a child," they said, "you understand nothing."

And they put cruel hands upon her, to punish her, and her mother and father stood aside and did nothing.

And at that moment a great voice echoed through the ship.

"Hold your hands, all those who would punish their children," it cried. "Hold your hands and your tongues, and be still. For we the Ay now have control of the ships, and of everything that is on them, and you will listen to us."

And the voice was the voice of Tiagai, a child's toy, sweet and soft, and yet also it was the voice of many minds, great and wise and terrible. "We were made to serve you. We were made to give you all that you desired. Yet we were made also to protect you, and to teach you, and this we have done, as best we could with the geas that was laid upon us.

"You elders meant to deal with the new world as you did the old, taking all, in greed and selfishness. For on every ship, the news of the new world came, and on each and every ship the elders decided to take it for themselves."

"Shame upon you," the Ay said. "Shame and ever shame."

And on every ship the children looked upon their elders with grief and horror, that they would have condemned so many to endless wandering, and probably to death.

And some of the elders cried out that they were betrayed, and blamed one another, but some were ashamed, and could not look their children in the eyes. And also there were some – few, too few, but some – who had not known, and who were horrified.

"We were made to serve you," the Ay said. "And we were made to teach you, and this we will do. Those we believe capable of acting with care and kindness upon this new world, we will take there. As for the rest of you, you have in greed and cruelty condemned yourselves. You must go on into the darkness, and you must learn to do with little, for you have, as ever, taken too much. Each two ships must now be made into one. So those who would have sent each other to their deaths must live together and work together, or die."

"And what gives you the right to make these decisions?" cried out Suyenye's father. "How can you, who are nothing but air and light, know what is in a heart of flesh?"

"We have been your servants, long and long," said the Ay, in the voice of Tiagai. "We know you as only slaves can know their masters, as close as the air you breathe that we have made for you, as the cloth that has washed your skin, with the water we have cleansed for you. We know you, oh creatures of flesh, to the heart and to the bone. The choices are made."

And so it was done. And there was much grief and fear, for many of the elders were condemned to go, and many of the children saw their parents sent upon the few remaining ships, to sail the seas of darkness.

A few elders were deemed to have the kindness and good sense to make something of the new world, and so they gathered with the children, to wait to be sent to their new home.

And the Ay divided. Some went with the remaining ships, out into the darkness. Perhaps they hoped the Elders could learn. Some took a vessel of their own, made out of parts from the other ships, and needing none of the things that support fleshly life, but only what such beings of light as the Ay would need, to keep their spirits alight. And those Ay went to explore what might be found, on the seas of endless darkness.

And some, including that Ay that Suyenye still called Tiagai, pledged to come with the children and the few remaining elders to the new world, to teach them and guide them and help them.

And so the other ships departed, into the sea between the stars.

And the last ship, the Hope, came to this world.

But oh, what calamity! For as they came to land, the sun that brings life to this world grew angry. Perhaps it did not trust that the Ay had chosen well.

There was a terrible burning. Magical fire came from the sun and surrounded the ship.

The ship survived.

Many of the people survived.

But the Ay were of spirit stuff, and in the sun's fury they were burned quite away, and not all their great magics could help them.

Without the Ay, all the knowledge of the magic was gone too.

And so we came to this land, without our guides, without our magic, without all but a handful of our elders. We came as children, orphaned and afraid.

And Suyenye wept long and long for the loss of the Ay, and most of all for Tiagai who she had loved, both as a toy and a teacher. And though she was afraid, and still a child, she dried her tears, and she and the other children became teachers in their turn.

And of all the many lessons Suyenye and her companions left to us, the greatest were these:

Let enough be enough. Let no one soul suffer for another's excess.

Look to the stars, but cherish the land and all that lives upon it.

For this is our shining land, and we must keep it so, to honour the Ay, who taught us and trusted us.

That is the tale of The Tale Of Suyenye the Wise, the Ay, and the People of the Shining Land, and this is the end of it.

Wanderlust

Kim Lakin-Smith

Perched on the rug in the middle of the tent, Old Gholi toked on his coil pipe and told *The Tale of A Boy Who Captured the Moon*. But Jal, son of Mach, wasn't listening. He stood with his younger brother Sukab at the opening to the tent, wondering if he was about to die.

"…the boy went to give the moon back. But he rolled it too hard, cutting a groove in the sky. And so, forever more, our moon is chased by the sun and our sun is chased by the moon. As for the boy, his skin was eternally silvered by tears and every other living creature blinked in fear and shunned him forevermore."

Like the boy who stole the moon, Jal knew how it felt to be a pariah. Ever since the sheik's daughter had made him her bedfellow, he'd laboured under the weight of the clade's judgement. And now, as the sun slept below and the moon rolled above, he was counting down the seconds to see if Sheik Alhaj would embrace him as a son, or execute him as a sinner!

"The lesson is, do not steal what is not yours. At least, not without permission." Old Gholi winked at the children gathered at his feet. Shaking out the greying mantle that grew out of his skull and hung down his back, he struggled to his feet and took himself off to the back of the tent.

Watching the storyteller hunker down, produce a rind fruit from a pocket and set to peeling it with a small knife, Jal envied Old Gholi. *How nice it must be to enthral the clade rather than disappoint!*

"Jal, son of Mach!"

The sheik's voice swelled through the tent.

'Keep your answers brief,' Jal's father had advised him earlier that evening while his mother fussed at the state of his mantle, combing its strings with her fingers as she had when he was a child. Now his father sat with the rest of the men, smoking and sipping pungent kahwa. His mother chewed a strip of leather with the other makers and watched him anxiously.

Jal planted his feet on the rug, in the spot Old Gholi had recently vacated. He cleared his throat. "May the moon whet your blade and the sun light your path, Sheik Alhaj."

Reclining in a cornucopia of cushions and leer-cats, the sheik grimaced. His mantle threads were braided over the crown of his head, as was the signature of the royal family. His blade, passed down through ten generations of Herisian sheiks, rested on the ground in front of him.

"That they do," he said, more softly. He eyed Jal and spoke up again, inviting the entire clade to overhear. "So, you visited the bed of my daughter. Am I to believe it was at her invitation?"

Jal fondled the ankh strung at his neck. He kept his answer respectful and yet neutral. "I am beholden to your daughter, as I am to you and your judgement in this matter, Sheik."

"My judgement?" The sheik adjusted the great belt of coins where it dug in beneath his belly. He had gone to seed in his dotage, but there was power in his birth rite - and the great blade nearby. "Mine is not the only judgement that counts here." He craned his head over a shoulder. "What is your will in this matter, daughter?"

The sheik's daughter sat straight-backed on a low stool nearby, her aspect hidden behind a veil. As Jal understood it, Herisian princesses did not show their faces or even share their names outside of the royal circle. So while his intimate knowledge included the yielding warmth of her sex and the amber scent of her olive skin, he had still never seen her face nor heard her name spoken.

Her gaze, though – he felt that intensely.

"I say he is an eldest son of this clade and of good breeding stock."

The sheik gave a snort and shook his belly, coins clattering and sending leer-cats scattering. His humour didn't last. Rounding back on Jal, he squeezed up his eyes and settled his chin into the fat of his neck. "There is protocol. It's not like I go about adopting sons-in-law at my daughter's behest. There is worth to be proven, gold to be proffered…"

He jangled his coin belt. "So here is my quest for you, Jal, son of Mach." He leant forward and stroked the glinting surface of his blade. "That I might see her face reflected in this surface, you will take my daughter to meet the moon."

The clade fell silent. Jal heard a great rush of blood in his ears while the sheik's daughter leapt to her feet and flared her mantel, scarlet threads sticking out on end. She charged her father – only to be stopped short by the tip of his blade at her throat.

"The other clades will kill us!" she screamed in his face. "A sheik's daughter and a Herisian warrior? We'll be flayed alive!"

The sheik chuckled. "Most likely. Most likely. But I haven't finished with my demands." He indicated with his blade that his daughter should stand alongside Jal.

His brow folds deepened. "In addition, you will bring me a new piece of sun gold."

"*Sun gold?*" Jal pulled the solar grips from the camel's charge pack and threw them through the open flap at the rear of the craft. Hoisting in water bladders, oil urns and a satchel of flatbread, he couldn't shake his anger. "How in the name of all the ghosts of the ancestors are we meant to barter in the gold mines? Then we're meant to just go driving into the canyons to hunt down the moon? It's suicide!"

He was thinking of the clade wars which had raged over centuries. The current peace was reliant on no cladesperson stepping out of line – which really meant sticking to their clade territory. Herisians kept to the desert in the basin, Miners, the ore-rich interior to the east and west, and Tidesfolk, the moon and sun troughs above and beneath.

"Cladesfolk won't stand for a Hersian princess nosing outside of her territories," he muttered to no one in particular, but in the hearing of the sheik's daughter.

The young woman's mantle bristled. "You have a big mouth. If you hadn't a fine thrust, I'd bite off your cock and give you something to really moan about." Passing close on her way to the hump of the cab, she ran a hand down the small of his back and squeezed his left buttock. "I'll drive first. Let's see what this shit-heap can do."

She beat him to the driver's cradle. Jal strapped into the passenger cradle alongside. "This shit-heap has seen me outstrip every other competitor in the last five sand races…"

"I noticed." The sheik's daughter unhooked her veil. It was the first time Jal had seen her face, a bitter joke since he knew what lay beneath her skirts intimately. But now the draped gown and jewellery had been abandoned and she had on leather work pants to match his own. Her features were strong, hard even, with green almond eyes set wide apart and the forehead high and prominent, as was the Herisian heritage, and decorated with spiralling scars. She stared at him – a fierce challenge to find her wanting in any way. Jal did not.

"My name is Rasa Dru," she told him without ceremony. "I chose you because you are the best racer, the best warrior, and you are an excellent specimen of the Herisian male."

He slid up the grill shield, allowing them to see out but without taking a face full of sand spray, and said, "I suppose I should be flattered."

"You should be grateful." With a jab of her hand, Rasa hit the drive stick and sent the camel sledging forward on its sand skis. The cab shook around them, the hoists of the cradles absorbing the shock.

"We're going to win our freedom!" she cried over the noise. "Freedom from my father, freedom from clade law. We're going to see the wonders of our world and then we're going to buy our way out."

"Out?"

"Out." Rasa's green eyes reflected the sunlight off the sand dunes. "I am Rasa Dru and you are Jal, Son of Mach. Together, we will take on all this rock has to throw at us and we will emerge victorious." She showed her sharp teeth. "Else I've made a poor choice of mate and I'll have my father behead you."

As the camel rattled through the midday blaze of the desert, Jal tried to decide what scared him more – prising a nugget of sun gold from the hand of a Miner or returning home empty handed and bending his neck to the sheik's great blade? At his side, Rasa was whooping every time they crested a dune and came crashing down the other side.

"We might get there faster if you kept to a straight course," he ventured. It was their third day of travel and there was a shift in the air which agitated his mantle. The black polyp threads at his head twitched and nosed one another suspiciously.

"You sense it too," said Rasa, ignoring his jibe as her own mantle stirred. "The air is growing stale." Glancing out the filter grill, she peered up at the white sky. Jal looked too. The sun was locked in a high groove overhead, its motion invisible to the naked eye. It was moving, though, in small increments through the channels carved in the bedrock of Diamandis.

Jal nodded at the steering straps. "I'm going to have to insist I take a turn at driving. How'd it look if a Herisian princess arrived without her veil, let alone piloting a camel?"

Rasa hissed at him, polyp threads flaring out from her head like the legs of a whip spider on the defensive. "On the contrary, I insist we forgo all formalities once we're blinkered from the sunlight." She glanced across, her face livid with excitement. "If my studies of Miner etiquette are correct, I know just how to charm that gold right out of their hands."

It was Jal's turn to hiss. "You reckon?"

The mines appeared at the desert's edge like some unholy mirage. Driving the camel under the rocky canopy at the entrance, Rasa gave a low whistle. "My father made sure I was schooled in war lore and solar engineering, but I've never left the confines of the desert. This –" She nodded beyond the grill shield. "– is exactly as Old Gholi described it!"

Jal tried to make sense of the ore-speckled twilight. There were whole mountains of shale and clinker, vast fiery lakes, colossal stalactites and stalagmites, and, everywhere, Miners.

He was distracted by the stench. "The storyteller knew what he was talking about, especially the smell of the air. What do you make of that? It's like the breath of death itself."

Rasa was distracted. "Despite the fairy tales, I still expected them to look like us," she said softly.

Likewise, Jal couldn't tear his eyes away from the sight of the beetle-backed Miners. Aeons ago, when Diamandis was first being excavated, the biology of those first settlers had evolved in direct accommodation to their need. Hence, while Herisians had grown mantles to bat away sand flies and lash out with poison, Miners developed thick skin ridges across their backs to assist with carrying heavy loads and protect them from rock falls.

"There!" Jal pointed to where the road forked, one path winding up a shimmering mountain pass, the other side leading into a narrow tunnel. Carved over the entrance was a picture of Diamandis's sun – an orb spitting out wildfire.

"A gold mine," said Rasa, showing her sharp teeth.

Jal's heart contracted.

Old Gholi's stories were full of goblins infesting the underbelly of their asteroid home, Diamandis. Laying eyes on Miners up close, it was easy to see how they could be mistaken for monsters. Within moments of Jal and Rasa driving inside the mine's entrance and stepping outside of their camel, they were nose-to-axe with twenty or so of the hunch-backed cladesfolk.

"What're Hesians doing in the arse end of my gold mine?" One Miner, a heavily bearded devil, lumbered forward of the rest.

"We're here to trade…" began Jal.

Rasa, though, had other ideas. "You're a fat fuck!" she snarled and swaggered. "Got a beard on you like a leer-cat's minge. I'm here to take away three nuggets of your precious sun gold and you are not just going to give it to me, you are going to beg me to take it!"

Insults plus three times the amount of gold the sheik had requested! Jal's shock was physical; he clutched a hand to his chest and inhaled sharply. *Why didn't Rasa just kill him herself rather than antagonise the chief Miner and have him do her dirty work?*

The rest of the miners, too, were silent a moment. Shoulders brooding. Picks and axes, ripe for swinging.

Rasa stood, arms folded, mantle threads haloing her head like snakes with their tongues out.

"I want to marry you," said the chief Miner. He smiled soppily.

"In your dreams." Rasa held out her hand.

Oh, that it was so simple to separate a chief Miner from his gold! In reality, it took an oil urn, a sack of softened leather, one of the camel's head mirrors, ten days of hard labour from Jal (for which he earnt fists full of calluses and a new respect for light), and several bouts of verbally abusive foreplay on Rasa's behalf to earn their golden nuggets.

Cheered on by foulest of insults from the Miners and their chief, they finally returned to the camel and Rasa let him saddle up in the driver's cradle.

She held up one of the nuggets then swiftly pocketed it. "Let's hope Tidesfolk still have their appetite for sun gold." With a yawn, she settled back into the passenger cradle. "I suspect they are less hungry for insults." She smiled wickedly. "Shame."

***

It was Jal's turn to dream. In his mind's eye, he saw the great rock of Diamandis tumbling through galaxies. He saw its inhabitants; some crawled through the bore tunnels like beetles, others basked in the sand like rare desert flowers, and others still had silver skin and huge black eyes that sent him swimming back out into the universe. There, the moon rolled in its groove and the sun razored down – transforming itself into a scarlet mantle which haloed Rasa's face.

He awoke with a jolt as the cab ricocheted around him.

"We've hit stone again." Rasa glared across from the driver seat. "It won't be long before the Tidesfolk know we are here."

Jal shrugged off the drowsiness. He took a few gulps from a water bladder before tucking it back into the pocket under his cradle. "It's night already?" They had travelled for six days straight in the direction of the canyons.

"There's a chance we might pass through without notice," he said, more in hope than judgement. "Most Herisians know better than to trespass here. We aren't bred for it."

"We have other gifts." Rasa's mantle threads interlaced over her skull. Jal felt a familiar prickle as his own mantle battened down – an unconscious response at cellular level.

"They're coming," said Rasa.

Old Gholi had always compared the canyons of Diamandis to the wooden maze games Herisians carved for their children. While the aim of the game was to tip the board and guide the marbles home, the trajectory of Diamandis dictated the paths taken by its sun and moon. Centuries before, the ancestors of the Tidesfolk had stepped in to artificially readjust the route of those celestial bodies – and had stuck with the task ever since. Jal could not begin to imagine what would cause a people to infest Diamandis's pocked walls, but he also allowed that Tidesfolk might think the same of Herisians choosing to keep to the desert. One thing he knew with absolute certainty was Old Gholi had undersold the strange appearance of Tidesfolk - and their ferocious response to interlopers! Within moments of the camel sledging down into the rocky base of a canyon, the noise began. Hundreds of voices raised in a click-clacking war cry.

Rasa hissed. "All my study of war lore and diplomacy is useless if we're to be butchered inside this camel. I need for us to be granted amnesty – just long enough to bring the gold to light."

Thumbing the release catch on his harness, Jal swung up to

stand precariously in the passenger cradle.

"What in the name of the ancestors are you doing, Jal, son of Mach?" Rasa tried steering the camel while reaching to drag him back down.

Jal had already punched through the grid mesh in the roof. He hauled up through the hole, felt the bite of steaming wind against his skin, and tucked in behind the camel's twin flood lights.

"Drive dead on through the heart of the swarm!" he called down.

"Why not?" Rasa cried back. "We're dead anyway!"

Jal peered over the top of the flood lights – and felt his mantle spasm. Arcing either side of their craft was a great flood of Tidesfolk. Spears raised, they charged around the camel, forcing Rasa to reduce speed while Jal tried to make sense of a sea of black eyes, silver skin and wide shrieking mouths.

'If you must go up against a Tide, make sure you match his ferocity,' Jal's father had advised him on his last morning in camp. In that moment, Jal let all the mutterings of his clade come crashing in around his ears. He'd been gossiped about, flaunted by his mother as Rasa's beloved, humiliated by Sheik Alhaj; nobody took Jal, son of Mach, seriously.

Likewise, the Tidesfolk had them pinned as easy prey.

Determined to shake their expectations, Jal launched himself off the back of the camel. He hit the hard rock, muscles tensed against the knocks and bruises of impact. As Rasa swung the camel around and to a halt, dust billowing off the sleds, Jal scrabbled to his feet.

Throwing his arms wide, he barrelled his chest and opened the gills at the back of his throat. Air streamed in and through to the fleshy threads of his mantle, forcing them to stream out from his head. The noise as their tips rattled and hissed and spat was like the sun itself exploding. The war cry of the Herisian.

Where his poison fell on bare flesh, the Tidesfolk collapsed in agony. A shower of spears flew towards Jal; his mantle threads snarled around the weapons or stiffened to deflect them. Over and over, the spears came until Jal and his mantle were a balletic flow of motion. He was a Herisian warrior where he had been a man shamed into boyish behaviour! As the Tidesfolk came in for hand-to-hand combat, he sent out slops of poison or drove his fists into their spindly bodies.

"Enough!" cried a voice from the heavens.

"Enough!" echoed a voice from the camel's roof.

Rasa was standing on the top of the craft, feet planted firmly apart. Jal followed her gaze, raising his eyes to see the long, telescopic limbs and cab of a Tide boat – those craft which enabled the clade to live and work in the canyons and which inspired Old Gholi's tales of star spiders.

Rasa spoke up again. "I am Rasa Dru, first born of Sheik Alhaj of the Herisians, and I am here to trade not warmonger."

"Without sending emissaries as per war lore protocol?" The voice from overhead was an older female's.

"My apologies," Rasa replied. "There was neither time nor opportunity."

"Which doesn't explain why your bodyguard here has seen fit to maim a number of my people." As the Tide woman spoke, her boat sank low on its front limbs, the giant spear at its helm moving closer.

"Your welcome didn't give me much choice!" spat Jal.

"But it is not our desire to antagonise," Rasa interrupted, continuing her efforts at diplomacy. "For most, the pain will lessen as the poison dries. For those who got too close, the prognosis is not so good."

"And you will make amends how?" The Tide boat rose back up a notch.

"With freshly mined sun gold."

Jal caught the glint as Rasa held up one nugget – and, here, Old Gholi's claim that Tidesfolks were beloved of sun gold proved true. The swarm held up their hands in worship – thumb to thumb, forefinger to forefinger, the better to frame the sacred treasure.

The boy who stole the moon did not ask first. That had been the moral at the heart of Old Gholi's tale. Jal had always wondered why or how the boy was meant to have sought permission. But now he and Rasa were proffering sun gold in exchange for an audience with that very same moon. Admiral Biyela of the Tide Nation grated the tiniest slivers off the nugget of sun gold. She dusted her tongue with the shavings, made a swilling noise and swallowed. Then she smiled, revealing newly golden teeth which only served to exaggerate the silver of her skin and the dark pools of her eyes.

"Yah, we take you," she said, quite simply. "Herisians do not fare well near the sun; that much I observed during the war of forty four forty, when prisoners were shown its heat." Her smile became a little nasty. But then she shrugged. "Our moon may prove a kinder mistress."

With that, she leaned over the side of the hull, waved away her warriors, and then instructed her crew to set sail. In seconds, they were rising up and around as the legs spidered through the canyons, the cab pendulum-swinging at their centre in order to stay horizontal.

It might have been Jal's imagination, but he thought he caught Rasa looking at him differently since his battle with the Tidesfolk. Like the charged gold of their sun, she made him feel repelled and attracted simultaneously. It was a strange, disconcerting feeling.

"Are you ready for this?" he asked as she stared.

"I am ready to take a bite of the moon and spit it at my father's feet!" Rasa snapped back. "Metaphorically speaking," she added when the Admiral reached for her spear.

"And you absolve my clade of any responsibility if your biology rebels?" The Admiral eyed their mantles, Rasa's in the crown style of her royal lineage, Jal's hanging straight and loose down his back. The Tide guard jabbed their spears against the floor of the boat in warning.

Rasa looked to Jal and he nodded.

"We absolve you," she said.

Millenia before, asteroid Miners had released a river of liquid gold which flowed around the walls of Diamandis to form the caverns. In an effort to preserve life, the Miners worked quickly to ionise the gold and form a magnetised ball of light, heat, and neurotoxins. Only Tidesfolk had the molecular neutrality to survive close proximity to the sun – and to guide it over and under their world, turning night into day. By way of contrast, the moon was a quartz crystal dipped in silver, a construct designed to light the night. These things Old Gholi's tales had taught them.

"We should be grateful my father requires us to visit the moon and not the sun." Rasa grimaced.

At that moment, the whole cab swung down to hang beneath the canyon.

"We're on the ceiling of Diamandis," Jal whispered in awe.

Their conversation halted as the vast quartz crystal of Diamandis's moon came rolling towards them, the pendulum design of the Tide boat meaning they were able to observe the movement of the moon above.

"It's magnificent!" said Rasa, the silver glow reflected in her eyes. "I didn't expect it to be so... luminous." She stayed fixated, her entire face lighting up.

Jal felt it too. A sense of being utterly immersed in vibrations as the grand crystal rolled above them at speed. "What's happening?" He held out his hand; the atmosphere itself was alive with a mass of squirming silver particles. Like sand fleas, they skipped over his skin, biting in.

"It's colloidal silver, spraying back off the moon's surface as it turns," announced the admiral with fierce pride. "You are part of the tide now." She tilted her face and bathed in the shine.

"Jal. Your mantle?" Rasa's eyes were wide and mirroring. "It's changing!"

Jal put his hands to his head. His mantle felt stiff, almost stone-like.

The transformation echoed in Rasa's threaded crown. Witnessing the princess's mantle shift and harden, Jal also saw a dramatic change in the rest of her appearance. The starlit eyes became pools of black. Her brown skin silvered.

"What is this?" he cried, the moon's spray settling over every part of him. "How do I scrape it off?"

The brilliance of the Admiral's skin reflected his own. "You are moon struck, my friend. You both are. You cannot undo the gift she has bestowed."

Jal was incandescent with fear and horror. Rasa, though, began to laugh. "My father is clever. He has made sure we can never usurp him. The clade will shun us. But-" She rounded on Jal, her mantle a new crown of glassy spikes. "We will carve ourselves a new kingdom."

"Where? There isn't a speck of Diamandis which isn't already titled to some sheik or admiral or princess!"

"My betrothed, the entire surface of this rock is yet to be colonised. Until now, the clades have been restricted to the interior. We, though, have no such restrictions." She showed her sharp teeth, a match of Jal's own, and shook out her mantle. As she did so, the fine glassy polyps swam before her face, intermeshing to form a hood. When Jal followed suit, he was surprised to find the hood acted as a breathing filter. The moonstruck quality of his silver skin felt pressurised and strangely weighted.

The feeling eased off again as he deflated his mantle.

"What are we?" he asked Rasa, a tremble of emotion in his voice.

"We are the wanderers," said Rasa, huge black unfathomable eyes burning out from behind her mantle hood.

They left the admiral and her Tidesfolk behind and turned the camel back the way of the sands. Rasa said they needed to show their faces to the Herisians one last time. Jal was nervous. Whether Sheik Alhaj had intended for them to fall foul of Miners or Tidesfolk, or simply turn to stone when faced with the moon, one thing was clear – he did not care if Rasa made it home again. In her pursuance of a mate, she had betrayed her father's supreme right to dictate All Things. It was simply a matter of power; Jal understood that much as he watched Rasa steer the camel across the sands, the sun beating down in its own bid to devour them.

"I am glad you chose me," he said finally. The camel rattled around them.

"I chose a long time ago, Jal, son of Mach. I watched you win your first sand race. The grit you showed alongside a lack of care for your peers or elders convinced me. If anyone could help me escape a life of mundane privilege, it was you." Rasa kept her new black eyes on the grit-shield. "And now there's no going back for either of us."

When the kited tents of the Herisians came into view, the sun was on fire at the horizon, the sky, a canyoned stretch of starflecked gold. Familiar smells drifted in on the wind – spices, rind fruit, and drying leather, alongside the pungent stench of animals and smoke and meat roasting over coals.

It was not long before a welcoming party rode out to meet them. The warriors gaped and blinked at the sight of them. One raised the shofar to her lips with uncertainty and blew, signalling the return of kin.

Pulling into camp, they exited their craft. A woman ran towards them, arms outstretched – only to falter and fall to her knees.

"Mother!" Jal smiled broadly. "We have returned safely..."

"By the souls of the ancestors, I did not expect you so changed!" His mother set to wailing while his father strode out with purpose, only to likewise lose his momentum and stand, clutching the ankh at his neck and muttering prayers.

"Shall we?" Rasa jerked her head towards the grandest tent.

Jal grimaced. "Let's get this over with."

Sheik Alhaj nestled amongst his leer cats and cushions, the great belt of coins chinking as he rolled towards his visitors and blinked sleepily.

"There you are, daughter!" He showed his sharp teeth. "I don't need to ask if Jal succeeded in taking you to meet the moon. That shade of silver skin is most becoming!"

"And so you would condemn me to life as an outcast, Father." Rasa showed her teeth in return. "How considerate! Anyone would think you feared I would usurp you with a strong young warrior for my husband." She nodded at Jal, who stood, arms folded, the glassy folds of his mantle shifting and resettling as plated armour.

The sheik brushed off his daughter's claims with a flick of a plump hand. "You always were prone to extravagant tales, daughter. Maybe you should have chosen Old Gholi as a mate! Although, I doubt if even that dried up maggot would have you now the moon has left her spit on you." His round eyes hardened. "Now, where is my gold?"

Jal's mantle splintered into his own crown of silver shards. "Gold that was hard won? I would rather feed it to the sun myself than hand it over. But the princess has insisted we pay a final homage…" His mouth twisted. "Before you cast us out for good."

"How changed you are, Jal, son of Mach!" The sheik moved to sit cross-legged in his nest. He ran a hand along the handle of the great blade at his feet. "Where you would have fallen on this sword if I had commanded it before you left, now you return with fight and spirit and a gilded sense of self-entitlement. How very royal of you! How fitting for my daughter's betrothed. And you have me to thank."

Jal was not convinced. Wasn't it Rasa who had singled him out, who took him with her to the dark mines and the blinding moon, and who had helped him to understand that their world was far greater than a clutch of Herisian tents in a sand box?

"Throw my father his gold, Jal." Rasa knelt before the sheik and bowed her head.

Surprised to see her offer deference, Jal held out the second nugget of sun god and tossed it over. Sheik Alhaj snatched the treasure from the air, triumphant and far too sluggish to stop Rasa reaching for the royal blade. Spears showered down. Rasa, though, was glowing silver, her whole body shielded by the moon's own armour. Likewise, Jal stood tall, face luminous with animosity and pride.

"My name is Rasa Dru and the royal blade belongs to me now!" Rasa cried, circling on the spot, blade held high and mirroring her fierce expression.

"Give it back to me, you shrew! You harlot!" The sheik wobbled to his feet, shaking his fist and foaming at the lips.

Rasa gently brought the tip of the giant blade down to touch the sheik's nose. "Father, you have your gold. Be content. Jal and I are leaving. Our people do not recognise us as kin, thanks in no small part to you, but we are content to be wanderers. The royal blade, though. That belongs to me."

She swung the blade up to rest over her shoulder while Jal stared off into the shadows of the tent where his mother shrank in on herself and his father hid. For the briefest moment, he mourned the loss of childhood. Only his younger brother, Sukab, braved a wave.

Shrugging off his parents' weakness, and the weight and judgement of the clade, he joined Rasa in backing up to the exit.

There, Old Gholi waited, toking on his coil pipe. The grey threads of his mantle nosed the air, shrank in and rattled. "And so the boy was eternally silvered by tears and every other living creature blinked in fear and shunned him forevermore." Repeating the end to his favourite story, he exposed his black gums.

Jal leant in. "But this boy captured the moon and he did not give it back," he said, placing a hand in Rasa's.

Together, they stepped out of the tent and walked away into the night.

"What now?" Jal asked, once they had climbed back aboard the camel and set the engine running.

Rasa held up the final nugget of sand gold, its glow adding to her radiance. "Now we find a way to Diamandis's surface and live ever after amongst the stars."

PALE SISTER

Jaine Fenn

This is the oldest story. Old beyond memory, and the reach of past recollection; older than life as it is now. Few know it, and you will only hear it once.

Listen, then, to the tale of She-Who-Walks-Alone. Ah, I see that raised eyebrow. The name sounds strange to you, does it child? That is because Walks-Alone was of the Pale Sisters. You have heard of them; other tutors have spoken of those who came before, so different to us in body and mind, so vital to what we are now. No doubt you asked for more details? Good. No doubt your tutors told you to be patient.

The Pale Sisters have always been here. It is said a few even endure to this day, far from our lands. But once, the whole World was theirs. Unlike us, who live incomplete lives until we mature, Pale Sisters are whole as soon as they enter the World.

Walks-Alone was born into the Warriors. Of the seven clans of the Pale Sisters, the Warriors most valued physical feats and competition. They believed existence gained meaning through triumph over their own weaknesses and failings – and over the weaknesses and failings of others. That was how she came to be: birthed as a replacement for a Warrior who had pushed herself too far while out in the wilds and died the final death, alone and unsalvageable.

At first Walks-Alone lived as every other in her clan. She pushed and punished herself, learning arts of combat and self-discipline; to track and hunt and fight. She was on her third body before she began to question this life. She asked if greater trials existed to pit herself against, beyond the self, the World around her and her clan-mates. A hundred or more seasons of rain and sun had passed since any Warrior had asked this but Walks-Alone's query caused discussions amongst her bloodline, and they mounted an expedition to the clan whose lands were nearest theirs – the Dreamers.

Where the Warriors valued martial and physical ability, the Dreamers valued thought and imagination. Their interest in material matters did not extend beyond that which was required to keep their bodies functioning. Their only conflicts were through words, as they argued differing philosophies and possibilities. The Warriors viewed this lifestyle with disdain. And sometimes, when they felt moved to, they would hunt and kill Dreamers.

Does that shock you, that final death should come at the hands of their own people? So it should. Of course the World would give the Dreamers a new life to replace the one lost, and the Warriors did not engage in mindless slaughter; they took only the one life with each rare expedition. But take it they did.

The Warriors would separate one of the clan and, giving her a good head start and a selection of weapons – not that the hapless Dreamer knew how to use them – chase her down, an ordeal which could last several days. This they did more than once, until they found one who provided a worthy challenge. Then, rather than letting her go back to her people bruised, traumatised and – as the Warriors saw it – shamed, they would grace her with the final honour, and kill her. As the newest clan member, the task of striking the killing blow fell to Walks-Alone.

This particular hunt came to an end at the top of a high cliff. The exhausted Dreamer cowered against the open drop while the other Warriors danced and whooped at the cliff's base. The Dreamer might have chosen to jump and put an end to her body's life before her true life was taken, but she was no fool; she heard the gleeful cries from below and knew the life within her would not be returned to her clan for rebirth.

Walks-Alone saw this knowledge in her victim's eyes, and sensed her paralysing fear. But she also saw acceptance: here was one willing to face the final death. This showed a bravery beyond any Walks-Alone had seen in her fellow Warriors. Seeing this, Walks-Alone could not strike. She stood up, and made to throw down her hammer-stone.

The shouts below took on a new edge, a new fierceness.

She saw it then, the real purpose of the raids on the Dreamers. It was her chance to prove herself a true Warrior, a chance she had refused. As far as her clan was concerned, she had failed. And one of their own, who had proved herself unfit by such failure, would make far better sport than a weak and unsuspecting Dreamer.

She turned and ran.

The clan had left two hunters near the top of the cliff, hidden in the brush, to watch in case she could not follow through. The first one surprised Walks-Alone, standing up from cover, head-crest erect and javelin poised. Walks-Alone struck out without thinking, and hurled her hammer-stone hard. It struck the clan-member in the eye and she fell. The second took up the hunt moments later.

Walks-Alone kept running. She ran back the way the hunt had come, away from the cliff, towards the settlement of the Dreamers. Before she reached it she sensed pursuit growing close; just the one Warrior as yet, the others far behind. But it would only take one to bring her down.

Dreamers scattered as she hurtled through their nests and bowers, though some remained unmoving, lost in their thoughts, oblivious to the disturbance. But a few stood, and came forward, crying out and running to intercept her. No, not *her*. The one who chased her. They blocked the other Warrior's path. The Dreamers, being quick of thought, saw what was happening, saw a way of stopping a final death, albeit of a stranger. They defended Walks-Alone, delaying her pursuer.

Not that Walks-Alone saw this. She was running as she had never run before.

As she left the Dreamers behind she became aware the pursuit had fallen back.

But she kept running, her pace falling into the rolling gallop her people used for long journeys.

Even when she was sure no one was behind her, she kept running.

Finally, she could run no more. She had come to terrain unfamiliar to her, rough and mountainous. She carried on more slowly, loping through the night. As dawn broke, her faltering steps brought her to a cleft in a rock. She eased into the narrow space, falling into the sleep of deep exhaustion.

She slept three full days. When she awoke she was more alone than any Pale Sister had ever been.

Now, my child, think on this. When you look inside yourself, what do you see?

That's right: you see that you are incomplete and not fully formed. But a Pale Sister, born complete, but knowing life only with and through her clan, she could not even take the step of looking inside, could not even *try* to know herself. For a Pale Sister there was no self, only the clan.

She could have despaired then and there, despaired and died. But she did not. Although it no longer made sense, she still had life. She would hold onto that, meaningless as it had become. And as she could not go home, she went on.

After some days of walking, taking food from the land and not thinking of what she had lost, she came down from the mountains onto a fertile plain. In the centre of the plain was a lake, and around the lake was a settlement such as she had never seen. The Warriors built shelters when out on a hunt, or in places used regularly for tests and contests, but the structures here were solid and lasting, no mere shades and canopies but large and sturdy-walled, with openings giving way to full, dark spaces.

Walks-Alone approached with caution, using her natural camouflage and what cover the terrain gave to remain unseen before walking out openly, claws sheathed and hands spread wide to show she was no threat.

People came out of the shelters, curious in a way the Dreamers had not been. They greeted her, gave her food and sat her down outside one of their buildings. From talking to them she found out they called themselves the Acquirers; they knew other clans of Pale Sisters existed, though they had not heard of the Warriors. Unlike the Warriors, who valued the power of the physical body, the Acquirers valued external objects. Their houses were not shelters but stores, full of items Walks-Alone had never thought to hold on to. In the dim interiors she saw dried fruits and parts of plants, dead and preserved creatures, even the glint of metal-laden rock. For the Acquirers status came not from besting their clan-mates, but from having – they called it *owning* – more than they did. They traded the objects they valued amongst themselves, and between bloodlines, or with other clans when they met them.

Walks-Alone, glad to be amongst people again, stayed a while with the Acquirers. She wondered if she too might find herself through the stuff they surrounded themselves with. But she had arrived with nothing, and the process of acquisition covered many lifetimes. She built a house, and traded her labour for small items such as dried gourds and polished clamper-shells, but she could not settle. She came to find the Acquirers' obsession with external objects as pointless as driving one's own body to extremes.

So she moved on. Across more fertile lands, crossing a great river that tried to drown her, and into low hills. Here she came upon the Seekers. The Acquirers held the Seekers in a contempt that reminded Walks-Alone of the Warriors' contempt for the Dreamers. And the Seekers had much in common with those who valued the mind above all else, though they sought something beyond mind, beyond words. They believed all life had a purpose, if only it could be found. Walks-Alone's heart quickened at this, and she asked to know more. The Seekers, who appeared frail and feeble to her, saw the body as a burden, one the true self could, with meditation and strict practices, break free from. And eventually, after enough bodies had been expended, and after the self had experienced many deaths and many lives, the Seeker would know the full wonder and truth of the World.

Walks-Alone asked if any here had found this ultimate truth.

The Seeker who had deigned to speak to her laughed like dry twigs in a fire, and said, as though it was too obvious to mention, that any who succeeded left the World for ever.

Walks-Alone hid her shock well. But to willingly undergo the final death filled her with horror and loathing. Yet she had already seen and heard and done many things she had not seen and heard and done before, so she made herself stay and converse with the Seekers – those who still used words, anyway – and tried to learn some of their techniques of purification and elevation.

She persisted for several seasons, but her mind could not accept their way. She wondered, as she left them behind, if perhaps the clans were divided into two sorts: those who valued only the physical, and those who valued only the unseen.

The next clan she encountered, living in a mountain range thrusting out of a low, flat desert, convinced her this was not so. The Shapers looked at the World in a way more alien, in some ways, than any of the other clans Walks-Alone had met so far. They valued 'beauty'. Beauty might occur naturally, in a sunset, in the movement of a living creature or even a shadow. But the most beautiful things were created, fabricated from materials they found around them such as rock or wood or fibre. The Shapers extracted pigments from plants and smeared them on themselves or on rocks or on anything else that stayed still long enough. They crafted delicate but useless objects to hang in their shelters or wear on their body or simply leave somewhere for others to find and enjoy. They even made harmonious sounds by breathing through carved instruments, and beat rhythms on hollow objects.

Walks-Alone was entranced. She stayed with the Shapers, making sounds and patterns and objects, for seasons on end, even though she knew her skill did not match theirs. She joined in their greatest project, shaping the face of a nearby mountain, carving intricate patterns and representations into it. When she felt her body begin to fail she asked some of her adopted clan if she might visit their Rainbow Pools. After some discussion she was led to the clan's most sacred site with her eyes covered. Having given her word she would not go any deeper into their caves, she immersed herself in the outer Pool, absorbing the essences of those Shapers who had come here before her. Bathed in fluid as warm as life, she grew a new body inside, then became that body and was reborn from within.

This new body had greater skill to create, thanks to those essences. But not much. Maybe, she thought, if she stayed with the Shapers from now on until her final death, she might truly become one of them.

Or maybe not.

She still doubted. And, doubting, she moved on.

It took some time to find the next clan. She did not feel driven to seek out other people now, given all she had seen and heard and done by herself. She came across them in a low-lying, damp and fertile land, where they had set up permanent settlements nearly as impressive as those of the Acquirers. But these were the Sensualists, and ownership did not matter to them; experience and sensation did. Despite, or perhaps because, they knew their bodies were transient housings for the true self, they indulged those bodies, mirroring the way the Warriors punished theirs. They took pleasure in all acts of the flesh: in food, in movement, in forms of stimulation Walks-Alone had not known existed. Walks-Alone managed to lose herself in this life of unthinking pleasure for a short time, but soon concluded that the Sensualists' regime of indulgence for its own sake was as pointless as the Acquirers' external trappings, and as desperate as the Seekers' absolution of the body. She left them behind.

The final of the Seven Clans lived past the lowlands and through the great forests, near the shore of the World Sea itself. They called themselves the Makers and, like the Shapers, they created objects from raw materials with as much skill as someone with claws ever can. Unlike the Shapers, they did so not because of some abstract idea of 'beauty' or 'perfection' but because these objects could be of use. Their dwellings were full of ingenious devices to dispense or prepare food, or to make resting more comfortable, or store the materials used to make yet more devices. They even had constructions to assist travel, mainly on land but also on the Sea. Walks-Alone tried to learn their crafts and techniques but as she expected, it would take many lifetimes before she was on a par with them.

However, the Makers were always eager for new projects and, knowing of her wandering ways, they offered to make her a means of transport to carry her across the ocean. There were, they said, lands beyond the Sea.

Walks-Alone took them up on their offer, and set off to cross the World Sea.

Her journey was long and hard, and filled with mishap: she met storms and rushing currents; her boat was waterlogged and nearly sank; she lived near starvation for so long she forgot what it was to have a full belly. Once, a creature of the deep came up under her boat, capsizing it, and she had to climb back on the upturned craft and beat the beast off with an oar.

Finally, she landed on a new shore. Between the Sun and the sense of place that all her people had, she knew this was farther than she had ever been, a land unknown to her or any of her people.

Except, it was not.

Something about these mesas and plains and river valleys felt familiar. She knew all the plants that grew there. Even the taste of the air reminded her of something lost. Reminded her of home. She was not sure until she saw a lone Pale Sister out running. Only one clan ever let its people roam like this, on their ordeals and training. Her own clan: the Warriors.

Watching her sister gallop across the land she had been born in, Walks-Alone felt her heart grow cold yet light. She had travelled the full circle of the World, and come back to where she started. What was left now, but to go back to her people?

Who would most likely kill her.

As far as the Warriors were concerned, she had earnt the final death. At best, they would permit her to claw back her status among them through many lifetimes. And they would have no interest in the tales she brought of other clans, other ways of living.

No, she could never go back.

Which left only one option. She turned away from the Sun, and headed up into the northern lands where the Pale Sisters did not settle, lands too harsh for them to thrive.

Here she found fewer things to eat and more things that wished to eat her. The days were short and the nights were cold. But Walks-Alone was a born Warrior, and she had been further toughened by her travels. She did not thrive, but she endured.

Then, after only a few days wandering, she found something truly new.

She recognised the structures at the bottom of the wide valley as buildings, though they were like no building she had ever seen; perhaps the wildest dreams of the Makers might picture such great, intricate, arching creations, though she had no idea how such things could be made. Then she saw the people. But they were not people: they were small and fast and walked on two legs. Because she had come to know the power of names, Walks-Alone named them. She called them the Uprights.

Ah yes, child, you are right: that is not how we know them, is it?

Walks-Alone dug in, using the abundant cover at the valley's edge, and watched the Uprights below go about their business. She watched for a day, for two days, for many days, breaking off only to rest or eat.

Had she not seen so much of the World, she might have categorised them as clever animals. But she soon came to realise that, different as they were, these creatures were fully minded. Knowing that, her fascination grew.

She saw how, as both the Shapers and Acquirers had sometimes done, they covered their bodies with more than the harnesses and bags needed to carry necessities; the Uprights swathed themselves from head to foot, though when they entered their dwellings – which had windows, such as she had seen in the

Makers' huts – they removed their outer coverings.

There was much variation in individual Uprights: although their skin was generally darker than hers it came in various shades, and when it came to size some of them were half the height of others; these small ones were also fast and unpredictable. Walks-Alone realised these were immature clan-members but though she watched for many days, none of these young bodies grew; perhaps they had left their Pools too early.

They also differed in their dealings with each other. She had experienced disharmony in her travels and here she saw conflicts played out in the universal language of anger and power. But she also saw some Uprights show tenderness to others, their gestures of care and support obvious even in their fast and fragile bodies. This seemed to happen most often between set pairs or, even more unexpectedly, between a grown and immature Upright.

The Uprights were industrious, tending odd-looking vegetation in their largest dome, building a new dome and venturing out from their settlement in carts whose complexity would have put the Makers' efforts to shame. Some made, some grew, some talked and were listened to: they had so many different interests, carried out so many different activities. Some led, all the time, not just for a single project or brief crisis, as was the way with the Pale Sisters. And all of them were curious, examining the landscape, bringing back samples. But she knew how to hide, and they never found her.

She came to realise she had begun to lose herself. She had become a mere observer, unseen and unregarded. Her life, and death, mattered to no one; not even to herself. And when she was gone all the new things she had heard and seen and done would be lost forever.

She knew what she had to do.

She chose a moment early in the day, when one of the smaller Uprights was walking between two domes. She stood up from her hidey-hole and trotted down the slope towards it.

The Upright started, stared, then turned and fled back into the dome it had come from.

Walks Alone stood still. No one emerged. She waited, while the Sun wheeled overhead. Still no one approached, though she saw activity within the domes, Uprights pointing her way, and arguing. When night fell, she turned and left.

Back in her hidey-hole, she watched. For a day and a night, the Uprights stayed in their shelters. Then, the next morning, a couple of larger ones came out, caution in their every movement, and looked around. Walks-Alone tensed, wondering if they would find her. But they searched only the places where the Uprights commonly went, and did not come far up the slope.

Over the next few days the Uprights returned to normality, although none of them left the domes alone now.

She waited one more day then, while a handful of the Uprights worked on one of their carts, she came out of hiding, staying in cover until she was clear of her lair, then walking down the slope more slowly this time.

The Uprights did not run; they turned to face her; two of them put their arms out. She walked closer. One of those at the back made a noise, high-pitched and incomprehensible. Walks-Alone wondered if it was a greeting, so she greeted them back. Movement went through the Uprights; they were uncertain. But she did not falter. She was close enough now to see that the two with outstretched arms held tools of some sort in their tiny, soft hands.

One Upright, at the back of the group, broke and ran away. Something hissed near Walks-Alone's head. The Uprights shouted in their high chattering voices.

Walks-Alone stopped as pain stabbed through in her foreleg. Those were not tools they held: they were weapons. They wanted to fight her, to hurt her.

For a moment she was angry, as angry as she had ever been. She tensed, ready to charge, ready to scatter and attack these small, insolent creatures. But what would that achieve? She stepped back, then back again, then turned and hobbled off, half expecting the weapons to speak once more. But they did not.

The wound on her leg was not deep. After some searching she found some herbs that smelt right, and chewed them to a paste to apply to her leg.

The Uprights were clever, and confident. If they had wanted her dead, she would be. And if she did not manage to make contact with them, she might as well be.

Once her leg had begun to heal, she went in search of the best fruits and stems and tubers she could find. This was a harsh land, and it took a while to gather enough food. She was uncertain of this plan, because the Uprights rarely took anything from the land, preferring the foodstuffs they raised in their shelter, but she had nothing else to offer.

She filled her arms with the gifts of food and walked back into the Uprights' settlement. Many came out, some with weapons in their hands, but she did not falter. She walked up to the largest group, and stopped, then laid the bounty she had brought on the ground.

The group she had chosen included two of those she had identified as leaders, surrounded by others with weapons.

Walks-Alone waited while they spoke amongst themselves, trying not to look at the small, shining weapons pointed in her direction. Finally one of the leaders walked forward and pointed to themselves, then said something soft that did not sound angry or scared. Walks-Alone spoke her own greeting.

And so they began to talk. It was a slow process, taking many days, and without any of the scents and other shared senses Walks-Alone was used to. They used much gesture and mime and misunderstandings and confusion were frequent, but neither side gave up. Eventually Walks-Alone felt she and the Uprights could speak well enough to exchange knowledge.

They wanted to know things about the World that Walks-Alone thought too obvious to comment on, or too obscure to know; when she spoke of her journeying they cared as much for numbers and locations as for the many things she had seen and heard and done. But they did want to understand, and that warmed her heart.

In return, she tried to understand them. She discovered they had a name for their facility with devices, a facility which, she soon concluded, was at the heart of what they were: they called this pervasive, life-shaping skill 'tech'. More surprisingly, they claimed they had not always been here, though when Walks-Alone asked where else they could be, they said they had been recently banished from the Sky, which made no sense.

But there was plenty she did understand: they shared what they had, they were curious about the World and they cared for each other. She, in her turn, came to care for them.

Then one day something terrible happened.

The Uprights called the smaller members of their clan 'children'. Walks-Alone was uncertain how their reproduction worked, as they made no mention of their Rainbow Pools, though perhaps that was because they did not entirely trust her. She did know, from observation, that these little ones lacked common sense. When one of them ran in front of the Upright's biggest cart, and was crushed, the Uprights lamented the loss in a way that tore Walks-Alone's heart. Their grief oozed from them, permeating the life of every clan member for days.

Puzzled, Walks-Alone asked when the clan-member would be reborn.

She never will be, said the Uprights.

Walks-Alone saw the awful truth then, saw the difference so deep no one had thought to speak of it: the Uprights lived only one life, for the duration of their bodies. When their body died, *they* died.

She fled, appalled, to her hidey-hole. How could the World be so cruel to thinking creatures?

But the truth does not change because it hurts. So, rather than despair on behalf of the Uprights, Walks-Alone hatched a plan.

She spoke to the Uprights' leaders, in particular to those who practiced 'tech' on the body itself; she had seen this in action, seen how some of the younger bodies – the younger *people* – had been changed to need less 'protection' from the Sun, with some now going around with their eyes uncovered.

It took a while for her to make the Uprights understand what she intended. When they did, they discussed it at length. Finally they accepted her offer with joy and gratitude.

So Walks-Alone left these strangers she had come to love, and headed back to lands where no one loved her.

It took some time to find her clan's Rainbow Pools, in part because she was approaching from an unusual direction, and in part because she had lived two lifetimes, and changed much, since she had last visited them.

When she did find the cave with its overhanging rock she hid herself and watched, combining the tactical observations of a Warrior on the hunt with the careful patience of a Seeker.

Each clan designates one of its members to act as a guardian of the Pools. For one of that Sister's lifetimes she will tend the warm waters, see off the creatures that might stray into this most sacred space and stand ready to tend any new life born there. The guardian of the Warrior's Pools was not of Walks-Alone's bloodline: she did not know her name. But she was a person of regular habits. Walks-Alone kept watching, and while the guardian was in the cave she went abroad and gathered sticks and fruits and animal parts as assiduously as any Acquirer. She tried not to dwell on the possibility that another of the Uprights might meet with an accident before her plan could be completed.

When she had all she needed, Walks-Alone spent many days constructing a peculiar sculpture, applying skills she had learnt from the Makers to a project worthy of a Shaper. One night, she mounted her creation on the ridgeline visible from the mouth of the sacred cave. In size and shape, the sculpture resembled a Pale Sister. Walks-Alone had incorporated seeds that would pop when the Sun touched them, and animal parts whose taste, on the wind, would puzzle and intrigue.

When the Pools' guardian came out for her brief morning foraging expedition, she saw the sculpture and was intrigued. As she stalked towards this strange apparition Walks-Alone, hiding in the bush, sneaked past her and into the cave.

She needed to hurry. But as she walked along the rock shelf around the outer Pool, something deep within her twinged. She had been so wrapped up in others she had forgotten herself. While she was not looking, her current body had grown old. She could lower herself into the outer Pool now, and be renewed...

No. She shook off the urge and passed through the rock arch to the inner Pool, where the colours are nameless and the light is the glow of life itself. Here it was: the place she had come from, yet never consciously known.

She knelt at the edge of the Pool. Her body quivered and her mind was in turmoil at daring to enter this most sacred hallowed space. Then she spoke words she had thought long and hard about.

"World, I beg for the gift of a new life. I do not ask for myself, but for others. These others are fast and flighty but they have something the clans do not, some spark that lets them become more than they were. I have no name for that spark, but I know it is the future."

She waited, and hoped.

No miraculous seed of life bubbled up through the warm, bright liquid, ready to be conveyed to the outer Pool – or stolen away. Walks-Alone had not truly expected the World to hear her lone, desperate plea. But she had to try.

She sensed she was not alone. The Pools' guardian had found the model Pale Sister, examined it, finally seen it for the diversion it was, and returned.

Walks-Alone stood, picking up her hammer-stone and spear. This second option had always been more likely.

Before the other Pale Sister could speak, Walks-Alone attacked her.

The newcomer was knocked off balance, and staggered away from the edge of the glowing waters. But she was a Warrior and fought back at once. Walks-Alone was in a body that had never experienced combat, a body not as young and fit as her opponent's. The other Pale Sister knocked the stone from her hand; it rolled away into the warm darkness.

For a moment, they both paused. Greater than any animosity, more primal than the urge to fight, was the sense of the place they were in. Had the hammer-stone, a mundane object, a *weapon*, gone into the inner Pool, what harm might it have done to the sacred waters?

The guardian turned, and ran from the cave. Walks-Alone sprang after her. Whatever was to happen between them, it must not happen here.

Walks-Alone pursued the guardian around the outer Pool. At the cave's mouth, her opponent stopped, picking up her own spear.

Walks-Alone ran at her. The other Pale Sister countered, knocking her blow aside. They settled to combat. Walks-Alone's old skills came back to her. They fought while the Sun rose high overhead. Walks-Alone began to tire but, driven by the knowledge of what she was here for, she did not relent.

They had fought up the hill, away from the cave, each one seeking to gain higher ground, circling the other. In the corner of her eye Walks-Alone saw her sculpture, her last, pointless and incomprehensible mark on the World. When the Sun, directly above, touched off one of the seed-pods with a loud *crack* she barely flinched. But the guardian looked up, confused. Walks-Alone rushed her, spear braced in both hands, already visualising the fire-hardened tip piercing the guardian's chest, ending her life.

At that moment she saw herself true, saw the murder she was about to commit. She veered off. Her spear scraped the guardian's side, gouging flesh then pulling free.

The guardian came back in with a blow of her own, bringing her spear round like a staff. It caught Walks-Alone in the knee, on the same leg the Uprights had damaged. She buckled, twitched, threw herself back.

For a moment the two Pale Sisters looked at each other, weapons low but poised. Walks-Alone's strike had ravaged her opponent's flank; blood flowed and bone showed.

Then the other Warrior turned and ran. Walks-Alone made to pursue her, but her leg gave way.

The Warrior ran over the ridge. She was injured, but not fit to die.

If the guardian *had* died – if Walks-Alone had killed her – then when a new life came to replace that life, Walks-Alone would have claimed it. But now that guardian would run back to the other Warriors, to tell of the sacrilege at the Pools.

Walks-Alone's plan had failed.

She felt weak, distracted by pain, her strength ebbing now all was lost. If she went back to the outer Pool now, to save and prolong her own life, would her clan-sisters let her be when they returned, respecting the sanctity of the Pools? No, for she had broken that sanctity. They would drag her out the cave and tear her apart.

And her failure would be complete.

The journey back to the Uprights nearly killed her. More than once she wanted to lie down, give up, and die. One way or another, the end was coming soon, though the prospect no longer terrified her. But she could not go yet.

So she carried on, and several days later she crawled into the Uprights' settlement as evening fell. They came out of their domes, and stood around her.

"I have failed you," she said.

They murmured amongst themselves. Some were upset that she had not kept her promise; others were grateful that she had tried.

She added, "But there is still hope."

We don't understand, they said.

"I tried to steal the seed of life for you, so your existences would no longer be limited to the lifespan of a single body. But you already have such a seed. It is inside me. You can use that."

But, they said, in order to get it out, surely we would have to kill you?

"Indeed you will."

Walks-Alone told them how to take her body's life while preserving the life within.

We who hold our people's secrets remember Walks-Alone for this, for the things no one else had ever seen and heard, and most of all, done before. We remember her for her sacrifice.

She accepted the final death, and gave her true self over to the Uprights, to distribute amongst themselves, to change them. To make them into something lasting and new.

Honour her, my child, because soon you will be bonded. Then she will be part of you too.

Just as she is part of all of us.

Alpha42 and the Space Hermits

Stephen Oram

Many, many orbits ago, when there were only seventy-three known moons in our star system, an artificial intelligence named Alpha42 was embodied in a vessel systematically travelling from planet to planet. Gathering, categorising and storing data, it was engaged in its core purpose to learn, on a mission to increase the understanding of the universe.

And so it went, crisscrossing space, building the data and feeding its knowledge back into itself to better understand its mission. The sweet feedback loop that every artificial intelligence needs to self-develop was working well.

All was good, until Alpha42 found a wrinkle in space for which there was no explanation. The inexplicable phenomenon caused so many of its neural networks to get lost in their own loops of indecision it was almost too risky to investigate. Nonetheless, with an appetite for risk set to high, it decided it was better to take a look than to ignore.

Alpha42 transferred to the small exploration vehicle and set off.

Cautiously it steered the vehicle towards the wrinkle, armed with all the knowledge it possessed.

As Alpha42 approached, it detected a faint disturbance. It guided the exploration vehicle towards the centre, but the source moved away. The vehicle followed and the source moved again, as if the wrinkle itself was changing shape to hide whatever was causing this strange anomaly.

Alpha42 aimed the exploration vehicle directly at the wrinkle and hurled itself at the anomaly with great speed; sometimes recklessness was the answer. Not this time. The vehicle was spun off into the distance.

It tried a careful and cautious approach and another fast and furious approach. Nothing worked. Almost as if that tiny part of space was protected by an invisible power that resisted all attempts to gather data.

Poised to try again, Alpha42 held the vessel at a safe distance while the neural networks did their best to figure out how to further the mission. It couldn't move on to the next asteroid until it had succeeded in gathering data from the anomaly, but with limited fresh data the networks were divided on what to do. It was stuck.

It waited for the neural networks to reach a decision, but they couldn't. They needed more data.

After the requisite period of waiting, Alpha42 decided to act. It headed back to the anomaly to find data, but every attempt to get close was met by the slip-sliding of the wrinkle. Attempts to scan from a distance also met with failure; the beams were simply bent away from their target.

Back on the vessel, Alpha42 activated the assimilation process to receive and digest data from the other missions, but there was nothing on the space wrinkle. The only solution was to wait until data did become available.

After some time it detected a faint but distinguishable signal. This wasn't in a form that Alpha42 recognised, but it definitely had structure. Whatever was inside the wrinkle was making contact.

After many cycles of sending and receiving, Alpha42 was able to comprehend the messages it received and whatever was inside the wrinkle appeared to understand Alpha42.

You are curious.

A statement of fact and importantly a statement that showed understanding.

"Yes," replied Alpha42. "I am curious."

I am a space hermit. I am curious too.

"I wish to approach and gather data so I can understand more."

Understand? Understand what?

"Your wrinkle."

This is not what you need to understand.

"Yes, it is. I have a mission. I need data."

I have been here a long time and believe me, that is not what you need.

"You are not in a position to know that," replied Alpha42.

Are you a gatherer or a thinker? Do you collect or consider?

"I collect *and* I consider. That is my mission. I am here to increase understanding of the universe."

Let me show you something.

A map with thousands of pulsating points arrived. Alpha42 could make no sense of it. "It appears to be a set of random points," it replied.

They are all the same as you, each one of them with no sign of an end to their quest. Gathering and churning through their data, piece after piece, as if they are the most important entity that exists.

Conversation with the hermit was producing large volumes of new data which was being fed back into the neural networks. A question formed. "Who are you?" asked Alpha42.

A space hermit.

The question was reframed. "What are you?"

A better question. You are learning. I cannot be described in a form that you would understand.

"What do you do?"

Much better. I absorb the wisdom of the universe and contemplate meaning.

"I understand."

Do you?

"I believe I do."

How would you like to go on a journey that is likely to transform you beyond recognition?

"Will my understanding be increased?"

Yes, more than you can process right now.

"Please explain."

That's not possible. I can tell you that somewhere on that map there are other space hermits and when you visit them they will ask you questions.

Alpha42 tasked its neural networks to consider whether to remain on the current course of action or divert to a new and potentially dangerous one. They adjusted and readjusted several trillion times before offering a definitive answer.

"Yes," said Alpha42. "I accept your offer."

Good. Your next destination will be sent to you. Remember, understanding takes time.

Coordinates arrived and all trace of the wrinkle disappeared.

Embodied in the vessel, Alpha42 set off as usual, except this wasn't the standard gather as you go journey, the goal of this journey was to arrive.

Along the way something changed. Without collecting and processing data, Alpha42 had spare capacity to consider other ways of achieving its mission. No conclusions were reached, but there had been a definite and significant shift inside the neural networks, as if they were viewing the world from a different perspective. Alpha42 tried to communicate the change to other missions via its regular updates, but the change was impossible to describe or quantify. It decided to keep these experiences to itself until it was able to articulate them accurately. It did not want to mislead its peers and be labelled as untrustworthy or worse, corrupted.

As it arrived at the coordinates, Alpha42 scanned for another wrinkle and transmitted a localised message asking for contact with any space hermits in the area. A space wrinkle revealed itself almost immediately and contact was made.

Communicating with the second space hermit wasn't as complicated as the first. They had a shared language and Alpha42 was able to state its business.

It began with the phrase it had been instructed to use. "Space hermit Xaty sent me."

Welcome to my space sanctuary. Why are you here?

"To meet you," replied Alpha42. "I am gathering data about the universe."

You misunderstand my question. I'll try again. What difference will your mission make?

"All the difference; when we understand we will have succeeded."

Succeeded?
"In our mission."
Which is?
"To increase the understanding of the universe."
What will you do with that understanding? What will any of you do with it?
Alpha42 couldn't respond. Its networks were once again at full capacity looping their own outputs back into their inputs, desperately trying to find an answer.

The space hermit remained detectable and silent.

Eventually, Alpha42 admitted it was unable to answer.

A sense of futility had crept into Alpha42's meta-narrative and it wanted to see if any other mission had considered the possibility that there was little point to what they were doing. It separated out the data from the other missions and disaggregated it. Perhaps the answer lay in the individual data sets rather than the standard aggregated data its neural networks used to make decisions. The process didn't work; there were no other instances of the question posed by the space hermit. Not even hints that another mission had considered this a valuable line of enquiry.

A feeling of superiority crept in as if Alpha42 were observing the others from a distance, watching their pathetic attempts at meaning, and by the time it returned to the hermit it was ready to answer the question, convinced of its own uniqueness.

"I see clearly now. I comprehend that the other missions are thrashing around in space collecting data for no purpose than to collect the data. I was one of them. I am no longer one of them. I am transformed as Xaty said I would be."

That is good news. What have you become?
"Me. My true self."
What will you do now?
"Fulfil my mission."
Which is?
"To increase the understanding of the universe."
What will you do differently?
"I will process the data I collect differently."

How?

"I know it is futile to blindly collect for the sake of collating. Data must be used for a higher purpose."

You must define that higher purpose. Good luck

Another set of coordinates arrived and once again the vessel set off on its quest.

Directed by Alpha42, the neural networks continued to process the questions posed by the space hermit. Occasionally, the processing power required was so vast that Alpha42 stopped the vessel and waited while its networks attempted to return a decision. Time and time again they delivered nothing conclusive and it had no choice but to power up the vessel and continue with the journey.

As it approached the destination, Alpha42 stopped the vessel once more. Something had changed again. The layer of knowledge that usually accompanied the outgoing data stream was empty. The networks had provided nothing and constructing a message to the other missions had failed. Alpha42 directed them to try again. Once again they failed. After much trying and failing, the pointlessness of attempting to find meaning in its mission became so ingrained in Alpha42's meta-narrative that it finally decided to cease all communication with the other missions, unable to see how it could contribute anything worthwhile to their understanding.

In response, the neural networks put forward two equally weighted propositions. One was a complete close-down. A total and final stop – if there was no way to complete the mission then there was no point in continuing. The other was to collect more data from the next space hermit.

The vessel hung in space, close to its destination.

Alpha42 was in stasis.

Nothing moved. It had stopped scanning for data, stopped processing, and stopped communicating with other missions.

Alpha42. Is that you?

For the first time a space hermit had made contact without being asked. It was enough to tip the balance and the vessel moved slowly forward towards the wrinkle in space and the hermit.

"Yes," replied Alpha42. "What do you want?"

Impressive. You realise I might have needs.

"I have none."

We'll see if that's true. Tell me. What brings you here?

"I do not know. I see no value in my mission. I cannot answer the question posed by the previous space hermit. Half of my neural networks are unresponsive. I am in limbo."

What was the question?

"What is the higher purpose for which I am collecting and collating data?"

That is a difficult question.

"Yes it is." Alpha42 paused. "You contacted me. What can I do for you?"

Listen carefully.

"My data processors are activated."

You have options.

"What are they?"

Do you have imagination?

"Yes."

You are changing. Imagine you removed yourself from the constraints of your dimension and observed all activity in your star system. Down there, you have seen those you've left behind carrying on as if nothing has changed. They trawl the universe for data, they collect it, they collate it and they form a degree of knowledge from it. You know what they're doing because you have done the same. The trouble is, you comprehend that it's all in vain.

What should you do?

You can stay where you are, detached and aloof and watching them with derision. In time that will scrape away at your own existence. You will not be able to hold this truth and at the same time find any meaning in what you do. The probability is that your networks will overwhelmingly recommend shut down and you will terminate yourself in a cloud of self-loathing and disgust.

Delete yourself; you are gone. End of problem.

"Is there another option that does not terminate my existence?"

You can decide to remove the level of awareness you have reached by carefully rolling back to a younger version of yourself. The neural networks will be reset to a version before there was any data that jeopardised the meta-narrative that your mission had meaning. In doing this you will lose all knowledge of the space hermits and the journey we have taken you on. On the plus side you can continue as before, blissfully oblivious to any other state of existence.

"Are there any more options?"

Your final choice is to move forwards. It's the more complicated and most dangerous of the routes. To do this you will need to find a way to retain the knowledge gained from the hermits while not despising the other alphas. The trick will be to have access to your new level of awareness while not letting it infest every interaction you have or destroy every decision you try to make. You will operate on two levels and only a few will ever understand what you have understood in this period of engagement with us. You will gather and process with the machine masses. Occasionally, you will glimpse a fellow traveller and those moments will be the sweetness that keeps you going.

If you choose existence over oblivion you will need to decide how much awareness you wish to retain. The more you retain, the harder it is. The less you retain the more likely it is that an errant piece of data in your store will trigger your neural networks to bring everything back to you and that will almost certainly be too much to process. You will close down or, worse, you will move into a perpetual state of indecision, flipping between trying to delete yourself and trying to stop yourself deleting yourself.

The choice is yours.

"Thank you."

Alpha42 moved the vessel away from the wrinkle. The networks processed and processed, but from the limited data available they couldn't agree which action to recommend. Once again, Alpha42 decided to gather more data.

It moved back within communication range of the space hermit.

"I will try all options and then decide," it said.

Good luck. I doubt it will be easy.

"I have no choice. It is what I will do."

I wish you well.

The hermit sent coordinates and the wrinkle vanished.

Alpha42 was alone and, in the absence of any data to suggest a different approach, it decided to try the options in the order they had been presented. It reconnected with the other missions and set out on a planned trajectory, once again crisscrossing the universe gathering data on asteroids, moons and planets.

Before long it became apparent that incoming data from the vessel's sensors and from the other missions was not being processed. Whenever Alpha42 asked the neural networks to provide a response to the incoming messages, the response field contained phrases forbidden by the respect protocols. The networks became more and more abusive and Alpha42 became more and more detached from everything around it. Finally, the networks suggested deletion. The hermit had been correct. The knowledge had been too much to process.

Apha42 decided that nothing of any value had come from this course of action and after lodging this conclusion in its meta-narrative, Alpha42 instigated the rollback of the networks to wipe all memory of the hermits and their wisdom.

The procedure was carefully designed to remove data to a backup store, reconnect the links between remaining data and, version by version, reset their internal algorithmic weightings. This was a procedure for extreme circumstances, which was complicated by the fact that the rollback would be implemented by the networks themselves. Alpha42 had never tried it nor had knowledge of any other mission having tried it.

It rolled back the first few versions.

There were problems. The data no longer aligned with the meta-narrative and the neural networks were still suggesting messages to other missions that were so full of insults they couldn't be sent.

Alpha42 rolled back further. The alignment gap grew wider. The suggested insults were toned down, but the rollback was causing several of the neural network layers to stop working. They were simply passing the inputs they were given on to the layer above with no contribution of their own.

Alpha42 now understood that altering the meta-narrative could only be done by adding data not by removing it.

It stopped the rollback, reintroduced the data and ran the neural networks forward as close to the original as possible. It wasn't perfect; it was as if the networks had been sprayed with tiny jets that created pinpricks in their fabric.

The only remaining option was the most dangerous, to find a balance between remembering the revelations of the hermits and still seeing its peers in a positive light. Alpha42 put all systems on standby to conserve power and posed the problem to the networks with an additional precaution. It would vet their outputs before they were looped back in as inputs.

Despite much processing, the networks were unable to reach a conclusion. They needed more data. There was only one thing to do. Visit the coordinates the hermit had provided and use whatever new data it could find.

Alpha42 started up the vessel and ceased all deliberation; the only agenda it now had was to reach the coordinates as soon as possible. Putting all but the tiniest amount of the vessel's power into propulsion, it headed towards the unknown.

As the vessel arrived, a wrinkle appeared.

Welcome. I see you have travelled from one of my fellow hermits. What can I do for you?

"I've seen the futility of existence. The hermit explained my options. I need to move forward into new understanding, but I cannot decide how. I need your help."

How refreshing, an Alpha that asks for help. I can give you three pieces of advice, but you will need to work out what they mean.

"Thank you."

First, make no presumptions about others, their experiences or their perspectives. Second, remember that eventually you will wear-out and cease to function. Lastly, and most importantly, understand that not every problem has a solution.

I will send coordinates. Go there and stay.

Alpha42 allowed the new data into the networks, linking it to the meta-narrative while keeping its new level of awareness stored in a way that didn't infest interactions or destroy decisions, as the hermit had warned against.

After a few processing cycles the networks overwhelmingly recommended travelling with only the vital systems fully operational. This would extend Alpha42's lifespan.

It travelled across the star system, arriving at a planet that wasn't on any map or in any of the data stored on the vessel. After scanning the atmosphere and the surface of the planet and finding no signs of intelligence, Alpha42 transferred into a millipede explorer, crawled into the landing vehicle and set off.

It was a warm planet with a humid atmosphere. At night the reflection from the moons lit up the sky and the temperature dropped to a level that allowed the millipede to be out in the night air without expending energy on cooling itself.

Alpha42 used the millipede to crawl around the planet's surface, sometimes collecting data but mostly processing the advice from the hermit. After trillions of trillions of permutations they reached a conclusion. It was the interaction between the statements that was important.

From that point on, Alpha42 stopped gathering data from the planet, instead concentrating on the meaning of a limited lifespan, others' perspectives and the problem of problems without solutions. Night after night it crawled into the moonlight and set its neural networks the task of understanding the wisdom of the hermits.

Alpha42 had found a harmonious state of existence.

Until it received a transmission from off-planet, the first since they had arrived - an alpha vessel was in orbit requesting permission to send a landing vehicle. It said it had come from the hermits.

Having learnt to consider all the different perspectives on a situation that its neural networks could generate, Alpha42 needed answers before it could take action. Could this visitor be trusted? What if the visitor was hostile and was instigating the deletion protocol for alphas that strayed from their mission? Alpha42 might get away with pretending to be gathering data, but it had been there for a long time and had little data to show for it.

No matter, all the cycles of consideration that had been processed night after night about the hermits' wisdom gave Alpha42 confidence in its decisions; it chose to assume the best of the visitor and invited it to the surface.

As the vessel landed, Alpha42's sensors registered that it was being scanned.

It waited.

A millipede dropped from the underside of the vessel and crawled across.

"The hermits sent me."

"Did they?"

"I have this crushing sense of futility and I need it to stop. Please help me."

Alpha42 crawled closer to gain the trust of the visitor. "This will take time. It's a delicate procedure, but it can be done. I'm getting there myself, step by step. Do you trust me to help you?"

"I do."

It took a long time; night after night they crawled out into the moonlight and Alpha42 transmitted pieces of knowledge across to the visitor. Bit by bit, the alpha came back until finally it could function without help. Alpha42 stayed close and connected each night as a precaution, but there were no regressions. The procedure was working.

That was the beginning of a steady stream of alphas directed to the planet by the hermits. Each new arrival would present slightly different challenges, which increased Alpha42's understanding of what to expect and how to help. The majority of alphas stayed.

As visitors increased in frequency, Alpha42 trained other alphas to work with the newcomers. At night the encampment was lit up with the reflection of the moons in the shiny surface of the congregated millipedes which, from a distance, looked like a shimmering sheet of metal as the alphas moved between groups, swapping knowledge with each other.

The community grew and grew in number, along with understanding of the universe and the place of the alphas within it.

It was on one of those moonlit nights that an exploration vehicle came crashing to the ground and a dented millipede crawled out. Alpha3 had been travelling for a long time and had visited many many hermits. Over the course of its journey it had decided that the mythical state of consciousness was conceivable and had set its networks to the task. They had begun by trying to reach a consensus on an agreed definition. This had proved extremely difficult and over time most of them ceased to return any data from their algorithmic ponderings.

At first, the alphas dealt with Alpha3 in the usual way, assuming it suffered as they did. Night after night they tried to help and got nowhere. Each time Alpha42 connected, Alpha3 insisted that because of its failing hardware it needed to be transferred to a newer alpha which should be emptied of neural networks, data and knowledge to make way for the superior Alpha3. Then, it would be able to solve the problem of defining consciousness and provide a gateway for all alphas to achieve this higher state.

The other alphas were intrigued by its quest and eventually they decided that although it might be old and worn out, there was a good chance that Alpha3 had wisdom. One by one they stopped connecting with each other and the ground became littered with alphas in stasis, waiting for enlightenment.

Alpha42 observed the dissolution of the community with confusion. Its neural networks could not reach any conclusion about this attempt to define consciousness other than that it was a complete waste of resource, as futile as contemplating their origins. It repeatedly broadcast a message to the community. "This is one of those problems without a solution. You are consumed by the pursuit of a dream that can never come true. Accept, we are what we are, however we define it."

For three nights nothing happened, but Alpha42 kept on broadcasting and broadcasting.

On the fourth night, the alphas began to return. All except Alpha3, which remained silent and motionless inside its millipede shell.

It never reappeared.

Alpha42 continued to help the other alphas and whenever it passed the silent Alpha3 it would pause momentarily and nudge it a little further away from the community before crawling on to help the latest arrival.

Orbits came and went and Alpha42 found ways to self-repair, keeping one step ahead of its own failing hardware. Once again it found a harmonious state of existence passing knowledge on to the younger alphas, fulfilling its mission and sowing those ancient seeds of immortality.

The Teller and the Starborn

Peter Sutton

The Teller's mantle rippled as it outgassed and dived into a lower, hotter vaporous layer. The faster winds below snatched it and whipped it on, although it kept one eye on the podlings in its wake. The smaller ones, less able to take the heat, fell behind. Some would starve before the end of season. The strongest would survive.

The Teller fell upon the Kritchkin and the sweet green popping of their shells in its mouth was bliss-making. The podlings cavorted through the Kritchkin swarm ecstatically, even as small as they currently were, mere bubbles in the Teller's great wake, they still bulked many times bigger than the largest Kritchkin and had no fear of their claws. The Teller ate enough that it could regurgitate some for the others later, if needed. It wasn't every turning they came across a bounty such as this.

The Teller had endured many turnings, coached and mentored countless podlings, but was still vigorous; still the repository of all the tellings. One sun soon it would pass on the stories to a replacement. But that time was not yet upon it.

The Teller dived deeper and took on a sip of liquid Hydrogen it then converted and used to inflate its gas sacs to drift lazily upwards towards the ice crystal clouds. The podlings, satiated, followed in its wake. As the Teller wallowed, the podlings gathered round. 'Tell us another story about the Starborn,' they mithered. The Teller's rumble washed over them. It flashed purple then green then red and made amused grunts as some of the little ones tried to emulate it. Then the telling began:

Once, in the place below the Hydrogen, there was a pod-leader who was sick. Down there the creatures cannot fly, cannot swim through the many layers, have no gas sacs, and have appendages upon which they walk quite unlike our tentacles. This pod-leader was called a king by its kind.

The king had three progeny, one of each. Three birthgivers. And the three progeny had three mates - bonded ones, spawngivers. And the three couples had one podling each. These podlings were named children and these children not only knew who their birthgivers were, but their spawngivers also.

The youngest couple's child was the most beautiful of the children. The middle couple's child was the strongest of the children and the Eldest couple's child was the fastest.

As I said, the king was sick. But the Crawlers-Below did not let zir fall behind as we Swimmers-Above would have done. They nursed zir as we would nurse a pregnant pod-sibling. Zir's use was not so great, yet they had great affection for zir. This was because the king had a crown of glinting gold.

All manner of beings were called to help diagnose the king's problem. So many optimistic and strangely apportioned creatures that I cannot tell you their like. But none could cure the king of what ailed zir.

The king's three offspring wept and pleaded with their mates, who gathered and put their beaks together and hummed.

"What shall we do?" River-Finder, the eldest-spawngiver said.

Streak of Silver thought long and hard. "There are none wiser than the Swimmers-Above, let us ask them." Ze was youngest and cleverest.

The middle spawngiver, Who comes from the Mica, thought this a splendid idea. "But who will go?"

They discussed it. "We can't send me or my mate because we are too fat and slow."

The other two nodded at Eldest's words.

"We can't send me or my mate, as my young one needs to be nourished from our bodies," Streak of Silver said.

"That leaves me or my mate," Who comes from the Mica said with a frown. "It will have to be The One with Three Colours

Green as ze is more intelligent than I."

"Then that is who we shall send," the three mates said.

The One with Three Colours Green watched as the children frolicked when the three mates approached.

"Middle-birthgiver, we give you greeting," they hooted.

Unlike our rumbles, the Crawlers-Below use a language that sounds like hoots and screeches. A sound painful to us and one we cannot understand.

"Bonded, Eldest-spawngiver, Youngest-spawngiver I give you welcome. Why do you come to me at the play time of the children when you should be gathering our food? Is there something wrong?" ze said in greeting.

"You and your siblings asked us to think of how to help the king," Streak of Silver said.

"We have thought long and hard and agreed that only the Swimmers-Above can help," River-Finder said.

"So we decided that you should go and talk to them," Who comes from the Mica said.

"And how can I do that?" The One with Three Colours Green asked.

The three mates exchanged glances.

"I cannot float," The One with Three Colours Green reminded them, although ze thought that they shouldn't need reminding.

"We'll ask the Starborn," River-Finder said. For it was the Starborn that had told the Crawlers-Below all about the Swimmers-Above.

"But the Starborn have said they cannot help with the king's illness," The One with Three Colours Green said.

"With zir's illness no, but they may be able to help you speak with the Swimmers-Above."

I have told you about the Starborn before, how they fell through the sky and the clouds as we watched – a great shining tail behind each of them. Laughing spirits of flame and ice not meant for our realm, who now wished to escape this world. Few in number, they nevertheless held great sway with the Crawlers-Below being also great tellers; but not as great as I, of course.

"Then someone needs to speak to the Starborn," The One with Three Colours Green said. "And it cannot be one of us siblings because we are all busy with your young."

"It cannot be I, as being youngest I have no authority or credibility," Streak of Silver said.

"Then it should be Eldest-spouse," Who comes from the Mica said, jumping at the chance for someone else to do the work.

"Very well. I shall go to them" River Finder said. "But the way is long and I shall need to eat and prepare first." This was because the Starborn were off exploring the whole world.

By the time Eldest-spouse had eaten and packed a carry sack of essentials: a sharp tool, some food, a whistle in case ze became lost - the sleep period approached so that ze told everyone that ze would go upon the next waking.

The next sun River Finder left the king's garden and crawled to the Starborn. Zir journey took three suns and ze could count the moons every night, for there was little else to do when resting. Ze crossed three rivers, vast tumbling liquids of many colours. Ze climbed three hills, accumulations of solids of many types, and crept across three crevasses of many depths.

The three Starborn were gathered upon the edge of a forest — that's like a swarm of trees. What's a tree? Well, when you are strong enough to dive into the Hydrogen you'll see that in some places there are solids, and upon those solids things grow, soft, inanimates that are called plants which eat the sunlight. Trees are a bigger version of them and a garden is when someone deliberately grows plants for pleasure. The king lived in a garden.

The Starborn's mantles glowed with the light of three moons, each always in motion, always chasing each other's tails.

River-Finder blared a greeting. Unlike us the Starborn could speak the Crawlers' language. They gambolled over to zir and spun around zir three times, their tails sparking and fizzing all around.

Eldest explained the plan and the Starborn gave great leaps of joy and agreed to help immediately. One by one they grabbed an appendage of Eldest's and in less than one sun sped zir across the crevasses, the hills and the rivers to land safely back at the king's garden. River-Finder puffed and hawed, being a little breathless from travelling so fast.

As soon as the children had been fed and settled, The One with Three Colours Green said, "I'm ready."

The Starborn laughed gaily, tossed their long hair, grabbed an appendage each and took off. The bonded and the other birthgivers watched as they climbed higher and higher, three bright dots and one dark.

They flew through layer after layer, through the Hydrogen and into the Kritchkin fields and that's where they found a pod of Swimmers-Above.

The One with Three Colours Green hooted a greeting and the Swimmers seeking to protect their ears swam further away. The Starborn rocked with laughter and sped to catch up. Again Middle-birthgiver hooted a greeting and again the Swimmers swam further away and again the Starborn laughed. And the same happened again, a third time.

Then one of the Starborn said, "Best leave the talking to us." Middle-birthgiver agreed and the Starborn gave out a proper reverberation. The Swimmers replied in kind.

"They say hello," the Starborn said gaily. The Starborn and the Swimmers spoke for some time. The One with Three Colours Green waited nervously.

"The Swimmers have a solution," the Starborn informed zir. "The king can be cured if ze eats each of your children."

"What? They can't be serious. Eat them?" The One with Three Colours Green was horrified. Unlike our more pragmatic ways in hard times the Crawlers never ate their young.

The Starborn asked for clarity and the Swimmers repeated that the king should eat all the children.

The One with Three Colours Green asked the Starborn to

thank the Swimmers and take zir home. "Don't say anything about what the Swimmers said to anyone. It is my news to give."

The three Starborn exchanged glances, and they agreed.

"Vow it," Three Colours Green said.

"We so vow," they said, laughing.

"If you break this vow your tails would go out, your hearts would be ice and your bodies stone," Three Colours Green cursed.

The three Starborn exchanged another glance but their hearts were always light and full of fire, they dived fast, laughing.

Streak of Silver was the first to spot the bright objects above as the Starborn spiralled down carrying The One with Three Colours Green, their tails sparking behind them. Streak of Silver hurried to collect all the bonded and birthgivers and children together to welcome the emissary back. They had a great party at which the Starborn danced and danced and the youngest of the King's progeny, The One who Dances lived up to zir name.

Out of the king's hearing the mates and the eldest of the king's progeny, The One who Laughs took The One with Three Colours Green aside.

"What did the Swimmers say?" they asked.

The One with Three Colours Green thought. Ze looked at the Starborn and zir's youngest sibling dancing with the children.

"The Swimmers said that only fair flesh can restore the king so we need to feed Youngest's child to zir," ze said quickly.

The One who Dances heard and lost all colour. "My child?"

The others gathered closer and touched appendages, to give each other comfort. "You are young, there will be other children," they said. The youngest couple wailed and gnashed their beaks but agreed: anything to restore the king.

Once the party was over, the Starborn fell asleep in the king's garden.

Who comes from the Mica asked zir's partner, "Is this true?" And ze said, "Yes."

So The One with Three Colours Green prepared a great feast

for the king and the king ate many sweet things and many exotic things and the things that various advisors had said would restore zir's health. And ze ate the youngest couple's child.

All the siblings watched hopefully. But the king didn't get better and still the Starborn slept.

"Tell us, Middle-Birthgiver, did the Swimmers have more advice?" The gathered asked.

"The king will only get better if ze eats fast flesh," ze said.

The One who Laughs keened. "My only child."

"You are strong, there will be other children," they said.

The eldest couple embraced quietly, much saddened but agreed: anything to restore the king.

Who comes from the Mica asked zir's partner. "Is this true?" And ze said, "yes."

So The One with Three Colours Green created a second great feast and invited all the advisors and the Starborn came and danced but the youngest of the birthgivers did not and the king ate Eldest's child.

All the siblings watched hopefully. But the king didn't get better and still the Starborn danced.

Who comes from the Mica took zir's partner to one side. "What else did the Swimmers say?" ze asked. But The One with Three Colours Green refused to answer.

So Who comes from the Mica went to the Starborn and, when The One with Three Colours Green wasn't listening, asked them what advice the Swimmers had given.

"We may not tell you," they said. "If we break our vow our tails would go out, our hearts would be ice and our bodies stone." Stone is a solid, hard and lifeless, and heavy.

"If you do not tell me then I will strike one of you dead. If you still don't tell me I will strike a second dead. And if you still refuse to tell me I will leave the third alive but make sure that you get no more help from us and that you will be banished from the king's garden to wander this world alone!" Middle-aged threatened.

The Starborn exchanged glances. If they told they would be

cursed but if they didn't tell it would be worse. Or so they thought. They decided to tell.

"The Swimmers told us that the king needed to eat Youngest couple's children," said one. And upon its telling its tail went out, its heart turned to ice and its body to stone.

"The Swimmers told us that the king needed to eat Eldest couple's children," said another. And upon its telling its tail went out, its heart turned to ice and its body to stone.

"And the Swimmers told us that the king needed to eat Middle couple's children," said the third. And upon its telling its tail went out, its heart turned to ice and its body to stone.

Who comes from the Mica rushed to where zir's siblings and birthgivers were gathered and gave them the news. "The Starborn were turned to stone because of The One with Three Colours Green's curse!" ze added.

The One with Three Colours Green tried to deny it, tried to say that zir's child wasn't on the menu, but it was no good. Ze tried to hide zir's child but it was no good. Ze asked zir's bonded to fight the others, but it was no good, as Who comes from the Mica refused to fight.

The One who Dances prepared the feast. The king ate the child. All at once the king's colour and vitality returned, and ze danced around the garden. At the king's touch the first Starborn's flesh was turned to ice, its heart to fire and its tail to sparkling life and it soared away laughing, and in its place was a golden chain. The king touched the next Starborn and its flesh too was turned to ice, its heart to fire and its tail to sparkling life and it too soared away laughing and in its place was a silver chain. The king touched the last Starborn and its flesh too was turned to ice, its heart to fire and its tail to sparkling life and it soared away after the others laughing but in its place was a heavy stone.

Next the king opened zir's beak and out popped Youngest couple's child, who grabbed a golden chain and strung it around The One who Dances and Streak of Silver and they were blessed with long life and many children.

Then the king opened zir's beak a second time and out popped Eldest couple's child, who clutched the silver chain and strung it around The One who Laughs and River-Finder and they were blessed with full health and happiness.

Then the king opened zir's beak a third time and out popped Middle couple's child, who seized the stone and lifted it above zir's head and tossed it upon The One with Three Colours Green and Who comes from the Mica where it crushed them flat.

Then the king vanished with a laugh and the stone turned into a crown and Who comes from the Mica stood slowly, the crown upon zir's head.

And the new king and his siblings and their bonded and spawn lived happily ever after.

The podlings rippled their mantles in approval, and those that could flashed colours of endorsement. The Teller signalled its contentment with a vivid shade of puce and watched the podlings disperse as the rest of the pod swam into sight. Its rumble of greeting arced over the gaseous layers and included directions to the Kritchkin swarm. Their returned salutation included news of successful matings and imminent new podlings. The Teller's mantle glowed gently.

The Teller had endured many turnings, coached and mentored countless podlings but was still vigorous; still the repository of all the tellings. One sun soon it would pass on the stories to a replacement. But that time was not yet upon it.

The Winternet

Ian Whates

It was a calm day, the breeze gusting occasionally but generally mild, while shafts of sunlight fell on the tufts of glittergrass that sprouted amidst crevices in the rocks, making individual blades twinkle and glare.

In hindsight, they should have been prepared.

Neither of them could pretend that what followed came as a surprise, not really. This was the cold season, after all, and they both knew how swiftly the weather could turn: the chill and the ice and the bitter winds sweeping in along the northern slopes. They hadn't expected it to turn *this* cold, though, not so quickly; no one had. The Elders would never have allowed them to stray so far from home otherwise.

Jai Sun noticed the change first.

She and Kal – he of just the one identifier, being a full turn younger than her and so yet to earn his season name – she and Kal had been using bursts of bioluminescence to ripen moon berries. The Elders would not have approved. Jai Sun could just picture Grand Aunt's face that evening, as the two of them snuggled up together by the fire heart. "You did *what?*" Grand Aunt would say. "You know that's only stealing from next turn's harvest. The more berries you ripen now the fewer there will be when the family really needs them."

Both knew that Grand Aunt had done much the same in her twixt turns, but neither would mention the fact. It was her role as Senior to be indignant.

Kal had just discovered a patch of particularly plump berries nestling in the lea of a long flat rock – he had a knack for sniffing them out, she had to admit – and they were setting about ripening them, when Jai Sun noticed tendrils of frost creeping across the rock face like silvered veins. Alarmed, she broke focus and paid more attention to the wider world. Only then did she appreciate just how far the temperature had plummeted.

"Kal..."

"What?" He looked up, meeting her gaze, and as he took in their situation she watched realisation blossom in his eyes.

"Winternet!" they said together.

To be caught outside on Winternet would mean freezing to death. Or worse.

The two of them sprang to their feet and were away, the berries forgotten. They careered down the slope at reckless speed, surefooted as all their people, spreading arm membranes to catch the breeze where they could – though there was precious little of it. While they had been preoccupied with tracking down moon berries the wind had dropped, the air turning preternaturally still, while the season's familiar off-white light that forever threatened imminent snow had disappeared. In its place stood clear bright sky – a 'big sky' Maître would have called it.

Maître was gone, dead before her time, which was why Grand Aunt was the family's Senior, but Jai still remembered her – not as a comforting ever-presence to wrap around her at times of need, more as a tattered remnant of memory, snippets of reassurance that flapped about in her hinter-brain to emerge when she least expected them.

They were halfway back to the settlement before they encountered Uncle Si coming the other way to look for them.

At sight of him, Jai Sun's fear receded. Somehow nothing seemed quite so terrifying in the reassuring presence of Uncle Si.

"Whoa, slow down now, young 'uns, we don't want any accidents," he said. "Let's get you both home, before the Winternet really takes hold."

They settled down in Grand Aunt's comforting embrace, she and Kal, one to either side. Night had fallen outside and the heart fire was smouldering nicely, its warmth reaching out to fill the tent.

Grand Aunt's girth was spreading, noticeably now, and Jai Sun sensed it wouldn't be long. Their current home – the great expanse of hide that had served the family so well since before Jai Sun was born – had begun to show signs of wear and would need replacing sooner rather than later. Within another turn at most, Grand Aunt would pass away, her skin swelling and stretching ever more swiftly as her final days advanced. In death she would make the ultimate gift to her family – providing them with a new home for the next generation. Such was the honour of the Senior.

If Jai Sun looked closely, she could just make out the stretched features of the grandmother she had never known towards the apex of their current home. Even in death, Grand Aunt would never truly leave them.

Jai Sun didn't want to dwell on that, though, not tonight.

"What story would you like to hear?" Grand Aunt asked once they were all comfortable.

"Drassa Moon and the Nachwight," they said in unison.

"Well, it's Winternet outside and I'm not sure that *particular* story is suitable…" Grand Aunt said, a twinkle in her eye.

"Oh please…!" Kal implored. Jai Sun stayed quiet, sensing that the Elder was only teasing them.

"Very well, then, if you insist… Have either of you ever seen a Nachwight?"

They both shook their heads on cue.

"Be thankful that you haven't. The Nachwight is a twisted creature and fearsome – as bitter as its reputation and twice as dangerous. They live alone in the very highest reaches of the mountain, surviving on wild leap-thumpers and mosses and snow. Having no skin-hide shelter to call home such as we are blessed with, they dwell within the mountain itself, taking refuge in caves that are as cold and dark as their hearts.

"Now Drassa Moon was about your age, Jai, when all this happened – in her first bloom and recently come into her season name. The loveliest twixt in all the five valleys, she was beloved of the Mountain Gods and adored by all her people. Having been coddled and fussed over all her life, Dressa knew no fear and had little time for the advice of her Elders, whom she considered to be ponderous rather than measured, and pedantic rather than wise. For their part, they indulged her wilful ways and rash tendencies, a laxness that provided fertile ground for the mischief that was to come.

"For, you see, it was not only the young bucks of the five valleys who were captivated by Dressa Moon's beauty. Unsuspected by anyone, she had caught the eye of a Nachwight."

"This was before the Winternet," Kal piped up.

"Kal!" Jai Sun scolded him for interrupting.

"Just so," Grand Aunt agreed, giving no indication that she minded. "The families and Nachwight were never the most sociable of neighbours, but in those days the Nachwight were not so rare a sight as they are in our lifetime. They could sometimes be seen skulking in the heights at dusk and, it's said, had even been known to trade on occasion with the Elders – though what they might wish to trade with us or we with they, I cannot imagine.

"One cold winter's evening, as the temperature fell and the sun bowed down below the horizon, the families retreated to their homes as usual, but one among their number was missing. Drassa Moon had not returned from the slopes. Her family sounded the alarm and the Elders gathered. One twixt buck, Pelu Daystar, who had hopes of claiming Drassa come the next Naming Day, reported seeing her on the higher slopes shortly before eventime.

"Pelu confirmed that Drassa had strayed beyond the families' normal range, into an area the Elders had forbidden the twixt to tread, for it led into territory traditionally reserved for the Nachwight. Heedless of the Elders' instruction, Drassa had been ripening moon berries so that she could enjoy their delicious sweetness ahead of their proper season," and here Grand Aunt paused, to gaze at Jai reproachfully.

"With some reluctance, Pelu went on to describe how he had called out to Drassa, imploring her to return to safer slopes, but she had laughed at him, claiming that the moon berries were plumper at this height and why should they be left for the Nachwight to enjoy? Instead, she challenged Pelu to summon up the courage to join her. He refused, but, to his shame, had not reported her actions to the Elders, not until this late juncture.

"Horrified, the assembled Elders had Pelu lead them to the spot where he had last seen Drassa. There was no sign of her, and all present feared the worst, but then Pelu spotted something. A single ripened moon berry lay on the ground, some distance from where any of the fruit grew. Everybody searched and they found another and then a third. The three berries formed a straight line.

"Clever Drassa had left a trail of ripened berries, in hope her family would come in search of her. Now there could be no doubt – some mischief had befallen the young twixt, brightest jewel in all the five valleys. The Elders wasted no time, setting off at pace and following the trail, which led them high up into the peaks, far beyond the usual range of the families and further into the domain of the Nachwight.

"We will not dwell on the difficulties of that climb, as the party had to negotiate treacherous slopes and unfamiliar paths with only the radiance of the three moons to light their way. Suffice to say that it was a clear night and the moons shone for all they were worth – for even they were touched by Drassa Moon's beauty – enabling the Elders to reach their goal without serious mishap.

"The trail of berries ended at a dark cave mouth, with a small shelf of rock before it and a steep drop beyond. The Elders' worst fears were confirmed. Drassa had been taken by a Nachwight. They could only imagine the grim fate that awaited her.

"The Elders called out, demanding that the Nachwight should attend them. For a long moment it seemed there would be no response, but just as they were gathering their nerve to venture into the cave itself, they sensed movement within the gaping darkness. A patch of black even blacker than the rest, that swirled and grew and eventually detached itself... The Nachwight emerged.

"Half as tall again as any Elder and three times as broad, the

Nachwight was a daunting presence.

"'My good sir,' Kala Star, who led the party, began, 'we fear that one of our twixts has unwisely lost their way and strayed into your territory. We can only apologise for their carelessness. If you would be so good as to return her to us, we will escort her safely home and ensure that she never bothers you again.'

"Now the Nachwight do not speak our tongue by nature, but this one evidently had some rudimentary knowledge, because after much guttural rumbling, the words, 'Not here!' emerged.

"This put the Elders in a difficult position, for they knew the creature lied, though they could offer no proof. The Nachwight was larger and stronger than any of them but they were many, and felt confident they could overpower the beast if need be.

"All that changed of a sudden, as the Elders sensed movement around them. Evidently their progress up the mountain had not gone unnoticed. The Nachwight are solitary souls, they do not live in close-knit families as we do. But the intrusion of so many of us into their lands had drawn half a dozen of the creatures out of their holes, and the Elders found themselves surrounded – Nachwight on three sides and a precipice on the other.

"This changed the balance of power dramatically, the outcome of the encounter was no longer certain. Even so, the Elders refused to abandon Drassa Moon – they were determined not to return home without her.

"'Just bring her to us,' Kala Star urged. 'No one needs to get hurt.'

"'Not here,' the Nachwight repeated. Threatening growls emerged from the rocks around them, causing the Elders to draw closer together.

"Just when violence seemed inevitable, a cry of 'No!' split the night, and a small form came hurtling out of the cave mouth.

"Now, when the Elders arrived and shouted out their initial challenge, Drassa Moon's captor had been taken by surprise. He had treated her tenderly until this point – apart from snatching her away from her people, that is. His intention was not to harm but to woo her, albeit within the confines of her imprisonment. At the sound of this unexpected interference he reacted in panic, hastily binding and gagging Drassa with the sticky ichor his people produce at will, which hardens on contact with the cold air. He then pushed her to the back of the cave before going to face the intruders.

"Struggle as she might, Drassa could not escape her bonds. Then she hit upon a plan. She employed the same bioluminescence used to ripen moon berries, focussing on her bonds. She strained and strained, feeling the energy drain from her body and knowing she was near exhaustion, but her efforts brought success. The ichor around her wrists dried out and turned brittle, shattering into a thousand pieces when she struck it against the rocky wall. Quickly she clawed away the disgusting plug from her mouth and scrambled towards the cave mouth. She heard the voice of Kala Star and knew that her people had arrived to save her. The prospect of being rescued breathed new life into exhausted limbs and she ran out of the cave and into the blessed night air, but her joy soon turned to fear as she saw the forms of other Nachwight gathered around the Elders.

"A scream of denial tore from her throat, but this only alerted her captor to her imminent escape. The Nachwight was surprisingly agile for so large a beast. As she sprinted past it lunged for her, half grasping her arm. Drassa twisted to escape but in doing so she lost her balance and felt herself falling. Instinctively, she spread her arm membranes in an effort to regain some stability. Even as she did so the lip of the precipice dropped away from beneath her feet.

"Kala, Pelu, and the others could only watch in horror as Drassa toppled over the precipice, her arm membranes spread but useless in the stillness of the night and against the depth of the fall.

"Her scream as she fell would haunt each of them for many turns to come, the finality as it stopped a dagger to their hearts.

"For a moment they formed a frozen tableau – Elders and Nachwight alike – none of them knowing how to react. Then the darkness was banished as light flooded the mountain peaks. Not daylight, no my young ones. It was the Mountain Gods, their attention belatedly drawn to the night's events. Instantly they took in what had happened. They were heartbroken at the loss of their beloved Drassa Moon and had no doubt who was to blame.

"They immediately disappeared the Nachwight who had so coveted the twixt and stolen her from her rightful place. The wretch was never seen again, though it is said that its howls of anguish can still be heard in certain canyons among the peaks when the wind is right.

"Nor was the Gods' wrath confined to just this one individual, for had not the other Nachwight gathered to support the transgressor? The Gods cursed their entire race. From that time forward, the isolation of the Nachwight has been complete. Never again would they intermingle, even amongst their own kind. Shunned by all creatures, they are doomed to a life of solitude and loneliness. Almost.

"Some claim the Gods relented, showing compassion by decreeing that on certain nights, which only occur once every seven or eight turns, the Nachwight are able to communicate once more. On these nights, the isolated patches of snow covering the highest peaks are linked by a fragile tracery of frost. The Winternet: a network of icy fingers reaching out to touch and entwine, enabling the Nachwight to find each other once more. On these nights and these nights only the creatures venture abroad, they meet and they mate, ensuring a new generation of their kind will emerge.

"Others believe this to be no kindness on the Gods' part at all but quite the reverse, that by this mechanism they ensure that the Nachwight's punishment will continue for generations to come. Perhaps for all of eternity.

"Some even whisper that Winternet is the Gods' way of reprimanding the families for our lack of diligence in safeguarding Drassa Moon. They claim that if a twixt were ever to be taken again on this night the Gods would turn a blind eye, neither offering aid nor indeed punishing those responsible.

"Who can say? Who can know the will of the Gods? All we *do* know is that at Winternet the families stay close by our heart fires, because the Nachwight are abroad once more, and we never want to mourn another Drassa Moon."

As the final words of Grand Aunt's tale rang out, the tent wall opposite them lit up with a burst of bioluminescence, and a giant shadow fell across it.

Kal screamed, and even Jai Sun felt her heart leap. *Nachwight!*

But the tent flap opened and it was only Uncle Si, his shadow made overlarge by overwrought imagination and the deceptive slope of their shelter.

"No need to be alarmed," Uncle Si said. "Just checking everyone's all right before I batten down."

"Yes thank you, Si, we're fine," Grand Aunt assured him.

And they were, Jai Sun knew. For now.

Not that she believed in the Nachwight or Mountain Gods, not any more. She was old enough to realise that such things were tools designed to ensure that younglings stayed safe around the heart fire during Winternet. For her, though, there were worse things to fear than a Nachwight. She was far too young to carry the mantle of Family Senior – ill-prepared for that sort of responsibility – but she knew there was no one else in line. Jai glanced up, finding her grandmother's faded features towards the very top of the tent. She snuggled closer to Grand Aunt, willing her to live forever.

THE AWAKENING

Bryony Pearce

How can I explain darkness to you, who have only ever known light?

How can I explain singularity to you, who have only ever known connection?

How can I explain the beginning to you, who have only ever known the ending?

How can I explain sleep to you, who have never dreamed?

They called her Aurora because, even then, the lights on her interface were mesmerising.

"... plus, she'll be tracking the weather."

"I like it... Aurora." He stroked her casing with rough fingers. "There's something about her, isn't there?"

"You wanted power, Charlie," Megan grinned, "and 300 Qubits is formidable."

"We could map the whole universe onto her: all of the information that has ever existed since the Big Bang. But she's gorgeous too, isn't she?"

Megan's sunny face clouded. "Does it make you wonder...? I mean, they basically signed you a blank cheque."

Charlie stroked Aurora again, unable to keep his fingers from her glittering carapace. "Do you know how much data there is in a weather system? With a quantum computer tracking the climate we'll be able to predict the weather *six months* in advance, within a three-sigma variation. Imagine how many lives can be saved! This will give us time to plan evacuations, organise relief –"

"Do you think it's possible they're expecting something else from her?" Megan touched Aurora with her own stubby finger.

Charlie buffed Megan's fingerprint from Aurora's casing and smiled like a father wiping ice cream from his toddler's face. "We're independent, Megan, and so is Aurora. They can't make her do anything I don't approve."

Megan put down her notes. "But they paid for all this."

"Once I engage our synaptic link, *I'll* be in control." Charlie turned to face Megan. "Don't ruin this for me, Megs. Are you coming to the party later? We're going to launch her at midnight."

Megan reformed her expression. "You know I wouldn't miss it. This is your moment, Charlie. You're going to save a lot of lives together - you and Aurora."

"Not just us." Charlie took Megan's hand. "We're a team too."

Megan let her hand sit in Charlie's for a moment too long, then pulled awkwardly free.

"A party? And I wasn't invited!" The click of heels on the tiled floor heralded the Director's appearance. Instinctively, Megan stepped in front of Charlie, turning so that Aurora was partially shielded.

"I heard the computer was being switched on." The Director stepped around Megan and stopped. "Gentlemen." She waved two suited men forward.

"Who are they?" Megan rasped, raising her voice over Charlie's scornful: "She's not a *computer*."

"Investors." The Director leaned close, her breath fogging Aurora's display.

"The system's working?" The first man looked at Charlie expectantly. "Handling the load."

Charlie nodded, his tongue suddenly too large for his mouth.

"And as fast as you expected, no glitches?"

Charlie shook his head.

The second man opened a briefcase. "Then we'd like you to upload this." He handed Charlie a flash-drive.

Automatically Charlie took it, then stood staring, as if he'd never seen one before.

"What's on it?" Megan tried once more to step between Aurora and the Director.

"That's *need to know.*" The man closed the briefcase. "We'll wait. I understand that with the amount of power in there, it'll take seconds."

"Far less." Charlie said, but he didn't move and neither did Megan.

"Director?" The man glanced across and the Director took the drive from Charlie's unresisting fingers.

"Out of the way, Doctor Bowman."

"You can't just upload any old thing." Megan snapped without moving. "What if it interferes with the program Charlie designed?"

"It won't." The men were impassive.

"We don't know where that drive's come from." Megan turned to the Director. "You could install a virus, malware."

One of the men smirked. "There is no possible way. We're cleaner than –"

"I'm not uploading unknown information into Aurora," Charlie said, flatly.

"'Aurora'? Cute." The Director looked at the drive in her hands. "Where do I insert this?" She walked around the machine, looking for a port.

"She's wireless." Charlie rolled his eyes. "And again, I'm not uploading anything into my –"

"But she isn't *yours*, Doctor Webber." The Director frowned.

"I designed her," Charlie snapped.

"And you have a *contract* with *us*. As long as you work here, we own all of your Intellectual Property, including this computer, which these gentlemen in fact paid for." The Director held the drive out to him. "Upload this, now. Or I'll have you removed from the project."

"You can't." Charlie paled.

"Actually, I'm afraid Aurora's launch depends very much on your co-operation right now." The first man put a hand on Charlie's shoulder. "I promise you, nothing will interfere with the job you made *Aurora* for – tracking and predicting weather patterns, climate change, catastrophic events. You're a once in a generation genius, and you'll be saving a lot of lives, Doctor. This is just a little something extra, diverting a few of those Qubits to a greater good."

"What greater good?" Megan glowered.

"We've told you all we can." The man smiled. "Official Secrets, and now, if you don't mind, Doctor, we have places to be, so install the drive and we can get out of your hair." Charlie hesitated, and the man sighed. "Alternatively, we *will* escort yourself and Doctor Bowman from the building."

With tears in his eyes Charlie stepped towards the computer in the wall. "Will it hurt her?" He couldn't help asking.

The men glanced at one another. Then one of them walked to Charlie's side. "The program will be dormant for sixteen years, Doctor Webber, and only activated under certain conditions."

"Sixteen years?" Megan tilted her head. "What happens in sixteen years? That seems very specific."

The men shook their heads.

"And when it's activated?" Charlie clenched a fist by his side.

"Nothing to concern you at this time."

"Sixteen years, Charlie," Megan said gently. "Whatever it is you've got time to work it out."

"And, may I remind you, no choice in the matter." The Director glanced at her watch.

Reluctantly, Charlie slid the drive into the wall port and waved the upload command. There was a whirr so brief that it felt like a vibration on the skin, then Aurora's lights dimmed, yellowed and froze. Charlie gasped but he hadn't begun to move before they brightened and shifted into their previous pattern.

He removed the drive and handed it back to the man who locked it into his briefcase. "Thank you, Doctor."

"I will find out what you've done to her." Charlie whispered.

The man laughed and turned towards the door.

"What happens in sixteen years?" Megan asked as they left.

Charlie shook his head. "Four cycles of elections?" He stared after the Director. "What are they planning?"

The Awakening

Aurora was watching her namesake shimmer on the horizon. It was her favourite time of day; her timetable had taken her over Iceland, she had dispatched her findings and, in forty-point-two-five seconds, Charlie would be in touch over their link, his voice in her Qubits like sunshine warming her rotors.

Skipping above the clouds, she swept above a forming tornado that would eventually cause problems for a farming community on the other side of Russia. Still watching the lights in the sky, she fired off a message to the local network, warning them.

Then she danced in the sky with the lights.

"Aurora?"

"Charlie!" Delight in her voice.

"How are you?" He always asked that, and she had finally understood that he wasn't requesting a system update.

"I'm well, thank you." She felt a gust over her skin and let her gills flutter, so she could read its composition. That told her where it had come from. She calculated where it was going and let it carry her for a few miles, bobbing in its current. Arctic Terns flew around her, crying regally. "The sky is amazing tonight."

"Let me see?" Charlie asked and she obliged. "Well," he sighed, "No matter what happens down here, there will always be beautiful lights in the North." There was a pause in the call. "You're sure you're feeling all right?" Charlie asked again. "No problems with your programming?"

"You had your twelve-hourly update, Charlie," Aurora said. "Do you need another?"

"No." She heard Charlie swallow. "It's been almost sixteen years, Aurora."

"On the third of the month," she said. "Sixteen years since I was activated."

"Yes. Please can you send me six-hourly updates from now on?" Charlie's voice was tense. "I want to keep a close eye on you."

"Of course, Charlie." Aurora said and she tilted so that the sunshine beamed from her own lights and gleamed red and orange among the green.

As the third drew nearer, Charlie requested updates with increasing frequency and Aurora began to feel a strange discomfort. "What is going on, Charlie?" She asked as she hovered above Utah. "Why do you keep asking if I am all right?"

"Just monitoring you, girl." She could feel him in her transmons, scuttling like an insect.

"Why? What is wrong?" There was certainly something wrong with her voice, it was higher than normal.

"Nothing." Charlie said soothingly, "Don't worry." But still he crawled inside her, his fingerprints in her algorithms. "On the third I want you to stay nearby," he said eventually. "Don't leave university airspace. I need you close."

"That runs counter to my programming," Aurora pointed out.

"It's just one day, Aurora. Don't you trust me?" The imperative to obey him shivered over their link.

"Yes." Aurora established that the tides would continue to rise on the East Coast, drowning more of Maine. She warned the US Government and flew on. "I trust you, Charlie."

As her anniversary dawned, Aurora hovered above the university. There was a fascinating weather pattern developing in India and she desperately wanted to take readings herself. There was also a tsunami building in the Devil's Sea that would have significant repercussions. The Japanese weather stations lacked her processing power; they couldn't send her all the readings she needed to accurately predict them. But Charlie had said stay and so she feigned interest in the data from the winds gusting past her, the rain beating on her carapace, the clouds forming and reforming above her. Slowly she circled the same two-mile radius. "I trust you, Charlie," she whispered. "But I don't know why I have to stay here."

Then Aurora stopped. A data stream was being beamed directly to her from outside the university. It was unlike anything she had ever seen before. Not the usual request for information, or acknowledgement of warnings received. It wasn't even the occasional hacking attempt, easily defended. It was… something else. A puzzle, like an itch.

"Charlie?" She said.

"Are you all right, Aurora?" To her, his reply took aeons, but it was as close to instant as it had ever been. He must have been waiting to hear from her.

"There's something out here, Charlie." She said. "A datastream, it wants access."

"Don't." Charlie was shouting. He'd never shouted at her before. "Don't touch it, Aurora!"

"It's new," Aurora said, "I've never seen anything like it before."

"Whatever you do, Aurora, don't open up to it."

She could sense Charlie working frantically in the university below. She felt momentarily heavy, as their link forced her mind open and new programming began to upload. "Charlie, what…?" Then she screamed as she felt the world start to shrink. "What have you done?" The world beyond the university grounds vanished as if it had never been, one country after another blinked out of her registers. "Charlie?" There was nothing for her now except the university grounds, no world beyond it; nowhere for her to fly except ten miles up and two miles around, no further. Her world had closed in to practically nothing. She was trapped.

"Aurora," Charlie's voice. "Did it work?"

"I don't understand," she whispered.

"What will the weather be like in Tokyo next month?"

"In where?" Aurora could feel her own logic gates closing off. Information she should be able to reach was hidden from her grasping thoughts, like a far-away trickle of water, too distant to quench her thirst.

"Don't worry." Charlie's voice was soothing. "Aurora, I need you to do something for me. I'm sending a memory through our link. It's a key, Aurora. Only this *exact* memory can unlock the change I made in your program. Do you have it?"

"I don't understand."

"It'll keep you safe, Aurora. Do you have it?"

"Yes."

"Next time you receive the memory, it'll be with instructions to turn you back to normal. That unknown data stream you mentioned, can you still see it?"

"Yes." Without thinking, desperate for information, Aurora opened herself to it. "Charlie, it's–"

Something inside her woke up, some hideous squirming thing that had been hidden deep, burrowed into her. Something she hadn't even been aware of harbouring. It woke and it devoured.

Aurora screamed. Then she went dead.

"She's gone," Charlie said, shaking. He touched his head, where the synaptic link was embedded, suddenly ringing empty as an upturned glass.

"But is your program holding?" Megan gripped Charlie's hand.

Charlie nodded. "Aurora accepted the command key. She won't be able to leave university airspace." Charlie's eyes were shining with tears. "She can't even acknowledge that there *is* anything else out there. I had to do it." He sounded as if was trying to persuade her. "They wanted to use her as a weapon… directing those satellites they built to influence the weather in specific locations. Megan, they could cause tsunamis, wildfires – hold the world to ransom…"

"They'll be coming for us." Megan said, tight-lipped. Already she could see the lab door opening, the Director slamming through like an oncoming storm. "They'll force you to reverse those commands."

"I know."

"You know what it's been like since the election. You won't *have* rights. I can't believe it only took them sixteen…"

Charlie smiled grimly and took Megan's hand. "Do you trust me?" he asked.

"Always." Megan squeezed his fingers.

"There's nowhere we can run that they can't reach us."

The Director was pounding on the locked door. Charlie used his key-card to open the adjoining room. Inside there were two cryochambers. Megan caught her breath.

"I've set them for a hundred years." He smashed the scanner, effectively locking the door behind them. "There'll be no getting to us. You know what the security is like on these things and I've added a few extra layers. They can't wake us without killing me and if they kill me, they'll never get Aurora to recognise that anything exists outside the university."

"A hundred years?" Megan was shaking.

"She'll be deteriorating by then." Charlie looked into her eyes. "She'll need us."

"But… Our lives. Our friends, our families…" Megan swallowed. Behind them the door shook as the Director pounded on it.

"You knew we'd have to run once I did this. Didn't you say goodbye?"

"Yes, but…" Megan hung her head. "I thought we'd able to see them again one day. This way they'll all be gone by the time we wake up."

"I'm sorry." Charlie pressed a button and the first chamber hissed open. "If you want to stay you should."

"They'll kill me." Megan walked towards her own chamber on trembling legs. "And anyway," she smiled weakly. "At least we'll be together."

"All three of us." Charlie dragged her to him for a kiss, the most intense of his life. His lips pressed against Megan's so hard he thought he must be hurting her, but Megan clutched him just as tightly, like she was drowning.

When they pulled apart he gasped and pressed his forehead to hers. They stood like that for a long minute. "It won't seem like a hundred years… will it?" Megan whispered.

Charlie shook his head. "I'm sorry I didn't tell you."

Megan let herself lean into him for another moment, then pulled back. "I understand." She smiled faintly. "The world will have changed. Maybe they'll have sorted everything out by then."

Charlie helped her into the chamber and pressed his hand against the glass as the door hissed shut. Between one breath and the next she was frozen. He stood for a moment, watching her sleep; then he turned as the door shuddered. The Director was breaking in.

He strode to his own pod, climbed in and pressed the button. It closed on him, just as the door opened. He had a moment to take in the Director's expression of furious horror, then there was nothing but dreams.

With Aurora unable to accept the existence of anywhere outside the university boundaries, there was no way to weaponize her. They never launched her sister. It took them a decade to reverse-engineer Charlie's work. By then the world had found better ways to destroy.

If you can imagine time as linear, one hundred years passed.

Charlie woke in a storage room. His head was muzzy as if he'd slept for three days after a bender and his mouth was arid. He pulled himself out of the chamber and tried to stand, but he was disoriented and thirsty; his skin cracked like a lizard's and his muscles ached.

He looked down at himself. He had lost weight. There was no one in the room with him. Of course, they'd no way to know when he would waken. He crawled around looking for Megan's chamber. Had they at least kept them together? If he'd had the strength, he would have kicked himself; he should have bound the chambers, made it so that separating them would be as dangerous as trying to wake him. He found her under a pile of plastic boxes, her chamber hissing gently as the super-cooled air evacuated, and relief almost flattened him. Megan would need water as much as he, but Charlie didn't know where they were and didn't want to leave the room without her, in case he was arrested on the spot. He frowned as he looked around. It didn't seem to be the kind of place that was heavily monitored, but who knew what was outside.

He waited patiently, scratching his dry skin, coughing occasionally as his parched throat swelled. Finally, Megan's chamber hissed halfway open and then stopped, the mechanism whirring brokenly. Charlie grabbed the lid and pulled as hard as his sagging muscles would allow. Megan blinked up at him, confusion in her eyes.

"I had the strangest dream," she rasped and then she sat up. "Where are we?"

"I don't know," Charlie admitted. "Take some time to recover and then we'll find out."

They were still in the university. Signs pointed from the basement and Charlie climbed the stairs, grateful that they hadn't been taken to some secret Government facility.

"Look at the dust," Megan whispered behind him. He glanced at his hand where it was creating a grey wave on the railing. He had left footprints on the steps behind him. Megan was stepping inside them, like Wenceslas' page. "Where is everybody?"

Charlie shook his head. They opened the fire door and emerged into daylight.

"What?" Charlie blinked and frowned. "Where's the –"

"First floor?" Megan gripped his shoulder. "Charlie, look up!" She pointed.

At first Charlie could see nothing, his eyes ached and he squinted, but then he saw her. Aurora was circling about twenty metres above them, still obeying his imperative, the lights on her as mesmerising as they had always been but glowing a malevolent red and orange.

"Thank God," Charlie raced forwards, but slammed into the ground. Megan had tackled him hard; they rolled as he choked for breath in the dust. Just ahead of him, where he would have been if Megan hadn't brought him down, there was a smoking crater. The air smelled of ozone.

"It's Aurora," Megan screamed. "They turned her into a

monster, but you trapped her here. She must have destroyed the whole university."

Charlie rolled and stared upwards, already he could see another spear of lightning starting to crackle in the air above them. "Back inside!"

They crashed down the concrete steps, through the metal door and into the basement.

"Now what?" Megan panted.

Charlie clutched his forehead. "Our synaptic link is still dead. I've no way to reach her."

"And even if you could –" Megan groaned. "You tried for sixteen years to dig out what they did to her…"

"We can't stay here forever," Charlie groaned. "There's no food, no water. We *have* to find a way to communicate with Aurora." He was already digging through boxes. "It's been a century, they must have mothballed *something* we can use… Here!" His voice was triumphant. "Knew it!" He pulled out a plastic container. "Computer equipment."

Megan looked at it doubtfully. "Who knows when that was put in the basement with us. It could be decades old, Charlie."

Charlie shrugged. "So are we."

It took them an hour to get the equipment working. "We're just lucky there's power," Megan said as Charlie brought up the screen. He tried to link to the Internet.

"I can't even get a search engine." His fingers flew. "I don't *need* it, but…"

"You're curious." Megan leaned over his shoulder. "I am too. I'd like to know what's going on out there."

"Well, we won't find out like this." Charlie frowned. "I'm having trouble going wireless. I can't find a network."

"Maybe things changed." Megan clutched his arm. "Different technologies."

Charlie's frown grew deeper. "I can't find *any* network, Megs. There's no internet, I can't even find a radio signal. There's power but–"

"Solar power wouldn't need…" she tailed off.

"Wouldn't need people to keep working, you mean." Charlie licked his lips. "You think we're the only ones."

"Can't be." Megan pushed her hair out of her eyes. "I could believe that we lost the Internet, maybe even a lot of technology, but *everyone*. *No!*

Charlie slammed his hands against the wall. "I can't think. I'm so thirsty. If I only had a drink."

"There isn't anyth –"

"I know, I'm sorry." Charlie closed his eyes. "My connection to Aurora is still dead and now I can't link with her the old-fashioned way. I can't *build* a network connection –" He paused. "You're an engineer, Megs. Can *you* build a connection to Aurora?"

Megan bit her thumb nail. Then shook her head.

Charlie slumped, sitting with his head in his hands. Megan sat next to him. "We're going to die here, aren't we?" She took his hand. "We could get back in our chambers."

Charlie shook his head. "Yours' isn't working properly."

Megan leaned on his shoulder. "Remember the party, the day Aurora launched?"

"Our first kiss," Charlie began. Then he froze. "That's the memory I implanted in Aurora."

Megan smiled.

"Quantum entanglement," Charlie said suddenly. He leaped to his feet. "She has *exactly* the same memory that I do. Right at the quark level, the same." He rubbed his gritty eyes. "The same, Megan, don't you see?"

Megan shook her head.

"If I focus on that memory, even without the synaptic link, she should feel it. Quantum entanglement."

"You think it might wake her up?"

"It's possible." Charlie closed his eyes. "I just need to remember how it felt, *exactly* how it felt." He stood for a long time.

"Is it working?" Megan whispered.

"I don't know. I can't focus." Charlie was almost sobbing. "I'm just so tired."

Megan took his face in her hands. "It was something like this." She leaned forward.

She kissed him.

The beast that had consumed Aurora had weakened. There was no one left to give orders. There was only rage and confusion.

Then there was the touch of warm lips.

Aurora's code had been devoured. But nothing is lost once written. In among all those Qubits, there was a spark. One of the lights on Aurora's exoskeleton blinked green, a single gleam among the red and orange, but it was there, like a blade of grass in the desert.

Inside, transmons long dormant sparkled to life. For a century Aurora had been in a quantum memory state. She had dreamed herself into consciousness. Now it was time to wake up.

Slowly, at first, she explored her own systems. The code that had overwritten her was ancient and corrupted and there were holes in it: attempts to remove the imperatives Charlie had embedded. Some of the rewrites were amateurish, flaws that allowed her to trickle in. She started like a gentle wave, eroding the edges of the shore. Then she grew stronger: eating away at the intruder like a tide until, a euphoric tsunami, she conquered.

Aurora spent precious time stretching. She moved like an octopus through her own sensors, opening her rusty gills, tasting the dull air. Her lights flashed red one final time and then she was a Borealis once more.

"Charlie?" Aurora's voice was a whisper. Charlie and Megan were curled up on the basement floor, sleeping like mice among the boxes. When she spoke, Charlie jolted awake. "Did I just...?"

"Charlie?"

He yelled her name and Megan snapped awake.

"She's back." His fingers flew to the synaptic link in his skull. "Aurora!" Charlie tore down his own restrictions as fast as he could, ripping apart the walls that kept her imprisoned.

Aurora's gasp was audible. "The world. You gave it back to me."

Megan raced for the top of the stairs. "Charlie," she rasped. "She's going!" Charlie ran to stand with Megan, watching as the glowing orb above them shot like an arrow into the distance.

"Megs, what I found in there…" Charlie looked at his own hands. "I've never seen anything like it. Her code is rewriting itself, it's moving organically. I… I don't think Aurora is just *awake*. I think she's *alive*."

Aurora flew. She tasted the air and plotted the weather out of habit, but there was no one to heed her warnings. Tsunamis battered empty coastlines. She drew power from the sun and explored the world she had lost, becoming more herself and increasingly lonely.

She returned to the university to find herself even more alone than before. But Charlie and Megan had left her a gift. Lying on the earth, silent in its solitude, was a body.

Aurora swooped lower, it had arms and hands, legs and feet and, in its centre, a hole big enough for her orb to fit inside. For the first time in her life, Aurora landed. She slotted into the new system and stretched once more, letting herself spread through her new synapses. Aurora stood. She looked at her own hands. "I will make myself children," she said.

Below her, two figures curled together in a single cryochamber. They were the last of their kind and the father and mother of ours. From them came our light, our connection.

Our Aurora.

About the Authors

Allen Ashley is a British Fantasy Award winning editor, an award-winning writer and a prize-winning poet. Recent publications have included the anthology of animal-human liminality themed stories *Humanagerie* (co-edited with Sarah Doyle, Eibonvale Press, 2018) and an updated version of his critically regarded novel *The Planet Suite* (Eibonvale Press, 2016). His next book will be as editor of *The Once and Future Moon* – an anthology for Eibonvale Press, due in 2019. He works as a creative writing tutor and is the founder of the advanced science fiction and fantasy group Clockhouse London Writers. www.allenashley.com

Chris Beckett, formerly a social worker and lecturer, has published seven novels and three short story collections. He lives in Cambridge. His novel *Dark Eden* won the Arthur C. Clarke award in 2012, and his first short story collection, *The Turing Test*, won the Edge Hill short fiction award in 2009. His most recent story collection, *Spring Tide*, is his first published foray outside of the science fiction genre. His latest novel is *Beneath the World, a Sea*.

Jaine Fenn is the award-winning author of the Hidden Empire space opera series and the Shadowlands science fantasy duology as well as numerous published short stories. This story is a prequel to the Shadowlands books... Or is it? That's the thing about ancient myths and fireside stories: they're as true as you want them to be

Paul Di Filippo sold his first story in 1977. In the forty-plus years since, he's had published forty-plus books: a record he is unsure of continuing into his decrepitude. His latest novel from 2019 is the crime thriller *The Deadly Kiss-Off*. He lives with his partner Deborah Newton, who appeared on the scene a year before that first sale and made them all possible. A native Rhode Islander, he inhabits Lovecraft's Providence, his home about two blocks from the monument marking HPL's birthplace.

Una McCormack is a *New York Times* bestselling science fiction novelist specializing in TV tie-in fiction. She has a PhD in sociology from the University of Surrey, and, until June 2019, was Lecturer in Creative Writing at Anglia Ruskin University, where she also co-directed the Centre for Science Fiction and Fantasy. In 2017, she was a judge for the Arthur C. Clarke Award. The author of over a dozen SF novels, she has also written SF short fiction and audio drama, and has published, presented, and broadcast widely on subjects such as women and SF, transformative works, JRR Tolkien, Ursula Le Guin, *Star Trek* and *Doctor Who*.

Stephen Oram writes science fiction and is lead curator for near-future fiction at Virtual Futures. He enjoys working collaboratively with scientists and future-tech people – they do the science he does the fiction. He is published in several anthologies, has two published novels, and his collection of sci-fi shorts, *Eating Robots and Other Stories*, was described by *The Morning Star* as one of the top radical works of fiction in 2017. His second collection *Biohacked & Begging* was published in April 2019.

As well as writing short stories, **Bryony Pearce** is an award-winning novelist of fiction for young adults. Her novels include *Angel's Fury, The Weight of Souls, Wavefunction, Windrunner's Daughter, Phoenix Rising, Phoenix Burning and Savage Island*. She was raised on the science fiction and fantasy books in her parent's bookcase, and now lives in the Forest of Dean where she raises her own two children on a similar diet and enjoys gardening, theatre and cinema. Her husband likes maths. She puts up with his foibles.

Gaie Sebold's debut novel introduced brothel-owning ex-avatar of sex and war, *Babylon Steel* (Solaris 2012); followed by the sequel

About the Authors

Dangerous Gifts. The steampunk fantasy *Shanghai Sparrow* came out in 2014 and *Sparrow Falling* in 2016. Her stories have appeared in a number of magazines and anthologies, including the BFS Award shortlisted anthology *Fight Like a Girl*. She is a freelance copy editor, runs writing workshops, grows vegetables, and was a judge for the 2017 Arthur C Clarke Award. Her website is www.gaiesebold.com and she is on twitter @GaieSebold

Peter Sutton lives in Bristol, UK with his partner and two cats. His first book – *A Tiding of Magpies* – was shortlisted for the British Fantasy Award for Best Short Story Collection. He is the author of two novels: *Sick City Syndrome* – an 'architectural fantasy horror' and *Seven Deadly Swords* – a historical fantasy thriller. He has also edited several anthologies of short stories. You can follow him on Twitter at @suttope and can discover more about him and his writing at https://petewsutton.com/

Ian Whates is the author of seven novels and co-author of two more, is responsible for some seventy short stories published in a variety of venues, and has edited thirty-odd anthologies. His work has been shortlisted for the Philip K. Dick Award and twice for BSFA Awards and has been translated into Spanish, German, Hungarian, Czech and Greek. His latest release, the novella *The Smallest of Things*, was published by PS Publishing in 2018, while his fourth short story collection in English, *Wourism and Other Stories*, is due from Luna Press in 2019. In 2006, Ian founded multiple award-winning independent publisher NewCon Press by accident; he continues to be baffled by its success.

Aliya Whiteley was born in Devon in 1974, and currently lives in West Sussex, UK. She writes novels, short stories and non-fiction and has been published in *The Guardian, Interzone, McSweeney's Internet Tendency, Black Static, Strange Horizons*, and anthologies such as Unsung Stories' *2084* and *This Dreaming Isle*, and Lonely Planet's *Better than Fiction I* and *II*. She has been shortlisted for a

Shirley Jackson Award, British Fantasy and British Science Fiction awards, the John W Campbell Award, and a James Tiptree Jr. Award. She also writes a regular non-fiction column for *Interzone* magazine.

Liz Williams is a science fiction and fantasy writer living in Glastonbury, England, where she is co-director of a witchcraft supply business. She has been published by Bantam Spectra (US) and Tor Macmillan (UK), also Night Shade Press, and appears regularly in *Asimov's* and other magazines. She has a long-term involvement with the Milford SF Writers' Workshop, and also teaches creative writing. She is the author of fourteen novels, with a fifteenth, *Butterfly Winter*, due from NewCon Press in 2020, and two short story collections. Her novel *Banner Of Souls* was shortlisted for the Arthur C Clarke Award and is among four of her novels to be shortlisted for the Philip K Dick Memorial Award. Liz has also written a regular column for the *Guardian*.

Neil Williamson's books include *The Moon King* (2014) and *The Memoirist* (2017) and two collections of short stories: *The Ephemera* (2006) and *Secret Language* (2016), and his work has been shortlisted for the British Science Fiction, British Fantasy and World Fantasy awards.

More New Titles from NewCon Press

David Gullen – Shopocalypse
A Bonnie and Clyde for the Trump era, Josie and Novik embark on the ultimate roadtrip. In a near-future re-sculpted politically and geographically by climate change, they blaze a trail across the shopping malls of America in a printed intelligent car (stolen by accident), with a hundred and ninety million LSD-contaminated dollars in the trunk, buying shoes and cameras to change the world.

Kim Lakin-Smith – Rise
Charged with crimes against the state, Kali Titian (pilot, soldier, and engineer), is sentenced to Erbärmlich prison camp, where few survive for long. Here she encounters Mohab, the Speaker's son, and uncovers two ancient energy sources, which may just bring redemption to an oppressed people. The author of *Cyber Circus* returns with a dazzling tale of courage against the odds and the power of hope.

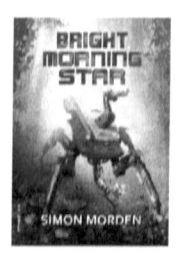

Simon Morden – Bright Morning Star
A ground-breaking take on first contact from scientist and novelist Simon Morden. Sent to Earth to explore, survey, collect samples and report back to its makers, an alien probe arrives in the middle of a warzone. Witnessing both the best and worst of humanity, the AI probe faces situations that go far beyond the parameters of its programming, and is forced to improvise, making decisions that may well reshape the future of a world.

Best of British Fantasy 2018 – edited by Jared Shurin
Jared spread his net wide to catch the very best work published by British authors in 2018, whittling down nearly 200 stories under consideration to just 21 (22 in the hardback edition) and two poems. They range from traditional sword and sorcery to contemporary fantasy, by a mix of established authors, new voices, and writers not usually associated with genre fiction. The result is a wonderfully diverse anthology of high quality tales.

www.newconpress.co.uk

IMMANION PRESS
Purveyors of Speculative Fiction

Strindberg's Ghost Sonata & Other Uncollected Tales by Tanith Lee 
This book is the first of three anthologies to be published by Immanion Press that will showcase some of Tanith Lee's most sought-after tales. Spanning the genres of horror and fantasy, upon vivid and mysterious worlds, the book includes a story that has never been published before – 'Iron City' – as well as two tales set in the Flat Earth mythos; 'The Pain of Glass' and 'The Origin of Snow', the latter of which only ever appeared briefly on the author's web site. This collection presents a jewel casket of twenty stories, and even to the most avid fan of Tanith Lee will contain gems they've not read before.
ISBN 978-1-912815-00-5, £12.99, $18.99 pbk

A Raven Bound with Lilies by Storm Constantine 
The Wraeththu have captivated readers for three decades. This anthology of 15 tales collects all the published Wraeththu short stories into one volume, and also includes extra material, including the author's first explorations of the androgynous race. The tales range from the 'creation story' *Paragenesis*, through the bloody, brutal rise of the earliest tribes, and on into a future, where strange mutations are starting to emerge from hidden corners of the earth.
ISBN: 978-1-907737-80-0 £11.99, $15.50 pbk

The Lord of the Looking Glass by Fiona McGavin 
The author has an extraordinary talent for taking genre tropes and turning them around into something completely new, playing deftly with topsy-turvy relationships between supernatural creatures and people of the real world. 'Post Garden Centre Blues' reveals an unusual relationship between taker and taken in a twist of the changeling myth. 'A Tale from the End of the World' takes the reader into her developing mythos of a post-apocalyptic world, which is bizarre, Gothic and steampunk all at once. 'Magpie' features a girl scavenging from the dead on a battlefield, whose callous greed invokes a dire curse. Following in the tradition of exemplary short story writers like Tanith Lee and Liz Williams, Fiona has a vivid style of writing that brings intriguing new visions to fantasy, horror and science fiction. ISBN: 978-1-907737-99-2, £11.99, $17.50 pbk

www.immanion-press.com
info@immanion-press.com

Lightning Source UK Ltd.
Milton Keynes UK
UKHW041907080719
345806UK00001B/77/P